NIGHT MOVES

There were just the four of them in the bunkhouse. Joe Dyer lay awhile with the gun in his hand. Cal Morgan snored, Dutch Hauser snored, Camargo's mattress rustled, and a coyote began to screech a long way off.

Joe got up and blew out the lamp. He said to Camargo, "If anybody tries to get me he'll have to do it in the dark, and I want to know he's coming. Anything moves in this room tonight, I shoot."

Robert MacLeod's meticulous research has earned him the reputation of being one of the most "authentic" of the top Western novelists. **The Appaloosa**, starring Marlon Brando, was based on one of MacLeod's Gold Medal originals, and another, **The Californio**, was made into the major motion picture **100 Rifles**.

THE RUNNING GUN

Robert MacLeod

PaperJacks LTD.

TORONTO NEW YORK

PaperJacks

THE RUNNING GUN

PaperJacks LTD.

330 STEELCASE RD. E., MARKHAM, ONT. L3R 2M1
210 FIFTH AVE., NEW YORK, N.Y. 10010

PaperJacks edition published August, 1988

This is a work of fiction in its entirety. Any resemblance to actual people, places or events is purely coincidental.

ISBN 0-7701-0952-7

Printed in the USA

To Laney

ONE

Joe Dyer's five feet ten of hard-muscled, flat-bellied frame was quite a colorful affair — thick black hair in ducktails around his red neck; black brows; gray eyes; his big hands and the area of his rugged face not hidden under the two-weeks' black whiskers also red from wind and cold. The rest of him would soon resume its normal stark white, but now it was a mottled blue as he sprinted to the fire. The bath, his first in two weeks, had been a shuddering ordeal in the icy waters of the creek. Through chattering teeth he muttered, "Jesus God Almighty!" and snatched up the grimy blanket to towel himself roughly, smoothing out the goosepimples.

His army shirt and worn socks and butt-sprung wool longjohns were draped on a rock by the fire, not yet thawed out from last night's freeze, after the laundering with the bar of yellow soap he had begged at the little ranch in the north end of the pass. The last of his bacon sizzled in the frying pan with the few doughballs from the last of his flour. The coffee boiled over and he set the pot aside, using a corner of the blanket for a mitt.

Mabel, the mule, came to the fire, expertly hopping with her hobbled front legs and walking with the hind ones. Joe gave her the bacon rind for her breakfast. Down on the bench, Brownie, the chunky little buckskin, had eaten a thirty-foot-diameter circle around his picket pin, in the high, sun-cured grass.

The sun peeked over a hill. Joe ate, and drank three cups of coffee as he toasted his bare shins and leaned back against the rock. He began to sweat and his hide now turned pink. He felt wonderful.

He got up and stretched, walked to his saddle by his bedroll, got a pencil and a dog-eared, canvas-covered notebook from the saddlebag, and came back to sit against the rock. Draped once more in the blanket, he began a letter to Mike Burnham, half-owner of the Kentucky Bar back in Prescott, Arizona:

December ?? 1915
Dear Mike,

I've been out almost two months now, and I still got $83.42 of the grubstake. Did you get my letter from Show Low?

I didn't hit any color where I found that placer pocket last year, so I kept going, poked around east of Bear Mountain, and I didn't find anything. I began to wish I had put my share last year into a good-paying saloon like you did, instead of buying the 640 up under the Mingus Mountain. I got supplies in Cluffs and worked on south through a mess of real bad canyons, and somewhere near Metcalf I hit a real good one. Maybe it is just a small vein and pinches out or runs back into the mountain, but I got a sack full of jewelry-store stuff you could pick the gold out of with a toothpick. And besides that, three sample sacks full of ore I crushed with my hammer. It really pans out. You'll find dust and a couple nuggets wrapped up inside one of the sacks. There's both placer and quartz, and maybe it is going to need a stamp mill and water, but there is plenty of water. It is awful rough country. Maybe have to pack high grade ore out on mules.

I will mail the samples to you so I don't have to pack it and won't have to answer fool questions like will I please show somebody where I found it. I will just be another saddle bum riding back to Prescott. But I bet you will be buying out your partner, and I am going to have 640 acres of the damnedest best white-face bulls and mama cows in Arizona, and fix up the house, barn, and windmill.

I didn't build any monument or set up any location notices. Two reasons. I don't want some crooked county clerk spreading the news. And second I don't know what the hell county I am in. I got the place spotted with landmarks, and I drew this map. I could find it again blindfolded, but getting out of those canyons, I got twisted up, and got over into New Mexico.

Fact is, I don't even know what day it is, but I think December 11th, and if I am right, it's my birthday and I'm going to have a big steak and a drink this afternoon. I ought to have twenty-eight of them, one for every year, and maybe I will. I been living on turkey for four days. You ever hit a hen turkey with a Winchester? It don't leave much but wings and drumsticks.

I stopped at a ranch yesterday, and they said it was Blue Creek I been following and the town I can see from here, down on the flat, must be Spanish Wells. I'll mail the samples and get a room and wait till I hear from you whether you want me to register the claim and come back, or wait for you if you want to come and have a look. If you don't come, I got enough grubstake to get me home. Tell the boys hello for me. Is Aggie still singing in the Kentucky?

Yours truly,
Joe Dyer

With his Arkansas stone he honed his skinning knife to an edge like a shard of glass and cut the pages of his letter from the notebook. Then he folded them with the carefully drawn location map and put them in the wallet in the hip pocket of his Levi's. He put on the slightly damp underwear and socks and got a potful of water from the creek. While it heated on the coals, he stuffed his few belongings into the two rawhide panniers which would go light now because his grub was used up. There were only the two blankets and a quilt, his cooking gear, the hand ax and prospector's pick and gold pan, an iron mortar and pestle, a spare shirt and socks, and a box of shells for the Colt's New Service Army revolver.

The water was hot, and he used the remnant of the bar of yellow soap to shave with the skinning knife.

The army shirt was dry, and he put it on, then got the buckskin and led him to the camp. He saddled and bridled him and hung his chaps on the saddlehorn. The notebook and the sample sacks went into the saddlebags which held a joined ramrod, rags, an oil can, nails, and four horseshoes. He shoved the Winchester '94 carbine into the boot under the off fender, its butt sticking forward through the coils of his grass rope.

Mabel always clamped her tail down like a vise when he put the sawbuck packsaddle on her and tried to get the crupper in place. He had to kick her skinny rump. He had to kick her in the belly, too, to make her quit swelling up when he tightened the cinch. He hung the panniers on the sawbuck and lashed the folded tarp over the load.

When he had drowned the fire, filled the canteen, and hung the shellbelt with its holstered revolver and sheathed skinning knife around his hips, he put on the Levi jacket and the battered Stetson, buckled his spurs on, and checked the saddle strings that held his slicker-wrapped sheepskin coat behind the cantle. Joe Dyer, cowman and sometime prospector, was ready to ride down to Spanish Wells and mail some very promising samples to Mike Burnham in Prescott, Arizona.

About noon, he rode out of a draw and saw the road. A Model T Ford rattled by with its brass radiator spouting steam, and Brownie and Mabel took it as an excuse to do a little bucking. This was fakery, because they had both seen automobiles in Prescott – not to mention electric streetcars – so Joe was harsh with the discipline, and they ignored the next car that overtook them, a shiny new Dodge with wooden-spoke wheels. There were buckboards and ranch wagons and many riders, all heading for Spanish Wells. It seemed like a lot more traffic than what went into Prescott on a Saturday afternoon, and Spanish Wells couldn't be a quarter the size of Prescott, from what Joe could see.

After a while he began to hear the uproar in the town – firecrackers and some Mexican-type coyote yells and a band. The banner explained it, stretched across the street that ran between two rows of adobe shacks and opened into a wide plaza seething with people and racket:

SPANISH WELLS SEMICENTENNIAL
FIFTY YEARS OF PROGRESS
PARADE – RODEO – JACKPOT ROPING
DANCING IN THE PLAZA, AFTERNOONS
(TRINI'S MARIMBA BAND)
DANCING EVERY NIGHT – ODD FELLOWS HALL
(BILL GALE'S BUCKAROOS)
BEARD GROWING CONTEST – JUDGING SUNDAY 2:30
FRI. SAT. SUN., DECEMBER 10-11-12

Over the heads of the people milling around in the plaza, Joe looked at the false fronts, the brick and adobe business buildings – the Grant County Bank, Emporium, Feed Store and Livery Stable; chili parlors and taco joints; the Longhorn Restaurant and Saloon; the Oasis Saloon; H. M. Norris, Attorney at Law; the Deputy Sheriff's office. Small boys chased each other, dogs chased small boys, cowboys guffawed and slapped backs, a few fashionably dressed men and women sat on benches under the wooden awnings and on the raised veranda of the Cattleman's Hotel. A few obvious cathouse girls strolled arm in arm trying to look respectable. A small brass band tuned up on a platform knocked together out of raw lumber. The saloon doors swung in and out as though actuated by clockwork. Saddled horses at the hitchracks shied nervously at the racket of shouting and the crackle of firecrackers.

Almost without exception, the cowboys and miners were bearded — an astonishing assortment of goatees, Vandykes, sideburns, and just plain bush.

Joe's gaze made a full sweep of the plaza and did not discover the post office. While Mabel jerked nervously at the halter rope, Joe reached down and touched the shoulder of a passing man, who looked at him inquiringly.

Joe said, "Where's the post office?"

The man said something unintelligible in the racket, and pointed. Joe looked down a narrow side street and saw the sign and pulled Brownie's head around.

In front of the adobe building was a clear space bounded by two signs — KEEP CLEAR and STAGE STOP.

There was no room at the hitchrack, so Joe got a Mexican kid to hold Brownie and Mabel, got his sample sacks from the saddlebags, and went in. He got shipping tags and a stamped envelope and addressed them to Mike Burnham, Kentucky Bar, Prescott, Arizona, and wrote the return address: Joe Dyer, General Delivery, Spanish Wells, New Mexico. He had everything ready just as the stage, a big Packard touring car, careened around the corner scattering kids and dogs and creating panic along the hitchracks. A placard behind the windshield said "U.S. Mail," and on the dusty tonneau was lettered SILVER CITY – DEMING – LAS CRUCES – EL PASO.

Joe stepped out into the heat of the street. The stage driver clashed the gears and wheeled out into the traffic.

Mabel plunged and reared and the Mexican kid jerked her down and called her a dirty name in Spanish.

Joe fumbled in his meager supply of Spanish and said, "*Guardar mi caballo?* Ten cents?"

The kid said, "Sure, I watch him. Two bits."

Joe gave him the quarter. "Where'll I find bacon and flour and maybe some underwear and socks?"

The horseguard said, "Emporium. They got everything."

Joe's impression of Spanish Wells was not favorable. He'd have a few drinks and a steak, buy what he needed, and get a room at the Cattleman's Hotel. He hoped Mike would show up in a hurry, or at least write soon and say what he wanted to do about the gold claim. Joe couldn't see hanging around Spanish Wells very long.

He pushed his way into the Oasis, where drinkers were two deep along the bar, and had to wait for a shot of bad whiskey. His sour face as he downed it seemed to annoy the bartender, who said, "Mister, you don't like it, you're free to go somewhere else."

"I will," Joe said. "Else I'll puke."

The bartender started a glaring match. Joe waited to make sure that was all the man intended to do, then turned and walked out. The heat hit him, and the noise of the hilarity in the plaza battered his ears.

A cowboy walked hurriedly past, surrounded by a jeering crowd of small boys. People stopped to watch him pass, grinning and catcalling. The cowboy, cleanly dressed and clean-shaven, was soaking wet. Water dripped from him, puddling on the gritty plank walk.

More kids came hurrying to catch up with those jeering at the cowboy. One of them yelled, "Here's another one! Yay! Yay! Here's another one! Get Dutch Hauser!"

Startled, Joe saw that they were gathering around him, capering and making faces and screeching at him. Cowboys and miners were joining the gang of children.

TWO

They grabbed his arms from behind and took his gun. Joe lunged and got one arm free and rammed his fist into a jeering mouth and a tangle of red beard. They hustled him into the plaza. Somebody yelled, "Cal! Hey, Cal! Over here!" Everyone seemed to be converging on him.

Four or five of them held him in the center of the plaza while the others made way for a skinny cowboy whose wispy beard was almost white, as was the lank and stringy hair hanging over his pale blue eyes.

"Man, where's your beard?" the pale cowboy said, laughing. The man holding Joe's right arm relaxed his grip and Joe wrenched the arm free and knocked Whitey flat. There was a roar from the crowd. Somebody slugged Joe in the kidneys.

The cowboy got up, patted his split lip, and looked at the blood. Those around Joe jammed his right fist up between his shoulder blades. The pale-haired cowboy worked his mouth and spat blood and said, "Mister, it's all just fun, see? You know the rules. Everybody grows a beard for the celebration." He was close enough so Joe caught the reek of booze.

Joe said, "I just rode in. I didn't know anything about your goddamn . . ."

"No excuses," the pale cowboy said. "Been in the papers for a month!"

The crowd began to yell, "The horse trough! The horse trough!" in a rhythmic chant. The bass drum on the bandstand began to thump, setting the cadence.

Joe wrenched at the hands holding him, but couldn't get free. A huge grinning cowboy bulled his way through to Joe, yellow teeth showing in the bird's nest of black beard.

"Outa the way there! Beard Committee! Make way!"

The crowd yelled, "Yay, Dutch! Yay, Dutch!"

The fat cowboy's shirttail was out and an expanse of fat, hairy belly hung over the buckle of his gunbelt. He grinned and waved his clasped hands over his head. His grimy Stetson rode far back on a clump of kinky brown hair.

"Turn him loose!" he yelled. "Gotta be fair, now! He ain't been tried an' convicted yet!"

They let Joe go. He touched his empty holster, then stood with his shoulders hunched and fists knotted. The slob lurched a little sideways, regained his balance and let go a windy belch. The crowd laughed. Dutch patted his bare belly and nodded around to the crowd like a politician after a speech, then faced Joe in mock seriousness, brows drawn down over his close-set, chocolate eyes.

"Mister," he said, "you're charged with non-growin' of beard, in d'fiance of th' rules of th' c'mittee."

Joe faced the men who had been holding him. Through clenched teeth he said, "Somebody hand me my gun. Then get the hell outa my way!"

Dutch's thick paw clamped onto his shoulder and spun him around. Joe tried to get a grip on his raging temper.

"Listen," Joe said, making an effort to keep it mild, "I just rode in. I just want to get a little grub and get the hell out. Now, if somebody'll give me my gun back . . . "

The slob wagged an admonishing finger and said, "Oh, no! You broke the rule, friend. You get ducked in the horse trough!"

"Mister," Joe said, "how could I know the rules? I never been here before. I never even knew Spanish Wells existed. Now, have your fun, but I'm going to . . . "

"Oh, oh! Now you insulted the whole town! Never heard of our whole goddamn half a century of progress?" He made a large gesture with his ham hand and almost fell down. "You hear that, fellow citizens of Spanish Wells?"

"Duck him! Duck him!" The crowd sounded as one voice.

When the racket let up a little, Dutch said, "Well, you got the verdict, man! Boys, do your duty! For th' Beard C'mittee, an' ol' Dutch Hauser, chairman!"

They grabbed Joe, but he shook loose and stepped close to Dutch.

"You goddamn bucket of hog fat," he grated, "get out of my way!"

Dutch's fat face went ugly. "Now you done contempt of court, too. Gonna fine you drinks all around. Grab him, Cal!" Dutch made the mistake of resting his hand on his gun.

Joe whipped out the skinning knife and put the point against the overflow of hairy belly. He said, "Any man touches me, I shove it in! So grab on, boys!"

Some kids laughed and there was a dogfight somewhere, but otherwise, not a sound in the plaza of Spanish Wells.

Joe said, "Everybody move back!"

Nobody moved. Joe pushed a little with the knife. Dutch tried to suck in his fat gut. He squalled, "Do what he says!"

Men shuffled backward, and there was a clear space of ten feet or so around Joe and Dutch. Joe turned the blade over, moved it down until it stopped against Dutch's gunbelt, and ripped downward. The severed belt dropped and the holstered gun thumped on the ground. Joe switched the knife to his left hand and picked up the gun and shoved it into his own holster.

He passed the knife to his right hand again and grabbed Dutch's beard and made a sudden swipe with the knife under the fat man's chin, clipping off a great fistful of whiskers.

"Dutch," he said, "you're not wearing enough beard. Go jump in the trough!" Dutch began to back away with Joe following close, crowding him with the knife an inch from his belly. Dutch turned and trotted to the wooden trough, where the main street entered the plaza. The crowd parted to let them through.

Dutch climbed in, barely able to squeeze his great rump between the mossy sides of the trough.

"All the way down!" Joe ordered, and he pushed down on Dutch's head with his left hand, shoving hard while the water overflowed. He jammed Dutch's head down between his knees and held it under water while the great arms thrashed. He seized the thick hair and pulled Dutch's head up. He let Dutch take a breath and shoved his head under again.

Behind him a man said, "Let him up!"

Joe didn't like the harsh arrogance of the voice. A cold recklessness began to rise in him, a calm rage that had scared him before, and scared him now. He sheathed the knife and let the fat man raise his head. While Dutch gasped and shook his head, Joe pulled the gun and turned around. The crowd began to jeer.

Ten feet away, the sheriff faced him, a big man, not as fat as Dutch, but going to seed in his late middle age. He was pretty far over the hill, but Joe didn't underestimate him.

The sheriff said, "You some kinda hard nose can't take a little fun? You git the hell out of this town!"

Joe said, "With my gun, or this one?"

The sheriff said, "Cal! Give him his gun!"

Cal walked out of the crowd and tossed Joe's gun at his feet.

Joe said, "Pick it up!"

The sheriff said, "Boy, you're askin' for trouble."

"Yeah, I know," Joe said. "Cal, pick it up."

Cal picked up the gun by the butt and looked as if he wanted to use it. Joe didn't say anything. Cal flipped the pistol in the air, caught it by the barrel, and handed it to Joe. He backed up three steps and stood glowering with his fists on his hips. Joe walked toward him and he didn't move. Joe kept coming, and Cal's stare wavered, and suddenly he swore and stepped aside.

The crowd made way for Joe. Behind him, the sheriff said, "Don't ever come back, tough boy, 'less you figure you got *me* bluffed."

When Joe walked up the side street to where the Mexican kid held his horse and mule, his hands were shaking. He handed Dutch Hauser's gun to the kid and said, "Give it to Dutch, will you?"

The kid took it, and asked, "Why'n't you cut his guts out? Somebody gonna do it."

"You, maybe?" Joe asked.

"Maybe. Some Mexican gonna cut the *tripas* out of that fat one!"

Joe rode west out of town.

The thing to do was just keep heading west till he hit a town, write Mike Burnham another letter, and wait for the reply.

That was a fool thing to do, back in Spanish Wells. Hadn't had that steak. Hadn't even got his flour and bacon. All he'd got out of it was one slug of awful whiskey and a queasy stomach — not from the whiskey, but from thinking about what could have happened, there in the plaza. He should have taken his ducking and kept his mouth shut.

But he never could stand being pushed around.

THREE

The road climbed out of the sage and creosote flats into low foothills studded with scrubby junipers. Didn't look like much for cow country — nothing like his 640 acres north of Prescott, where the grass was belly-high to a tall horse. It looked better ahead, though, the land still rising and piñons beginning to show. He could head south and hit Lordsburg, but he was of a mind to get back into Arizona, get as far as Duncan, and go on tomorrow and wait in Safford for Mike's letter.

As he kept climbing, the country got better, and he wondered why he didn't see any sign of cattle. The day was getting along, and this time of year it would be dark by six. Already there was a bite in the air. He stopped Brownie and got down and changed the Levi jacket for the sheepskin. Riding again, he began to worry about where he'd stop. Then, way ahead, he saw a windmill.

When he came to the ranch gate, he could hardly read the name painted on the plank overhead between the two peeled poles. It had been there a long time — THE SPADE BIT. He didn't have to turn Brownie; the buckskin was as eager as he for food and rest.

It was a quarter of a mile before he came to the buildings, and he hadn't seen man, horse, or cow. This was a big outfit, judging from the wagon shed and the blacksmith shop, the big barn, the cookhouse and corral, but mainly from the size of the bunkhouse. There were two horses in the corral and only one man in sight, in the doorway of the bunkhouse watching Joe ride up.

Joe kept both hands on the saddlehorn and waited to be asked. They looked each other over. The man was a short, broad Mexican in well-worn, clean clothes – faded blue wool shirt, Levi's, good boots, vest without buttons, and a heavy Mexican sombrero of straw. Maybe forty years old, with a little gray in the black hair, the face dark mahogany, the eyes as black as the heavy brows. The man grinned and said, "What you waitin' for? Get off!"

Joe grinned and got down and held out his hand. "Joe Dyer," he said. "Been up in the hills to make my fortune in gold. Didn't find anything. I'm starving."

"Santos Camargo. At your service." His handshake was only a brief clasp of fingers.

He helped Joe strip the buckskin and the mule. "You got eye for good horse," he said.

"Well, I been around 'em some," Joe said. "All right to get a little hay?"

"In barn," Camargo said. "Bring can of barley, too."

Brownie and Mabel were rolling, raising the dust, when Joe got back with a big forkful of hay. He went back to the barn for the barley, and when he came back, Camargo was watering the animals. As Brownie began to feed, Joe got a grain sack from the fence rail and rubbed him down. Camargo got another and began to work on Mabel.

Joe said, "She isn't used to being pampered."

"Pamper? What that mean? She good girl. Good girls, you gotta treat 'em good, eh?"

Camargo picked up Joe's bedroll and walked into the bunkhouse. "Any place you want," he said, as Joe looked around.

There was a pine table with playing cards scattered on it, and in the back of the barnlike room was a cold, potbellied stove and a stack of wood. A swift glance showed Joe twelve bunks. Nine of them were not in use, their thin mattresses bare.

On the right side, two bunks had dirty, wadded-up blankets on them, and wooden boxes nailed to the wall above, holding razors, dirty socks, and a few sacks of makings. Levi jackets and chaps hung from nails in the wall, and work-worn boots and dirty underwear had been kicked under the bunks.

The bunk by the door on the left side was neatly made up, covered with a brilliant blanket that didn't look Navajo — maybe Chimayó or Tarahumara. Beside the bunk was a small, painted dresser on which stood a plaster Virgin of Guadalupe. Above the dresser hung a framed photograph of Pancho Villa, not in his accustomed dress of breeches and leather puttees, suit jacket and campaign hat, but in full charro dress, with the big felt sombrero, the short jacket, hip-length leggings, and cartridge belts over his shoulders and around his waist. He sat a beautiful horse. The printed caption said, *"El Centauro del Norte, montado en su famoso 'Tragaleguas' (Caballo de Guerra)."*

On the wall at the head of the bunk hung a leather jacket, shotgun chaps, and spurs that must have weighed a pound apiece, with their silver inlay and five-inch rowels. A bone-handled, singled-action Colt's hung in a holster on a shellbelt.

"Take any bunk you want," Camargo said and sat on the neat bunk by the door. "Only three of us here, now."

Joe put his saddle, with the saddlebags and slicker and rifle scabbard still attached, under the bunk next to Camargo's, and hung the sheepskin and the Levi jacket on nails in the wall. He opened his bedroll and spread out his blankets.

Camargo said, "There's towel an' basin outside."

"Thanks," Joe said, and stepped outside. The sun was down and the chill struck through his army shirt. There was a tin basin on a bench under a faucet, and a clean towel on a nail. Joe washed his face and hands. As he was drying them, someone began banging a triangle over the hill behind the bunkhouse.

Santos Camargo came out and said, "Boss cut the crew a while ago. Only three of us an' him, now. So he close cookhouse, too. We eat up at big house. He doin' the cookin' himself."

Joe thought that maybe to be polite he ought to shuck the Colt's. He unbuckled the belt, stood there a moment, then fastened it again. Camargo said, "Sure, keep it on. I would, too. Come on."

He led onto a path that went behind the bunkhouse.

The adobe ranch house sat under tall, bare cottonwoods — a big place with a portal of pine-log columns along a veranda, clear across the front. Small, many-paned windows reflected the afterglow of a pale sunset. Camargo led him around to the side and opened a door into a vast kitchen, warm with the heat of a big, black range and the yellow light of four kerosene lamps in wall brackets.

A tall man wearing a flour sack for an apron turned from the range as Camargo and Joe entered. Camargo said, "This Joe Dyer. He gonna eat with us an' sleep in bunkhouse tonight."

The man said, "I'm Frank Pritchard. I bet this is the first time you ever had a ranch owner cooking for you. Don't worry, I'm pretty good. Glad to have you." He shook Joe's hand with a firm grip.

Joe said, "Looks like I hit bonanza," and nodded at the table, where there were hot soda biscuits in a clean flour sack on a platter, and a smoking pot of beans. He could smell the steaks frying.

Pritchard said, "Sit over there, Dyer," and turned to Camargo. "The boys come in yet?"

"No, Mr. Pritchard. They still in town, gettin' drunk."

Joe took a good look at Pritchard — a tall man, broad of shoulder, ruddy, graying at the temples, just shy of being too handsome. A pleasant and affable man, well dressed — and, Joe thought, maybe a little hard to figure.

Pritchard brought the steaks and a steaming coffeepot from the range and sat down and said, "Help yourself. You just traveling, Dyer?"

Joe slid a thick steak onto his plate and speared two biscuits and answered, "I've been up in the hills looking for color. Found a few placer pockets last year but couldn't hit it again."

"You look more like a cowman than a prospector," Pritchard said and waited expectantly.

Joe didn't like being questioned, but he supposed that if you fed a man and took him under your roof, you had a right to ask about him.

He said, "Everybody in Arizona gets gold fever once in a while. I hit a little color last year, enough to buy me a few acres, so I went out again hoping to get enough to stock it with cows. I got skunked."

"Whereabouts in Arizona?"

"A few miles out of Prescott," Joe said, and refilled his coffee cup.

"Prescott. I know a few people there," Pritchard said. "Does Kellog still own the Palace Bar?"

What the hell is this? Joe thought. Wasn't any Kellog ever owned the Palace.

"Never heard of him," he said — and thought, and you never did either!

"What do folks in Arizona think about Agua Prieta?" Pritchard asked. The abrupt change of subject was startling.

"Agua Prieta?" Joe asked. "You mean across the line from Douglas?"

"Pancho Villa's attack," Pritchard explained and looked at him expectantly.

"I don't know anything about it," Joe said.

"Villa attacked it with sixty-five hundred men, about ten days ago. General Calles slaughtered them.

Scattered the survivors into the sierra. A damn good thing, I say. Mean to say you haven't heard of it?"

"I guess you forgot," Joe said. "I told you I was in the mountains. Haven't seen a paper in two months."

"Oh, yes," Pritchard said. "Well, I just wondered what you Arizonans think about Villa. Personally, I think he'a rabid dog. Just a ragged bandit out of the hills, a brutal killer."

Santos Camargo said angrily, "Mr. Pritchard, you got no right to . . . " then shut up and resumed eating.

"Well, I never paid him much mind," Joe said. "I remember that picture of him and General Scott arm in arm that time in El Paso, and everybody cheering for him when he fought against that . . . Huerta, was it? I can't keep 'em straight — Díaz, Huerta, Madero, Carranza — nor who assassinated who. I'm not much interested in what happens down there."

"Every American ought to be interested, Dyer. Wilson has recognized the Carranza administration, and the Mexicans ought to accept that and settle down. Or we ought to take over the country and run it right."

"I'm too busy scratching for a living to get stirred up about Mexico," Joe said. "Let 'em knock each other off."

Santos Camargo shoved back his chair and said angrily, "Pancho Villa is very great man. He beat Calles there at Agua Prieta until dirty gringo army across line in Douglas, blind his men with searchlight, an' cut 'em up with machine guns. You wanna take Mexico, why you don't come 'cross border an' try it, 'stead of stay safe across the line an' murder good men? Maybe you get some surprise! Maybe Pancho Villa take back New Mexico when he finish Caranza!"

"Now, now, Santos! Nothing personal in what I said!" Pritchard seemed anxious to soothe the feelings of his hired hand. He went on, "Every man has a right to his opinion." He turned and smiled at Joe. "Only it seems

Dyer doesn't have one. Probably his interests are outside politics."

Joe was tired of the prodding, if it was prodding and not just simple curiosity. "I've got no interests at all right now, except getting a night's sleep and moving on," he said.

Pritchard smiled broadly at him. "And you're a little sore at the questions. Well, Dyer, I know the tradition . . . west of the Mississippi you never ask a man's business or name, you just take him in and feed him and don't bother about what he might be."

Joe's temper blazed, but he spoke evenly enough. "Mr. Pritchard, that was a good dinner, and I had hay and grain for my horse and mule. I'll pay up and move on. How much?" He shoved back his chair and started to get up.

Pritchard grabbed his sleeve and laughed.

"Now don't get sore! I never could see any sense in this tight-mouthed secrecy if a man's got nothing to hide. We're in a backwater here, don't get many visitors. You ride in and tell me you've been prospecting in country not as promising as your home diggings. You don't show any samples or dust. Nevertheless, you probably told the truth. But you might be anything at all – fugitive, gunrunner for Pancho Villa, Pinkerton bounty hunter. Is there any reason why I shouldn't try to find out?"

"Well, yes, there is, seems to me," Joe said. "Same reason I haven't asked you how come a bunkhouse for twelve hands only has three men in it, and how come there isn't a cow in sight. Only I don't ask you, because it's none of my goddamn business."

Pritchard's eyebrows went up. "You make your point very well," he said. "So I won't ask you whether those two little holes in the flap of your shirt pocket are where you pin your badge. Nor whether you're a detective for the Cattlemen's Association, or a deputy U.S. marshal."

"Listen, goddamn it!" Joe said. "I'm nothing but . . . oh hell! I fastened the pocket with a safety pin because the button's gone and I didn't want to lose my Bull Durham sack."

Pritchard laughed. "Just idle curiosity, Dyer. Have a drink before you turn in?"

"On top of that dinner it would be wasted. Thanks all the same." Joe got up and said good night. Camargo went out with him.

In the bunkhouse, Camargo lit the lamp — a fancy rig with a green shade that hung over the table and could be raised or lowered. He sat on his bunk to pull off his boots.

Camargo said, "Mr. Pritchard got no right sayin' bad things 'bout Pancho Villa!" He was still mad.

"Well, I don't know whether Villa's a hero or a traitor," Joe remarked.

"Madero, he was fine man," Camargo said. "He rich, but he work for poor people. An' that bastard Huerta murder him. An' now Carranza is president, but he not for people. He for Venustiano Carranza. And Pancho Villa, he fight them all. He win *revolución* for Carranza at Torreón and Zacatecas. Then Carranza set his big general on Pancho Villa . . . that's Obregón. An' Obregón, he sit behind trenches at Celaya. He got barb wire, he got machine gun, so Pancho Villa, he got beat. So he fight again, up here at Agua Prieta. An' he win, too. He beat that General Calles. Only goddamn dirty gringo army across the *línea fronteriza* in Douglas, an' they shoot with machine gun. United States president, son of bitch Wilson, he let Calles bring army through Texas an' go into Agua Prieta through Douglas. But don't you worry! Pancho Villa, he not beat. Nobody beat him! He gonna win!"

Well, Joe thought, you're so goddamn stirred up, why don't you go down there and fight for Pancho Villa? But he didn't ask. Instead, he asked why Camargo hadn't taken the day off with the other two hands and gone into Spanish Wells to get drunk.

"Oh," Camargo answered, "I'm wrong color. Them two son of bitch don't like Mexicans. They callin' me 'greaser' an' '*cholo*.' You got any Mexican where you live, over there in Arizona?"

"Sure," Joe said. "My next door neighbor, name of Chávez, he loaned me his men to dig my well. And I went to school with Eddy Murguía and Danny Quevedo. We worked together on the Cloverleaf Ranch. Had a Yaqui puncher, too, and two Apaches; they were all top hands."

"You like them all right?" Camargo asked.

"Hell, yes," Joe said. "Why wouldn't I?"

"Okay," Camargo said. "Put out lamp, okay?"

Joe hung his gunbelt on the nail at the head of the bunk and peeled down to his longjohns and blew out the lamp. He thought he'd be awake all night with Camargo's snoring, which started immediately.

The next thing he knew, he was sitting up wondering what had awakened him. He knew by the feel of the night that it was late, maybe four o'clock. Then he heard two horses coming, and mumble of voices, and a crazy-sounding laugh.

The riders stopped outside the bunkhouse, unsaddled, and turned their horses into the corral with a lot of staggering around and swearing, then came blundering in. One of them stumbled over to the table and lit six matches before he got the lamp going.

Joe swore softly and got the Colt's from under his pillow and held it under the blankets. The drunk was Cal, the pale cowboy from the plaza in Spanish Wells. Behind him, rocking on his feet, was the slob Dutch Hauser, with his black beard chopped off under the chin.

Hauser said, "Y'know, Cal, if that bastard with the knife hadn't cut off my beard, I'd've won . . . I'd've won th' . . . " His voice trailed off vaguely, his knees buckled, and he made a grab at the table. He straightened up and stared owlishly at Camargo, lying still in his bunk. "Hey, greaser! *Cholo!* You all tucked in your li'l beddy-bye, you nigger son of a bitch? Why'n't you git down an' pray t' your li'l plaster whore?"

Santos Camargo growled in his throat.

Cal grabbed Hauser's arm and said, "Look, Dutch! Over there!" and pointed at Joe.

Hauser lurched across to Joe's bunk and scowled, squeezing his eyes shut and opening them in an effort to concentrate. He recognized Joe and cursed and tugged clumsily at the gun on his hip. Joe, with the Colt's in his right fist, threw the blankets back, pulled back his right leg and kicked Hauser in the face with the flat of his foot.

Hauser staggered back, dropped his gun, crashed full length onto his back, and lay sprawled, with his eyes shut and his mouth open.

Cal Morgan called Joe a son of a bitch and bent into a crouch, with his hand on his gun.

Joe cocked the Colt's.

Cal stopped as though he had run into a wall.

Camargo, sitting up, laughed and said, "Go ahead, you white-eye piss ant! Jump him!"

Cal snatched his hand from his gun and backed away. Dutch Hauser snored raucously on the floor. Camargo said, "You' guts run out like the di'reah if that hog ain't backin' you up."

Cal picked up Hauser's gun and put it on the table, then stared down at Hauser and deliberately kicked him.

Hauser whimpered. Cal said, "Get up, you fat-ass hog!" but got no response. He spat on Hauser and walked to his bunk. He kept glancing over at Joe and the steady Colt's in Joe's fist as he straightened out his fusty blankets.

He then moved unsteadily to Hauser's bunk and pulled a blanket off, turned as though to carry it to the drunken hulk on the floor — then threw it back on the bunk and said, "So lay there an' freeze, you tub of guts!"

He unbuckled his shellbelt and hung it on a nail and took off his boots. As he climbed into his bunk, Joe got up and picked up his own boots.

"What you doin'?" Camargo demanded.

Joe said, "I'm leaving. I ran into those two in town, and we had a little set-to. I don't want to be shot in bed."

"They gonna sleep till noon," Camargo said, "an' wake up with head like watermelon, heave guts a few times an' go to sleep again. You have good breakfast, early, an' ride after." He nodded toward Cal. "That *hideputa* sleepin' a'ready."

Joe thought it over. He'd have a hard time packing in the dark, and he didn't know the road. He looked over at Cal, who was on his back, already snoring.

"All right, Santos."

"*No le hace,*" Camargo said. "Don't worry. Cal Morgan ain't no danger, only if he with Dutch. He got no guts."

Joe lay a while with the gun in his hand. Cal Morgan snored, Dutch Hauser snored, Camargo's mattress rustled, and a coyote began to screech a long way off.

Joe got out of bed and blew out the lamp.

Camargo said, "Hey, maybe better leave it on, eh?"

"No," Joe said. "He could draw down on me from over there. In the dark, he'll have to come to me. Santos, if you gotta go pee, you sing out. Because if anything moves in this room, I shoot. And if you're listening, Cal, you better believe it!"

He got back into the bunk and was asleep in five minutes.

The blast of the shot, the incredible, shocking detonation, seemed to blow him out of the bunk. He stood crouched with the gun cocked in his hand before he was fully awake. There was only silence, dead silence, with his ears ringing and the stink of burned powder in his nostrils.

Camargo said, "Wha . . . ? *Qué pasó?*"

Joe heard him climb out of his bunk. There was a spurt of flame as he wiped a match alight and took the lamp chimney off and lit the wick. Cal Morgan, sitting on his huddle of blankets with his pale eyes staring at Joe, yelled, "You *shot* the son of a bitch!"

Dutch Hauser's smoking pistol was on the floor beside him. The fat man still lay on his back as though asleep – but there was blood leaking from his left ear.

FOUR

Santos Camargo stared Joe, then swiveled his head to look at Cal. He walked back to his bunk with his chin on his shoulder and his black eyes darting from Joe to Cal, and felt for the gunbelt hanging on the nail. He got the gun and said, "I go get Pritchard."

He sat on the bunk and tugged his right boot on with one hand, shifted the gun to his other hand and got the left boot on.

Cal hadn't taken his eyes off Joe. He said, "Mister, drop that gun!"

"There's only one way you'll get it," Joe said.

"Santos!" Cal said, his voice high-pitched. "Get his gun!"

Camargo said, "I go for Pritchard," and got up and sidestepped to the door.

At that moment, Frank Pritchard shoved the door open and came in. He, too, had a gun in his hand. A striped flannel nightshirt was stuffed into his pants. He stared down at the dead mound of meat on the floor.

"You, Santos?" he asked.

"Not me!" Camargo said.

Cal Morgan, staring at Joe, said, "Him! Make him drop his gun."

"Why would *he* kill Dutch?" Pritchard asked. "Dutch get tough with him?"

"There was trouble in town yesterday afternoon," Cal said. "He was gonna kill Dutch with a knife."

"Now just hold on," Pritchard said. "Put your guns down, the both of you." He looked at Camargo. "You, too, Santos. It *wasn't* you, was it?"

"Not me, Mr. Pritchard. One of them two. Was in the dark."

Pritchard said to Joe, sharply, "Put that gun down!"

"Three of you with guns in your hands, and I lay mine down?" Joe said. He backed to his bunk and sat on it, with the Colt's cocked in his right fist. "You gonna take it, Pritchard?"

Pritchard's face went dark with anger. He stepped around the carcass on the floor to sit in a chair at the table.

"What's this about Spanish Wells yesterday afternoon?" he asked.

"Just a little fun," Cal said. "You know, the beard growin' contest for the celebration. Well, he rode in without no beard, and the boys were gonna duck him in the horse trough, only he got ugly and pulled a knife and was gonna cut Dutch's guts out. Tom Kincaid run him out of town. And he come here and laid for us and shot Dutch in the dark."

"That the way it was, Dyer?" Pritchard asked.

"Not by a long shot," Joe said. "I rode in to Spanish Wells to get some grub and they grabbed me and got my gun, and that pile of meat on the floor there said they were gonna duck me because I didn't have a beard. Only I wouldn't play. They were too stupid to get my skinning knife, and I cut Dutch's beard off and walked him to the trough and ducked him. Then that has-been sheriff horned in and I left."

"And came here and ambushed my foreman and shot him!" Pritchard said.

"How would I know he'd come here?" Joe said. "I never heard of him . . . or the Spade Bit Ranch, or you. Why single *me* out?"

"This isn't a trial," Pritchard said. "Somebody has to go for the sheriff."

"Me, I go," Camargo said and reached for his pants.

"No," Pritchard said. "Stick around, Santos. You saddle up, Cal."

Cal Morgan got out of his bunk and tugged his boots on.

Joe said, "Pritchard, how you know you'll ever see him again? Why don't we all ride in together, then nobody gets away till this is straightened out."

"Cal and Dutch had a few arguments," Pritchard answered, "but Cal wouldn't have shot him."

Cal buckled on his gunbelt. "I don't like leavin' you here with these two, Frank," he said.

"Now you're not so sure it was me, huh?" Joe said. "Might've been Camargo, huh?"

Cal said, "You both better hand your guns to Frank."

Joe laughed at him.

"Santos!" Cal said sharply. "You heard me!"

"Chíngate, güero!" Camargo said.

Cal's face flushed pink.

"I'll be all right," Pritchard said. "Santos will give me his gun, and I think I can persuade Dyer when you leave. He doesn't seem to trust you."

Joe said, "You want this Colt's, you take it off me. That's the only way you'll get it. But I'm going nowhere with a murder charge hanging over me."

Cal put on a jacket and went out, and they heard him swearing at his horse in the corral. The lamplight paled as gray daylight seeped in. Presently Cal rode out.

Pritchard glanced down at the carcass of Dutch Hauser. He said, "Hitch up a wagon, Santos, and take him out somewhere and bury him."

"No!" Joe said. "He stays right where he is."

"We can tell Kincaid what happened," Pritchard said. "He doesn't smell so good, lying there leaking at both ends."

"So let's get out of here," Joe said. "But he stays where he is."

Pritchard didn't like the tone. He stared into Joe's eyes without expression for a moment, then said, "Just as well wait up at the house. I'll get some breakfast."

Joe and Camargo pulled their clothes on, with Pritchard watching. Joe said, "What's the matter, you afraid we're going to run for it? Well, I'm not. Not till somebody gets nominated for a hanging. And I'll make damn sure Camargo stays."

Camargo grinned at him. "You saved me lotta trouble, 'cause I woulda kill him some day. About one more time he call me '*cholo*.' "

"Well, Pritchard," Joe said, "that's plain enough. What do you think, now?"

"I don't think he'd talk like that if he did it," Pritchard said.

Nobody had much to say at breakfast, until Pritchard said Dutch hadn't been too bad. Sure, he was loud and overbearing and he didn't like Mexicans, but he wasn't vicious, and he had been a hardworking foreman.

"Foreman of what?" Joe asked. "Don't look like much for a ramrod to do around here."

"Whole trouble was his mouth," Camargo said. "He don' know how to keep it shut."

Joe got up to go and feed Brownie and Mabel. As he tended to them, he was thinking that everyone sure wanted him disarmed. Only Camargo knew he had the carbine, and maybe he wouldn't notice if it was gone from under the bunk. He went to the bunkhouse and got his Winchester in its scabbard. He had no immediate plans for it. But it might come in handy.

The day was warming up, and flies swarmed around the carcass of Dutch Hauser. The stink was bad already. Joe carried the carbine around to the rear corner of the bunkhouse, where there was a space between the ground and the floor joists. He shoved the carbine back out of sight. There was a pile of lumber beside the blacksmith shop, and he got a weathered piece of one-by-ten to cover the opening.

When he went up to the house, Pritchard and Camargo were in the kitchen, and they all sat drinking coffee until about eleven o'clock, when they heard two horses coming.

Joe said, "Now, listen, Pritchard . . . Camargo . . . that sheriff doesn't like me worth a damn. Just tell it the way it happened, and don't go giving him any fancy stories or smart guesswork. Your weren't there when Dutch got shot, Pritchard, so you won't have much to tell . . . only what we all said after you got there. You go any farther than that, and I guarantee you'll regret it."

Pritchard's face darkened. He said, "Goddamn you, Dyer, don't threaten me!"

"I just did," Joe said.

Cal Morgan and Sheriff Tom Kincaid got down and came into the kitchen. Kincaid looked everyone over with those hard, blue marble eyes.

"All right, Dyer," he said. "I'll take the gun."

"No, you won't," Joe said. "Not unless you show me a warrant."

Cal shifted his feet nervously. Kincaid turned away, and said, "We'll all go down to the bunkhouse."

"So, no warrant," Joe said and got up.

The session in the bunkhouse didn't take long. Kincaid had, of course, had the story, with embellishments, from Cal Morgan. He asked questions and made notes on the back of an envelope. Cal and Camargo and Joe agreed as to the sequence of events, while Pritchard told about the shot waking him up at five in the morning, and his pulling on his pants and boots and running down to the bunkhouse. Joe walked over and leaned against the wall beside the door.

When Pritchard got through talking, Kincaid said, "All right. Take him out and bury him somewhere." He got up from the chair at the table and turned to Joe. "Okay, Dyer, saddle up."

"Why me?" Joe demanded. "Cal kicked him in the belly while he was lying there passed out. Camargo said if someone else hadn't done it, he'd've shot the bastard himself."

The sheriff said, "I saw you workin' on Dutch with a knife in the plaza, and heard you slingin' threats around. You'll do, for a starter. You hand me that gun and get ready to ride. It's plain enough you come out here after that ruckus in town and watched your chance and just plugged him."

"When I rode into Spanish Wells," Joe said, "I didn't even know what town it was. Ask the postmaster. I never saw Dutch before. Why the hell would I kill him?"

Kincaid said, "You got tough with me, too. I've seen a lot of you hotheads, ready to start shootin' just 'cause you figure somebody insulted you."

"Look," Joe said. "It was *him* that crawled. Not me! If I'd wanted to prove anything, why I guess I did it. I never even heard of the Spade Bit Ranch. How would I know he belonged here?"

"Anybody could've told you after I run you out of the plaza," Kincaid said. "Get a lawyer. Argue with *him*. But you're comin' with me, now."

"Hold on!" Joe's tone of voice stopped the sheriff. Joe said, "I could've run for it . . . any time this morning."

"You're too smart for that," Kincaid said. "Now quit wasting time."

Joe said, "Huh-uh!" He let his hand hang by his gun. "You swear out a charge, all legal and proper, then come get me. I won't be going anywhere."

He meant it, and everyone knew it. Sheriff Kincaid said, "Okay, Dyer. You're just fool enough to shoot it out. I'll be back with a warrant in the morning. I hope you make a run for it, so I'll have the pleasure of runnin' you down. Save the county the expense of a trial."

"Just bring the warrant," Joe said, "and nobody gets hurt."

Kincaid walked out and rode away.

Pritchard said, "Santos, hitch up a wagon. You and Cal take Dutch and bury him somewhere."

Santos Camargo said, "Mr. Pritchard, you do it you' own self." He walked out, too.

Pritchard cursed and said, "I swear, I'll fire him! Cal, get a couple of shovels. We'll take him to that draw behind the tank."

He stamped out angrily, and Cal Morgan got a blanket and threw it over the corpse. He leered at Joe and made the gesture of cutting his own throat. As he stepped to the doorway, Joe booted his butt as hard as he could swing his foot. Cal yelled and stumbled out and went to his knees. He glared back at Joe in fury. Joe leaned in the doorway, watching him get up and dust off his knees. Cal went toward the wagon shed, swearing under his breath.

After Pritchard and Cal came back from burying Hauser, the atmosphere was pretty strained, as the four of them sat in the kitchen drinking coffee. After dinner, when Joe got up to go to the bunkhouse, Santos Camargo gulped the last of his coffee and hurried to go with him.

The stain on the floor where Dutch Hauser had died had been covered with sand. Camargo lit the lamp and sat at the table.

Joe grinned at him. "When does the shift change? Midnight?"

Camargo laughed. "Yeah," he said. "Pritchard say we gotta keep eye on you. Cal gonna take my place."

"You think Cal's gonna stop me if I decide to ride?" Joe asked.

"Hell, no!" Camargo replied.

"What *did* happen in here last night, Santos?"

"Well," Camargo said, "if it was you, you crazy to stay around. That sheriff an' Cal, they gonna hang you for it."

"So that means you didn't do it, or you'd be long gone right now?" Joe asked.

"Sure. You right. I didn't do it, so I'm stay here."

"Then you're sure it was me," Joe said.

"I don't know, Joe. You got some sense, I know that. So why you gonna kill dirty *mugrero* like that an' hang for him? You coulda kill him when he try to pull his gun last night, but all you do is kick in face. But Kincaid, he gonna prove you do it, if you did or you didn't."

"Well, that leaves Cal. Why would he kill his partner?"

"They not much partner," Camargo said. "Not real *compadres*. Dutch, he pretty bad when he drunk . . . Swear an' wanna fight, an' he hit Cal sometime. Cal scared of him, you bet. But Cal, he take it, an' they go to Spanish Wells an' get drunk alla time."

"Doesn't anybody ever *work* around here?" Joe demanded. "What do you do? What's Pritchard keep three hands for?"

Camargo looked away, and Joe thought he was going to treat the questions as though they hadn't been asked. But at length he said, "Well, right after I come here, Pritchard sell all his steer, big herd; he got good cash deal. Then he was gonna buy more steer cheap, down in Mexico, but Pancho Villa been raise hell over there, an' take all cow an' horse from them big *hacenda'os*, so he can't buy no herd. He's fire everybody an' just keep me an' Dutch an' Cal. You know, cut firewood, fix fence, grease windmill, all that stuff."

Joe said, "One fifteen-year-old kid could handle that."

Camargo switched to the former subject. "You know, if Cal don't make sheriff think you kill Dutch, then he gonna make him b'lieve I done it. It gonna be you or me."

"Cal was maybe too drunk to do it," Joe said. "So how do you prove it wasn't you?"

"He not so drunk when I light that lamp," Camargo said. "After him or you shoot. He talk okay then. Now, how you prove *you* didn't do it?"

"The old Mexican standoff, huh?" Joe said.

"Well," Camargo went on, "if you did, I don' give a damn. But you watch out for Cal, he gonna lie you into hangman's rope. An' that bullhead sheriff, you couldn't knock no sense into him with pick handle. Why you don' get some sleep? I gotta watch you till Cal come at midnight."

"This is pretty stupid," Joe said. "If I was a mind to go, I'd just bend my gun over your head."

Camargo stared at him, the friendliness gone. "You got good chance, right now."

"Oh, crap!" Joe said and went and stretched out on his bunk. "Wake me up before Cal comes on shift."

"Sure," Camargo said, then grinned at him. "I hope you hide that carbine where you get it quick. Maybe you gonna need it."

Joe couldn't think of an answer. He closed his eyes.

When Camargo shook his shoulder, he was instantly awake.

Camargo said, "Pretty near twelve. He gonna come pretty quick."

Joe got up and sat at the table, and in a few minutes Cal Morgan came in, sleepy and surly. He sat across from Joe, and Camargo said, "Well, have nice dreams, you two *pelados*."

Cal turned to look at him, and when he turned back Joe had the Colt's pointed at his chest. Joe said, "Stand up and turn around."

Stupid with surprise, Cal obeyed. Joe got up and got Cal's gun and put it on the table.

He looked over at Camargo, who had rolled up onto his elbow and was watching him. Joe said, "I'm going to tie him up. Any objection?"

Camargo said, "Me next? Then you gonna saddle up an' ride someplace, eh?"

Joe said angrily, "I don't think you'd shoot a man in the dark unless it was Dutch Hauser, but I don't trust this goddamn albino not to kill me and say I tried to run for it. Do I have to keep telling you I'm not leaving until this is settled?"

"Okay, then," Camargo said. He got out of his bunk. His pistol was in his hand. "Because I was gonna tell you you not gonna tie up Santos Camargo."

"If I thought I had to," Joe said, "I'd do it. Get me some baling wire, will you?"

Cal Morgan said in a high voice, "Goddamn you, Dyer, I'm gonna . . . "

"Shut up!" Joe said.

Camargo opened the top drawer of his dresser and got a padlock. "Lock him in saddle room. It got no windows," he said. "You gonna tie his mouth?"

"If he starts to holler, I'll break his head," Joe said. "Come on, Morgan."

Together they locked him in the saddle room beside the blacksmith shop, with the blankets from his bunk. When they returned, Camargo said, "Mr. Pritchard gonna be awful mad. Okay, we get some sleep, eh?" He pulled off his boots and got into his bunk. "You gonna blow out lamp?"

Joe slept soundly and woke with the crack of dawn.

Santos Camargo was gone, along with his leather jacket and dress-up boots, the plaster Virgin of Guadalupe, and the photograph of Pancho Villa.

Joe got up and pulled on his boots and went to the door, his breath smoking in the frosty morning. Brownie whinnied at him and Mabel hung her hammerhead over the corral gate. Camargo's saddle was gone from the fence rail, along with Pritchard's personal mount, a big sorrel that had looked as though it could run forever.

FIVE

When Joe unlocked the saddle room, Cal Morgan stepped out blinking and shivering. He said petulantly, "Goddamn you, you didn't have to lock me up! I was only gonna see you didn't get away. Pritchard said to. I wasn't gonna do nothin' to you."

"I'd trust you like a sidewinder," Joe said. "I didn't run away, see?"

Cal mumbled something and walked past, trailing the blankets draped around his shoulders.

"But Camargo did," Joe said. "On Pritchard's sorrel."

"Aw, bullshit!" Cal said. He went into the bunkhouse. "You tryin' to be funny? He just went up to the house for coffee."

In the doorway, Joe said, "Oh, sure! And took that plaster Saint Mary and the picture of Pancho Villa and his best boots up to the kitchen with him?"

Cal whirled and stared at Camargo's bunk. "Jesus!" he said. "Now you done it! You sure got the gift for gettin' in trouble. Pritchard's gonna throw a fit!" He picked up his gun from the table and trotted out, heading over the hill to the big house.

Joe washed, then fed the stock in the corral. Pritchard, unshaven and with his hair on end, came scurrying around the bunkhouse. "Cal says you locked him up and let Camargo get away!"

"Sure I locked him up. You think I want to get murdered in my sleep, like Dutch? But *I* didn't let Camargo go. That was his own idea . . . while I was asleep."

"Don't you see what this means, Dyer? Kincaid will have your scalp! Camargo shot Dutch!"

"Did he?" Joe said. "Yesterday everybody voted for me."

"Obviously we were wrong," Pritchard said. "You could have got away last night, but you didn't. Camargo has convicted himself."

Cal came running from the house, cramming food into his mouth. He carried two carbines and a belt of cartridges. Joe put up the gate bars and started to walk to the house.

"Hey!" Pritchard said. "Come on! Saddle up! We're going after him."

"Not me," Joe said. "When you lose him, come on back. I'll keep the coffee hot."

"I guess you're right," Pritchard conceded. "We'll have some breakfast and ride in and tell Kincaid."

He walked to the house with Joe, Cal trailing along. In the kitchen, Pritchard put wood in the stove and began to slice bacon.

Cal and Joe sat at the table. Joe said, "Cal, you got the sheriff convinced I killed Hauser. How do you figure that made Camargo cut and run for it?"

Cal flushed. "Guess I was wrong," he said grudgingly.

"Obviously Camargo did it," Pritchard said. He laid bacon in the pan, and stirred hotcake batter in a pitcher. "When you dropped in, a stranger, it gave him the perfect scapegoat. He said he was going to kill Dutch some day. I thought it was just talk. I guess he had enough provocation."

He turned the hotcakes, put bacon and beans on the table, and poured coffee. "He's got a long start," he said, "and he's one smart Mexican."

Joe said, "I'm riding in to see Kincaid. If he wasn't an obstinate fool, he'd've held all three of us, me and Cal *and* Camargo."

"Cal," Pritchard said, "you ride in with him. Kincaid's got it in his head that Joe's guilty. He'll never listen to Joe alone."

"I hope Camargo gets away," Joe said. "And the hell with Kincaid. I wouldn't bother, except he's probably got the warrant. I'm expecting a letter in town. May have to wait over, a day or two. Mind if I leave my mule and gear here till I head for home?"

"Sure, Dyer. I'm sorry I didn't see you were telling the truth all the time."

"No hard feelings," Joe said.

Cal said, around a mouthful of hotcakes, "I can save Kincaid a lot of trouble. He can just telegraph, and they'll nail Santos when he shows up. He'll head for El Paso. Got a young wife there he's crazy about."

"It's worth a try," Pritchard said. "You better ride."

Joe got his sheepskin coat and his saddlebags and buckled on his spurs. He thought about retrieving the hidden carbine, but he'd be coming back to the Spade Bit for his bedroll and Mabel. When he went to the corral and saddled Brownie, Cal Morgan was already mounted, fretting to start.

They were at a trot, about a mile down the road from the ranch gate, when Joe said, "Hold up a minute."

Impatiently, Cal pulled up. He said, "Come on, man, move!"

"He can't beat the telegraph," Joe said. "They'll nail him in El Paso. Now listen. Why didn't Pritchard come with us? Kincaid won't listen to me, and he knows you're a liar . . . but he'd listen to Pritchard."

"Well," Cal said, "that Mexican's smart. He could be laying up in the brush, just waitin' for all of us to go hoorawin' off to town. He knows where Pritchard keeps the money."

"What money? Doesn't Pritchard trust the bank?"

"Well," Cal said, "there's been some kinda monkey business goin' on . . . I don't stick my nose into it . . . But Pritchard keeps a lot of cash on hand." He gave Joe an odd, sidewise glance, and hesitated.

"What monkey business?" Joe demanded.

"Maybe somethin' that ties in with why Camargo shot Dutch."

Joe grabbed the bridle of Cal's horse. Cal spurred it, and it slung its head and circled, but Joe hung on.

"Goddamn you, why didn't you speak up when the sheriff was there? Tried your best to get me hung, you bastard, and all the time you knew . . . "

Cal turned in his saddle. "Here he comes, now," he said, with obvious relief.

Ahead, the morning sunlight slanting through the piñons threw flickering shadows on a rider rounding a bend. Tom Kincaid had got an early start from Spanish Wells.

Joe spurred ahead to meet Kincaid. He pulled Brownie to a sliding stop and faced the sheriff. He said, "Santos Camargo pulled out last night. He's your man. Cal says he's heading for El Paso."

"I *knew* you'd do it!" Kincaid yelled. "I left you loose, figurin' you'd run for it!" Kincaid pulled his gun. "Git your hands up! This time I'll take that gun!"

"Now wait, damn it!" Joe said and turned to look for Cal Morgan, who sat his horse twenty yards back, making no move to approach.

Joe turned back to Kincaid. "You goddamn bullhead fool! I said . . . "

"I heard you! What some gutless greaser does cuts no ice. Gimme the gun! You can read the warrant after. It's for murder!"

He pushed his horse up to Joe's right side, with his six-gun pointed at Joe's chest. "Git them hands up!"

Joe put them up. Kincaid shifted the gun to his left hand and reached for Joe's Colt's with the right. Joe jerked his hat off and slashed it across Kincaid's face.

The sheriff's horse lunged sideways. Kincaid made a grab for the saddlehorn, and before he could recover, Joe had his Colt's out.

"Drop it!" he said. Kincaid dropped his weapon and began to curse, a vicious string of filth.

Joe looked back at Cal, wondering why the hell he hadn't backed him up. Cal was drawing a deliberate bead on him with his .45. Joe rammed his right spur into Brownie. The buckskin squealed and jumped sideways. Cal fired, and the slug hit the road and went wailing off into the pines.

Joe threw two shots over his shoulder, as fast as he could pull the trigger. He heard Cal scream behind him, and hauled Brownie to a stop and looked back. Cal was down. He kept on screaming.

Kincaid was on hands and knees in the road, scrabbling for his gun under his frantic horse, which reared and jerked at the reins clutched in the sheriff's left hand.

Joe fired under the horse's belly, not trying to hit Kincaid, but to keep him from his gun. The horse plunged and smashed into Kincaid, knocking him flat.

Joe really gigged the buckskin then, and it squealed and almost jumped out from under him. The cantle hit him in the tailbone, and he reined Brownie down a bank, sliding in a small avalanche of gravel. They went hammering down a long slope, jumping windfalls and twisting among the piñons, with Joe just hanging on, letting Brownie go full out while he fended off branches with his elbows.

SIX

He let Brownie run until he slowed to a walk, and stopped him then and let him blow. He listened for sounds of pursuit, but heard none. Kincaid must have gone back to Spanish Wells to raise a posse, or perhaps he was taking care of Cal Morgan — or Cal's dead body — because now Joe might actually be the killer Kincaid said he was. Questions boiled in his mind, and there were decisions to make, but he thrust them aside.

For the rest of the morning he put distance between himself and the Spade Bit, concerned more with tangling his trail than with his direction of travel. He hadn't decided what that direction should be, anyway.

When the sun was overhead, he and Brownie had a drink at a little creek. He slipped the bridle and let the horse glean what it could of the sparse grass.

Where would Kincaid figure he would head for? Prescott, perhaps? Kincaid would realize he wouldn't make such a stupid move. He would have the roads watched, and alert any town that had a phone or a telegraph — which meant that Joe must reconnoiter any such community and check for poles and wires. He would not be able to avoid all human contact because he had no food and no canteen and no blankets — and no carbine. He couldn't live off the country.

Perhaps the greatest shock of his life had been when he turned to see why Cal wasn't beside him telling the sheriff that Santos Camargo had convicted himself by running — and found himself looking down the muzzle of Cal's .45. Had Cal needed to shut him up before he could talk to Kincaid? Had Cal, himself, shot Dutch Hauser? Had he been afraid of what might turn up if Joe were tried; if a smart lawyer were to dredge up facts and implications that no one at the Spade Bit wanted dredged up? This didn't seem likely, considering Camargo's flight. But maybe Camargo had simply run from the whole mess, believing that no Mexican would get justice in an American court, but would have the murder hung on him by a prejudiced sheriff, a biased jury, and a gringo judge. That is, if Camargo was actually innocent. But hating Dutch Hauser, and suddenly presented with a scapegoat, Santos Camargo almost had to be guilty.

The thing for Joe to do was to lose himself in some big town, get in touch with Mike Burnham, and plan from there. And it might as well be El Paso, because Camargo might be there. If Joe could find him, maybe he could force him to talk — maybe even get him to come back and testify, if indeed he was innocent. Or, if he was guilty, perhaps he would talk anyway, because he could easily slip into Mexico. He had seemed to be a decent man. Maybe he would give Joe information that would help him defend himself.

The best thing would be to head east, pick up grub at some ranch or mine before word of his flight got around, and stick to the mountains until he hit the Rio Grande, then follow the river south.

That night, famished, he slept in a deep ravine, huddled in his sheepskin beside a small fire, shivering in the December chill. Having taken the roughest route Brownie could negotiate, he had seen no sign of human activity except a tall column of yellow smoke east and south —

probably the smelter at Silver City — that gave him a fix on his location.

Midmorning of the next day, he rode down to a small mine, where a man was pushing a small car on insecure rails to a dump. The man had a partner, and Joe told them he was lost, and his pack mule had spooked and gone south with his blankets and grub. They gave him two cans of beans, and a couple of pounds of flour already mixed with baking soda in an empty tomato can. They didn't charge him for the meal of bacon and biscuits and canned tomatoes. Joe said he had to get after the mule and left, following a trail they pointed out, then cutting into the pines again. He kept going east, figuring it was about two hundred miles, give or take fifty, from the Spade Bit to El Paso, and he could make it in four days.

He risked riding down primitive trails and old logging roads, but whenever he came to a traveled road, he shied off and blundered through the hills and canyons again, keeping his generally eastward direction.

It took him three days before he got out of the hills and saw the Rio Grande. This was flat land, sparsely grown with yucca and sage and cactus that moved hardly at all in the ceaseless, dust-laden wind.

He turned south then, trying to keep the river in sight, but was frequently forced away from his course by long washes and rounded hills. The mountains, south and east, rose sharply, thrusting up into the blue — abrupt declivities of bare brown earth and naked rock. He came at dusk to a well-traveled road and risked riding it eastward, and late at night crossed the Rio Grande and rode into Las Cruces.

In a Mexican restaurant he ate tacos and bean burros, and bought a dozen tortillas and a couple of pounds of dried goat meat. The cook directed him to a store where he bought Levi's as stiff as two stovepipes, a blue chambray shirt, a cheap black hat, and two sleazy blankets.

He changed clothes and slept in an abandoned adobe shack and started on the forty-five mile ride to El Paso very early.

He rode into El Paso at dusk, along the streets that bordered the muddy river, hoping to find the Mexican section, Chihuahuita, which he had heard about. Across the river in Old Mexico, Ciudad Juárez showed a few lights. El Paso was the biggest town he had ever seen, more Mexican than Tucson.

There was much traffic — wagons and horsemen and pedestrians. Ahead, he could see a bridge, with streetcars crossing the river into Ciudad Juárez. Three blocks farther along was another bridge, with the traffic coming north.

A street light came on, a single, bare bulb, and another shone dimly five or six blocks ahead. There was the smell of charcoal fires and spiced cookery. The residences began to run to unplastered adobe shacks interspersed with chile parlors and taco joints and cantinas. This had to be the Mexican quarter, Chihuahuita — Little Chihuahua. He swung Brownie into a hitchrack in front of a cantina that was overshadowed by brick tenements on each side. Saddle horses stood tied in the bitter wind. A sign over the door was banging in the wind, and Joe made out the peeling lettering — EL CENTAURO DEL NORTE.

Stiff with cold, he got down and tied Brownie and went into the cantina.

On the right was a bar, where a man wearing a huge sombrero stopped talking to the bartender and turned to study Joe. All talk in the room stopped. Joe took his time looking around. The heat from a cast iron stove in the center of the room was almost tangible. Several men sat around the stove, and there were five others at a table playing cards. Against the rear wall was a sink crowded with unwashed dishes beside which was a tile *brasero* radiating an incandescence of glowing charcoal. A fat woman stood in front of it, tending the bubbling pots. On a table by the sink was a clot of meat, a pile of onions, and a stack of tortillas. At a small table by the left wall, two Mexicans sat in a fog of tobacco smoke, with a bottle between them.

Joe stepped over to the bar. The bartender said, "Yes, *señor*?"

Joe said, "Whiskey. Can I get something to eat?"

"Sit at table. Âmparo will come." He nodded toward the small table where the two drinkers sat watching Joe. Joe walked across the room a little uncertainly. The men got up and took their bottle. One of them said politely, "*Favor de sentarse, señor*," and nodded to his chair.

Joe said, "I don't want to push you out. Maybe there's another chair."

"Is all right," the man said. "Sit." They walked to the bar, and Joe sat down. The fat woman waddled from the kitchen section. Strands of dark hair stuck to her forehead, and sweat beaded her upper lip. "What you want?" she asked.

"Anything," Joe said. "Whatever you've got."

"Okay. I fix." She waddled back to the *brasero*, and the bartender brought a bottle of Jim Beam and a glass. "A little water on the side?" Joe asked.

"Water?" The bartender looked puzzled, then said, "Sure." Joe poured a big slug into the glass and waited. The bartender came back with a glass and a chipped enamel pitcher of water and watched Joe throw down the drink and chase it with half a glass of water. Joe grinned at the bartender and said, "*Es costumbre*. Gringo custom."

The bartender produced the first smile Joe had seen since he had come in. "You gonna spoil that whiskey."

The fat cook brought a medium-size platter, insulated with a towel. "Is hot," she warned. She enumerated the menu, counting on her fingers — "Enchiladas. Chile relleno. Carne asada. Frijoles refritos. You want hot sauce, put on you'self, eh? You want beer?"

"You bet!"

She waddled to the bar and came back with a bottle of dark beer. "Dos Equis," she said. "Come from Monterey."

Conversation resumed, all in Spanish so rapid and colloquial that Joe caught very little of it, except some mention of the battle at Agua Prieta and a few names he knew – Plutarco Elías Calles, Alvaro Obregón, Pancho Villa.

When Joe had mopped up the last of the sauce with the last fragment of tortilla, Ámparo came to take the platter. "You got enough?"

"Plenty!" Joe said. He smiled at her and pushed back his chair. "*Muy bueno*!"

Ámparo beamed.

"Any more of that beer?" Joe asked.

She yelled at the bartender, *"Florencio! Otra cerveza pa'l señor!"* The bartender brought it and said, "Dinner thirty cents. Two bottles beer, twenty cents."

Joe paid him, rolled a smoke, sat back relaxed and comfortable, and examined the place. There were no gringos. The gamblers and drinkers were dressed for the most part in Levi's, two or three of them obviously *vaqueros*, the rest laborers. The bartender was short and broad but not fat, his mustache, a great drooping affair, turned up at the ends like the pictures of Zapata, the beloved *revolucionario* of Morelos.

Over the shelves of bottles that served as a backbar, was a greatly enlarged photograph of Pancho Villa, the Centaur of the North, on a fine horse. Behind Villa were mounted troops who wore wide-brimmed sombreros and white shirts and tapered, wrinkled, white pants like underdrawers, and were festooned with cartridge belts.

The bartender pulled out a chair and sat down. He said. "That Pancho Villa on the way to Zacatecas, with his Dorados . . . All them ol'-timer been with him since nineteen ten, an' some before that. They die for him any time. Pancho Villa, he's only man for poor people. He kill them big rancher an' give money an' land to *peones*. He fight them son of bitch Carranza an' Obregón. He gonna shoot all them general an' politico an' bloodsucker. I name my cantina for him."

"Yeah, I saw the sign," Joe said. "He's a great general! I understand they made him an honorary citizen of El Paso, once."

The bartender grinned — then suddenly his face darkened. He scowled at Joe and said, "What'samatter that goddamn Woodrow Weelson! He was back up Pancho Villa when he fight that butcher, Victoriano Huerta. Then when Carranza is president after Huerta, an' start givin' land to rich people, he's give oil well an' mines to Americans, an' Weelson say he gonna back up Carranza, so he don't sell no more guns to Pancho Villa! That's why Obregón beat him in Celaya. Obregón got all them American machine gun an' barb wire, an' Pancho Villa he don't got enough gun. Was just like murder!"

"That's right!" Joe said. "Exactly what my friend Santos Camargo said."

The bartender looked at him sharply, seemed about to speak, then clamped his mouth shut.

Several men had come to the table and were looking accusingly at Joe. He said, "Look! Some of us don't like Wilson any better than you like Carranza. He's going to get us into that war in Europe, where we've got no business being. And what he did to Villa was dirty!" Joe didn't actually know what Wilson had done to Pancho Villa, but he figured right now he'd better be an ardent Villista. "A lot of Americans would like to help. A lot of 'em do, too. Where you think Villa gets the guns he *does* get?" He didn't know the answer to that, either.

The bartender patted his shoulder and gave a fast translation to the men around the table.

Joe wondered how much they would swallow of overblown praise for Pancho Villa. He said, "Americans know

Pancho Villa is the greatest man in Mexico. I'll buy a bottle, so we can drink a toast to him."

The bartender's grin showed gold teeth as he translated. Ámparo hurried to the bar and got the bottle of Jim Beam and handed it to Joe. He handed it back to her and said, "Ladies first! A toast to Pancho Villa!"

Ámparo took a real slug and gave the bottle to Joe. He drank, and the bottle made the rounds. Ámparo said, "You good man!" and a couple of them shook hands with him.

Joe paid for the bottle, which cut his capital down to eighty dollars and thirteen cents.

The bartender said, "You livin' here in Chihuahuita? I don't see you before."

"I just rode in," Joe said. "I need a bed and a place for my horse."

The bartender said, "I'm Florencio Vidal, *a sus órdenes*," and stuck out his hand. Joe took it and said, "Joe . . . " and almost said "Dyer," but caught himself and said the first name that came into his head, " . . . Daly. I'm glad to meet you."

"Mucho gusto!" Vidal said. "I gonna fix you up." He spoke rapidly to Ámparo, apparently telling her to take over the bar and cash register. He got a kerosene lantern from behind the bar and held the door open for Joe. Several of the customers called out, *"Hasta pronto!"* as they went out.

Joe untied Brownie, and Vidal led the way down a narrow alley between the brick walls of the saloon and the tenement and through a gate in the back. There was a sort of patio where two horses stood jerking at the hay in a rickety manger, their eyes gleaming like pale moons in the lanternlight.

Vidal said, "In there," and pointed to a doorway in the side wall. Joe led Brownie over, and Vidal held the lantern while he inspected the stall. It was roomy and dry.

"You want hay, Mr. Daly?"

"Yes, please," Joe said. "What about me? You got a room?"

"Sure," Vidal said and began to unsaddle the buckskin. "We put saddle in your room, eh?" He put the saddle down carefully, keeping the sheepskin off the ground. "We rub him down, then I show you. Fifty cents for you, an' fifty cents for horse."

He went into the stall and came back with two grain sacks. While they gave Brownie a rubdown, he explained, "This my hotel, too."

Joe gave him a dollar and picked up the saddle and saddleblanket. Vidal took the roll of blankets and slicker and led the way back along the alley and into the building. The door opened onto a narrow hall lighted by an unshaded bulb. Joe heard talk behind several doors as they passed. Vidal took a key ring from his apron pocket and opened the padlock on the last door on the left. He gave Joe the key.

The small room was clean, lighted by a low-watt bulb hanging from the ceiling. There was a white-enameled, iron bedstead with an excelsior mattress and two U.S. Army blankets, one chair, and a dresser with a pitcher and a big bowl. In the corner was a suspended pole with two coat hangers hooked over it. Joe put the saddle down near the pole.

Vidal came in with a piece of soap and a worn hand towel. He said, "Toilet outside. Go through door at end of hall. Candle and matches in dresser drawer."

He went out and Joe fastened the door with the inside bolt. He stripped and had a fast hand bath, shivering in the chill. The towel was about as absorbent as a new bandana, and he was still damp when he opened the window six inches and fastened it with the spring-loaded pegs that plugged into the window frame.

He added his two blankets to the house equipment and got into bed.

A wave of depression swept over him. It all seemed like a story someone might have told him: Joe Dyer hiding in a third-rate Mexican rooming house in the slums of a town he had never seen before tonight, on the run from a murder charge — maybe two murder charges — his only hope the long chance that the one man who might clear him had fled to the same town, and that he could find that man and persuade him to confess the killing of Dutch Hauser. There was nothing else, except to change his name permanently, hide himself in a new place, and try to build a new life. Not that the old one was so great — nothing to his name but a good horse, a mule, and a two-room shack, barn, and well on 640 acres of prime grass in that beautiful flat under Mingus Mountain. But that was all Joe Dyer wanted, just that, and a bunch of good cows to get fat on that good grass, in that place, and nowhere else on earth. Then he thought of good old Mike Burnham, who had been smarter with his share of the strike last year. Mike was coining money with the saloon and gambling tables and with Aggie and the three other girls.

But Joe would never have been able to stand that life — up at noon, spend the day and night and early morning selling booze and women. Still, the thought of Mike Burnham was a comfort, because Mike would never let him down. If this hopeless hunt for Santos Camargo failed, as it almost certainly would, he'd get in touch with Mike and make his way back to Prescott. Then with a loan from Mike, and a good lawyer . . .

Joe drifted into sleep.

SEVEN

Joe woke early and dressed and went to see Brownie. Florencio Vidal had been there first, and there was fresh water in the trough. Brownie was concentrating on a full manger of hay and ignored Joe. Joe went to the cantina.

Florencio, seated at a table, looked up from his newspaper and greeted him glumly. "Sit down, Joe. How you sleep?"

Without waiting for Joe's reply, he bawled, "Ámparo!" The cook came in through a rear door, carrying a bucket and mop. She grinned at Joe and put them down.

"You hongry?" she asked. "I gonna make huevos rancheros for you."

"Hey, no!" Joe said. "Just scrambled eggs and some hash browns."

" 'Ash brown? I don' know no 'ash brown. Okay, scramble egg an' refry beans." She brought him a mug of coffee and went to the kitchen and began clashing dishes and pots.

Florencio Vidal swore and showed Joe the headlines in the El Paso Herald — VILLA RETREATS FROM HERMOSILLO. VILLISTAS ABANDON CHIHUAHUA AND CIUDAD JUAREZ.

Joe didn't give a damn what was happening to Pancho Villa, but figured he'd better be a good Villa partisan. He took the paper and pretended deep interest, shaking his head solemnly as he read that Villa's forces, after the defeat at Agua Prieta, had made a heroic march across the sierra into Sonora from Nueva Casas Grandes, and through Naco and Cananea and Nogales, and had been on the point of overwhelming Hermosillo, when the news reached them of Carranza's abject concessions to President Wilson's demands in exchange for vast military aid and reinforced embargo against Villa – a fatal blow to Villa's campaign. Villa's army was now fighting rearguard actions in a retreat east across the trackless Sierre Madre. His forces in Ciudad Juárez and Chihuahua had been forced to evacuate in the face of increasing Obregón strength, arriving – illegally – across American territory from Eagle Pass, Texas.

Joe made appropriate sounds of sympathy, then began to look for news of a search for Joe Dyer. He was distracted when he noticed the date – December 18, 1915. Had it been only five days since he shot Cal Morgan and ran from Sheriff Kincaid? Seemed like a month. And Christmas only a week away. Christmas would be pretty grim this year. He remembered Christmas, 1914, and the free dinner Mike Burnham had set up, and the sweet, high soprano of Aggie singing the old songs, with the off-key help of all the boys getting drunk in the Kentucky Bar. Whiskey Row had been bedlam all day.

Ámparo brought the scrambled eggs and refried beans and hot bolillo. While he ate, he went through the paper from headlines to ads and found no mention of Dutch Hauser's death, or of himself.

Florencio began to talk about the injustices and treachery that had been heaped upon Pancho Villa. Joe wasn't listening, but thinking how he would go about looking for Santos Camargo. He supposed Florencio Vidal was curious about him – he'd certainly begin to get curious if Joe hung round with no apparent reason. But again, maybe he wouldn't. The border towns were good hiding places for wanted men from both sides of the line, and probably the residents were used to strangers who didn't talk about themselves. So maybe he was safe enough, unless police came asking about him.

He almost said, "Listen, friend, I'm in a hell of a jam, and if you know a man named Santos Camargo, why . . . " But he knew it would be foolish to risk it. It would only arouse suspicion as to why he wanted to find Camargo. Maybe he'd try it later if he couldn't find Camargo, and if he could manage to get Florencio to trust him.

He paid twenty-five cents for his breakfast and pushed out of his mind the worry about what he would do when his money ran out. He'd better write to Mike Burnham, right away.

He borrowed a tablet and envelope and a pencil from Vidal. There were customers at the bar now, and a couple of his friends of the night before smiled and nodded. He sharpened the pencil with his skinning knife and started his second letter to Mike:

El Paso, Texas
December 18, 1915

Dear Mike,

A lot has happened since I wrote to you from Spanish Wells. I got in trouble with a couple of drunk cowboys in the plaza, and . . .

He set down the whole story briefly and told why he had to try to find Santos Camargo and concluded:

So about my only chance is to find him, and if I don't, I will have to try to get back to Prescott. I can't risk the train or the stage. I'll have to ride the owl hoot again. If they catch me, they'll railroad me in Spanish Wells. I'll sell the ranch if I have to, to hire a good lawyer. In the meantime, I could sure use a hundred dollars if you can spare it. You better send it

General Delivery and not to the cantina here, so they can't trace me. Address it to Joe Daly.

Sorry to bother you, Mike, but this is real bad trouble.

Yours,
Joe

He addressed the envelope and went over to the bar and asked Florencio, "Where's the post office?"

"Uptown eight or nine blocks," Florencio said. "Ámparo gotta go over there pretty quick, she gonna buy some things for Las Posadas. She take it for you."

Joe was glad not to have to walk around the streets outside of Chihuahuita if he didn't have to. There might be a wanted poster pinned on the bulletin board in the post office. He gave the cook the letter and two cents for postage and went out to start looking for Santos Camargo. In spite of the odds, Camargo might be hanging around waiting to see whether any hue and cry had been raised for him. If he was well known in Chihuahuita, someone might drop a careless word. Joe didn't know any other way to go about it.

He spent the day in a succession of dark saloons, stretching out a beer in each, and just listening. He didn't see a *norteamericano* all day. Several Mexicans talked to him, their curiosity and suspicion obvious. He responded politely and asked no questions. He understood little of what conversations he overheard, which seemed to be mostly about the surrender of the Villa forces in half a dozen Chihuahua towns, and the Mexicans were all gloomy. Chihuahuita was solidly behind the hero of Zacatecas and Torreón and a dozen other bloody frays.

When he went back to the Cantina El Centauro at about eight P.M., with the sheepskin pulled up around his ears against the bitter breeze, he was discouraged and a little drunk, and had spent two dollars and a quarter.

The cantina was crowded, and his friends of the night before welcomed him. He had to drink to Pancho Villa, and to a Colonel Fierro — El Carnicero — who seemed to be a bloodier killer than Pancho Villa himself.

It went that way for five more days, and he guessed he had covered every saloon in Chihuahuita, yet he heard no mention of Santos Camargo. Each evening, as he had made his way somewhat unsteadily back to the cantina, he'd seen groups of kids and a man and woman in long robes, singing a very pretty song, and stopping at door after door. The people where they stopped always turned them away. Joe asked Ámparo what it was all about, and she said it was Las Posadas, Saint Joseph and the Blessed Mary trying to find a place to stay the night. "She *embarazada, entiendes*? She knocked up. She gonna have baby Jesus, an' nobody let her come in house. So she gotta stay in barn."

This night, Christmas Eve — Novhe Buena, the Mexicans called it — as he sat drinking beer after another unsuccessful foray into a dozen saloons, the cantina was decorated with candles and paper flowers and pictures of the Holy Family, and Joe heard the singing in the street, and then there were firecrackers going off in long strings and skyrockets swooshing into the sky and bursting with a tremendous smash of sound and light. Florencio and a half dozen patrons flung open the door, and the kids and Joseph and Mary came in. There was more singing, with all the customers and Florencio and Ámparo answering with other verses. It was very beautiful, and Joe had a lump in his throat. With great ceremony, Florencio conducted the singers to the big table and served them a banquet.

Everybody got drunk, and Joe could hardly find his way to his room.

Christmas Day he didn't get up until noon, then went around to say hello to Brownie, who whinnied at him and moved around in the stall. Joe knew Brownie wanted to do a little running and resolved to saddle him the next day and ride him around. He counted his money and was dismayed to find that he'd spent fifteen dollars in four days. He guessed he'd better risk talking to Florencio Vidal about Santos Camargo.

He went to El Centauro and ate ravenously of Âmparo's cooking. There were only two customers, who left in a few minutes. Âmparo said everyone was probably "*crudo*" after the fiesta last night, but they'd be coming in soon for something to kill the hangovers.

Florencio came in and got two bottles of beer and brought them to the table. When Joe reached into his pocket for money, Florencio said, "No. Is on the house." He sat with his hands clasped on the table, studying them as though he had never seen them before. Then he looked at Joe and said, "What you want with Santos Camargo?"

Joe felt as if someone had thrown cold water in his face. "What are you talking about? Who's that?"

Florencio said, "First day you come here, you said you got friend was tellin' you Pancho Villa can't get enough guns. You say, "My friend, Santos Camargo."

Joe said, "Well, that's right. I've been looking for him. He's supposed to be here."

"Why you want him, Joe? You some kind of p'liceman, maybe Border Patrol or something? Everybody in Chihuahuita know you lookin' for somebody."

"Is he here, then?" Joe asked. "I'm no lawman! Camargo's in trouble. I only want to warn him. Maybe he doesn't know it, but . . ."

"Why you want him, Joe? What kind of trouble?"

"He killed a man in New Mexico. There's a warrant out for him. Maybe he doesn't know they're after him."

"He know it," Florencio said. "Only he din't kill nobody. Maybe *you* kill that man yourself. Your real name Dyer, eh?"

Again it was like a bucket of icewater in the face, and Joe could only say, "How'd you know that?"

Florencio pulled a folded paper out of his pocket and opened it out for Joe to see.

Wanted for Murder. Joseph Dyer. About 30. 5' 11". Black hair. Gray eyes. Last seen wearing khaki shirt, gray hat, sheepskin coat. Riding buckskin gelding, branded Lazy J D on left hip. Armed and dangerous. Reward. Hold, and notify Thomas Kincaid, Deputy Sheriff, Spanish Wells, N.M.

Joe read it twice. It was no more than he expected, but it still gave him a sinking feeling in the pit of his stomach.

Florencio said, "I gone to Post Office and read them notice on board. I think maybe I'm gonna find one about you, an' I see it."

"Yes," Joe said. "That's me."

"So why you wanna find Santos?"

"Camargo and me are both wanted for that killing. I didn't do it. I don't know if he did or not. I think he did, but he's safe, because all he has to do is slip across the border. *My* only chance is to get him to tell me what happened that night, and who else might have done it. If he'd just give me a line to go on, like maybe somebody wanted to shut Dutch Hauser's mouth for some reason. You know Camargo, I guess?"

"Sure, Joe. Everybody know him. Everybody proud of him, 'cause he keep on gettin' guns to Pancho Villa after your son of bitch president try to stop them. He was here when you come in, here in Chihuahuita. And when you say his name, I send somebody to Santos' house an' tell him was gringo here maybe lookin' for him. He come to see me that night, an' I tell him what you look like, an' he say, 'That Joe Dyer.' He say maybe you kill that man in New Mexico. He say if you did, he don' want you to get in no trouble. He say try to find out what you want."

"He's still here then?" Joe asked.

Florencio said, "Look, Joe, I gonna take chance on you. Santos say he don' wanna see nobody hang that shoot that bastard on that ranch. I find out if he will talk to you."

Joe felt a surge of hope. Santos Camargo, with safety for himself just over the river, could afford to be generous. He might sign a statement that would point to the motive for the murder of Dutch Hauser — and if Camargo had done it, he had nothing to lose by clearing Joe. If the law couldn't lay hands on him, it couldn't hang him.

Ámparo brought more beer. She had heard the talk. She grinned at Joe and said, "If you shot that bastard that make trouble for Santos, everybody your friend!"

Florencio and Ámparo had a loud argument about the cash register. He put on his coat and hat and said to Joe, "Every time I leave her runnin' things when I'm gone, she get cash all tangled up. She don't steal nothing, but I gotta work all night gettin' it straightened out." He went out.

Joe saddled Brownie and took him for a ride along the river and out into the country and got back about two in the afternoon. Florencio had come back. He led Joe to the rear table.

"He not gonna talk to you," he said. "He don' want no trouble for you, but he say he don' know you so good. He say maybe you an' that sheriff fix up something to fool him. Maybe you find out where he live, you gonna take police there."

"Didn't you tell him . . . ?" Joe began, and Florencio said, "Sure. I tell him I think you okay, but he can't take no chances."

Joe argued to no avail. Florencio gave short answers and no more information. He said, "You waste time here, Joe. You better go. I not gonna do nothin' Santos don' want."

Joe said, "What's he hanging around El Paso for, if he's so damn scared?"

"His wife gonna have baby," Florencio said. "He don' wanna go till she all right. Then he gonna join up with his cousin, is colonel in Pancho Villa's Dorados. He can't run no more gun for Pancho Villa, on account of that killin' in New Mexico."

"Florencio, what's it going to hurt if I just *talk* to him? Take me to see him!"

Florencio's face hardened. He said "No!" and that was all.

Joe said, "Well, I tell you straight, I'm not going to stop looking for him. If I could just talk to him, he'd understand I'm not going to do anything to hurt him."

"You go ahead," Florencio said. "Hunt all you want to. Nobody in Chihuahuita gonna help you."

For another week, Joe continued to haunt the saloons in Chihuahuita, with all hope of running into Santos Camargo down to about zero. He was desperate enough to have waylaid anyone he heard mention Camargo's name and beat some information out of him — also discouraged enough to quit. All that prevented his trying to make it back to Prescott now was lack of funds. He had about thirty dollars left. The necessity to stick to the mountains would make the winter journey long and difficult, and would require a good outfit. If Mike didn't send the hundred dollars very soon, Joe didn't know what he would do.

Warm-hearted Âmparo felt sorry for him and went to the post office every day to ask for his letter. He began to feel that everyone in Chihuahuita knew what he was after. Customers in the saloons pointedly turned their backs, a few got ugly, and two bartenders ordered him out of their saloons. Florencio Vidal was not unfriendly, but had almost stopped talking to him. To conserve his dwindling funds, he stayed in his room on New Year's Eve and listened to the uproar in the cantina and the racket in the streets.

On Monday, January 3, 1916, Ámparo served his lunch, and went to the post office for him. She came back very excited, and said, "I think is letter for you! Man at window look through bunch of letter and look at one and say, 'You don't look like no Joseph Daly to me,' 'an he won't give to me."

Joe knew he had to risk it — and there was no trouble at all. He saw the "Wanted" notice for himself on the bulletin board, but there was no photograph. The man at the General Delivery window scarcely looked at him when he gave him Mike's letter.

The hundred dollars was in cash, and the letter suggested that he risk returning by train and said that Clark Bellamy, the best lawyer in Arizona, was ready to defend him, even though Sheriff Kincaid and Cal Morgan and maybe Frank Pritchard weren't going to let a little perjury bother their consciences. Bellamy said Joe's big mistake had been to run away, like Camargo — and if Joe had killed Cal Morgan, it would really be rough.

Joe almost decided to risk the train, but he couldn't bear to leave Brownie, and now he had the money to buy a pack horse and good winter outfit. He hurried back to the cantina.

Florencio Vidal bought him a drink and sat at a table with him. He said, "Joe, why'n't you quit? You never gonna find Camargo."

Joe said, "I know it, Florencio. I'm leaving tomorrow."

Florencio beamed. "Hey, that great!" He didn't try to hide his immense relief. "We gonna have big dinner tonight! All free for you!" He turned and bawled, "Ámparo!" and when she hurried to the table, he began giving instructions for the meal.

It was a fine dinner, with half a dozen of Joe's acquaintances there — Lencho and Margarito and Hector, and three Francisco's distinguished only by their nicknames, Pancho, Paco, and Cisco — and there were toasts to Pancho Villa and to Joe and to the damnation of all Carranzistas.

Later, in his room, after the cantina was closed, Joe was making out a list of purchases for the next day, when there was a knock on his door. He unbolted it and Ámparo slipped in and put her finger on her lips and said softly, "Don't talk loud."

She sat in the chair and said, "They gonna catch you for kill that son of bitch on that ranch?"

Joe said, "I'm going to get a lawyer and give myself up."

"Tell truth," she said. "You didn't do it?"

"No, I didn't, Ámparo. I think Camargo did, but I'm not sure."

"Camargo, he could tell you something, maybe?"

"I think he knows why somebody had to kill that man. If I knew that, I could prove it wasn't me."

She said, "You tell anybody I said it, an' they gonna hurt me."

"Tell them you said what, Ámparo?"

"I think he oughta told you what he know," she said. "He safe. Nobody gonna touch him."

Joe waited while she stared at him solemnly.

"He gone, Joe. His wife have the baby las' week."

So the gamble had lost — and he guessed he wasn't any worse off than he had been. He said, "I'm grateful, Ámparo. You're a good friend. I guess it doesn't matter, now."

"But maybe he still in Cuidad Juárez," she said. "He gonna join up with his cousin, that Jesús Castro, is colonel in Pancho Villa army. But Castro, he s'posed to come to Cuidad Juárez. He gonna meet lot of men was fight for Pancho Villa before. They all gonna go with him. An' I don't know if Castro already been there or if he not come yet. So maybe you still got chance to talk to Santos Camargo, if he didn't go already."

"Do you know where he might be?" Joe asked.

"Them Villista, they stayin' in big brick house where Calle Anáhuac cross Avenida de los Insurgentes, if they didn't already go with Jesús Castro."

She stood up to go, and he bent down and kissed her.

She began to cry. "Nobody done that for fifteen year. You be careful; don't take no chance."

She went out and he bolted the door.

In the morning, he was waiting when Vidal opened the cantina. Ámparo grinned fondly at him and brought coffee to his table. Florencio put change in the cash register, then came to sit with Joe. He said, "Anything I can do, Joe? I'm sorry I couldn't help you none."

Joe choked back an angry answer — Vidal could certainly have told him that Camargo had been gone for nearly a week — but he remembered how well Vidal had treated a strange gringo when he didn't have to. He said, "Yes, there is, if you don't mind. I left my saddle and some gear in the room, and I'd like to leave my horse for a while. Will you take care of them for me?" He took a twenty-dollar bill from his wallet, and laid it on the table, with the padlock key.

"Sure," Florencio said. "You smart not to ride all that way. Nobody gonna reco'nize you on the train."

Ámparo brought a huge breakfast and sat with them while Joe ate. He put five dollars on the table and said "Here, sweetheart, buy yourself a new hat or something."

He thought she was going to refuse it, but suddenly she crammed it down the front of her dress and began to cry, and got up and trotted to the kitchen section.

Florencio said, "When you get that murder charge fix up, you come on back some day, eh? We be glad to see you."

Joe shook his hand and went out.

He wore the sheepskin because the evenings and nights were very cold. He left the cartridge belt and holster in the room and slit the bottom lining of the big right-hand pocket of the sheepskin and managed to cram the Colt's revolver in. He wouldn't be able to get into action very fast, but it was inconspicuous, and he hoped it wouldn't attract the attention of the Mexican immigration guards.

He walked to Stanton Street and got on a streetcar, and stood in the aisle jammed in with a lot of people, and five minutes later got off in Mexico and walked past a group of Mexican officers gossiping by the gate. They paid no attention to him. He thought about asking someone where the Avenida de los Insurgentes was, but decided the less he talked to people the better.

The Federal army was much in evidence — the forces of Carranza and Obregón — with neatly uniformed infantrymen crowding the saloons and restaurants and clustered on the street corners, and detachments of well-mounted cavalry clattering importantly over the cobblestones.

Joe walked along Avenida Lerdo and turned left onto what looked like the main street — Avenida 16 de Septiembre, according to a sign. There was a good deal of automobile traffic mixed in with wagons and a few elegant carriages and a lot of horsemen and strings of burros loaded with firewood. There were a lot of gringos, and the bars were already busy. Several blocks along, the avenue was intersected by Avenida Anáhuac. He turned right, walked three blocks, and found Avenida de los Insurgentes and the big brick building Ámparo had told him about.

Across the street and half a block away was the Hotel El Charro Tapatío, above a narrow flight of stairs which went up between a saloon and restaurant. A slatternly woman at a desk at the head of the stair rented him a room for twenty-five cents a day and led him down a narrow hallway and into a cubicle about eight feet by ten that had a bedstead, a small dresser, a chair, and a window that opened onto a dark areaway. Joe asked for the key, and she said there was none and the toilet was at the end of the hall.

For the next six days he took all three meals in the dirty restaurant beside the stairway, suffering stomach cramps and loose bowels, and lingering as long as he could over his meals, watching the brick building through a fly-specked window. Between meals, he sat at the end of the bar in the adjoining cantina, drinking the excellent Mexican beer and continuing his vigil through another fly-specked window. When customers and bartender began to take an interest in him, he would saunter out and lean on a wall opposite the brick building.

There was considerable activity there, a lot of coming and going, and often a group of men talking outside the entrance. Joe hoped that they were still waiting for the arrival of Colonel Jesús Castro on his recruiting expedition — but he saw nothing of Santos Camargo.

The waiter in the restaurant, and the bartender, began to question him and turned a little ugly at his noncommital answers. And late on Sunday afternoon, as he leaned against the wall opposite the building, he saw that three men in the doorway were taking considerable interest in him. He rolled a smoke and sauntered around the corner. As he turned the next corner, he glanced back. They were standing at the corner, watching him. Joe decided to give it up. If Camargo was there, surely he would have seen him coming or going, at least once in six days. He wished he could think of some excuse to ask one of those men if the colonel had come and gone — but that would be asking for trouble. He ate in a different place and went back to his room late. Tomorrow he would go back to Cantina Centauro del Norte, get his horse and gear, buy a mule and packsaddle and whatever he needed, and ride the back trails for Prescott.

Very early on the morning of Monday, January 10th, he had chorizo and fried eggs in the greasy restaurant, then walked to Avenida 16 de Septiembre and was crossing Lerdo to go on to Avenida Juárez and catch the streetcar that crossed the bridge to South Santa Fe Street in El Paso — and he saw Santos Camargo.

Coming back to Cuidad Juárez from El Paso, Joe thought. He's been to see his wife and kid.

Camargo dodged between a string of burros and a wagon and crossed Avenida 16 de Septiembre and went briskly along Lerdo. He wasn't dressed as Joe knew him, but wore a neat business suit and a derby hat and knob-toed button shoes, but there was no mistaking the set of the graying head, the thrust of the shoulders, the glimpse of the craggy face. Joe started to run after him, but thought better of that, and followed at a fast walk. He kept looking ahead for a good place to overtake Camargo, maybe shove him into an alley or behind a building and plead with him to talk. And if pleading didn't do it, there was the Army Colt's. Camargo began to walk faster and swung around a corner into a side street. Joe broke into a run.

He skidded to a stop when he got around the corner, and he began to walk again. For a moment, he thought Camargo had seen him, but the Mexican was still walking briskly.

Ahead was the station of the Mexican North Western Railway — a long, rambling, paint-peeled wooden structure, with a freight deck and a baggage room, and a few people coming out of the waiting room. Behind the station were cattle pens and a marshaling yard where a few empty boxcars and flats and many steel logging cars stood on parallel tracks. A Mogul with steam up was hooked to two boxcars and a flatcar. On the flatcar, six soldiers lounged around a parapet of sandbags enclosing a machine gun. The last car was a long, wooden passenger coach, its paint peeling like that of the station, its windows grimy. A conductor by the steps of its open platform yelled and waved at the people coming out of the waiting room, who picked up suitcases and packages and walked to the coach. Around the open doors of the boxcars, Mexican farmers milled about clutching bundles and crates of chickens. Kids ran around, and men were embracing and shaking hands and boosting women and kids up into the cars and tossing bundles in. Several men in white clothes that looked like pajamas with the ankles wrapped tight, climbed to the tops of the boxcars.

There was no feather of steam at the safety valve of the engine, and for a moment Joe thought it wasn't ready to go. Then he realized that leaking tubes and dried out packing lost enough steam pressure to prevent the valve from popping. The bell began to clang, and Santos Camargo broke into a run and went into the station. Joe ran after him and was about to go in, but suddenly stopped and waited, sweating and anxious. The hoghead pulled the cord, and the whistle hooted. Camargo came out holding a ticket and trotted for the rear of the coach. Joe turned away and didn't look at him. This was certainly not the place to grab him, out in the open with a hundred or so witnesses.

He ran into the empty waiting room and up to the ticket window. He got out his wallet and had the ten-dollar bill in his hand, but couldn't think of what to say. The ticked seller said, "*Adonde? Adonde?* Chihuahua? Nueva Casas Grandes? Madera?"

Joe wanted to say, "End of the line, wherever that is," but couldn't think of how to say it. He didn't know where the train was going, but the thing to do was get aboard and not lose sight of Camargo. He said, "Chihuahua!" and shoved the bill at the man.

The ticket man, muttering about stupid gringos, shoved a ticket and a handful of pesos at him, and Joe ran out.

The Mogul was blowing smoke rings. Steam spouted from the cylinder cocks and the loose packing around the piston rods. The drivers turned ponderously, and the train moved slowly ahead. Joe sprinted through the crowd of *paisanos* and caught the grab rail of the platform of the rear coach.

EIGHT

Joe shouldered the door open and went in, shoving paper pesos and copper coins into the left pocket of his sheepskin. The car was full, and people were putting bundles into the overhead racks. He looked along the aisle and couldn't see Camargo and thought he had gone right on through and jumped down from the front platform. And if he had, then he had recognized Joe and wouldn't be caught again. Joe swore, and people turned to look at him; then Camargo, on the aisle side of the front seat on the left, just behind the toilet compartment marked "Damas," stood and took off his jacket and stuffed it into the overhead rack. Joe took the only empty seat, the lengthwise one on the right at the rear of the coach, behind the last transverse seat. Across the aisle, the conductor was taking things out of a little satchel. He looked across and scowled at Joe.

The train rolled slowly through a district of hovels, scattering dogs and children and terrorizing hobbled burros. As it left the city on a long curve, with the Mogul coughing and the cars lurching on the uneven roadbed, the conductor went to the head of the car and began punching tickets.

Joe got a look at the passengers, most of them well-to-do Mexicans, and about twenty Americans. There was only one woman, by the window in the seat just ahead of

Joe's. She wore a fussy straw hat and her costume was in the height of style, with puffed shoulders and wide lapels on the jacket, and a long, full skirt. Her white shirtwaist had a choker collar of lace. She took off the hat and jacket and asked the man beside her to put them up on the luggage rack.

He got up and put them and his Stetson on the rack. He was a man with an ill-tempered expression on his red face, a lot of yellow hair brushed back from his forehead, and a drooping mustache framing a pursey, red mouth. As he sat down, he said, "Well, like Queen Victoria, you have a whim of iron."

The woman said, "Harry, you know very well I had to come!" Her face, olive skinned and black browed, was strongly modeled, not quite pretty, but certainly not ugly. She had a lot of black hair knotted into a big bun at the nape of her neck.

The man said, "It's a stupid risk, the way things are! You can still get off at Nueva Casas Grandes and catch the northbound . . ."

The conductor interrupted, asking for their tickets, and the man handed them to him. The conductor said, "You know we stoppin' at San Isidro? Track not open to Chihuahua."

"*Sí, sabemos*," the woman answered.

The conductor punched Joe's ticket and handed it back and said, "Chihuahua also, eh?" and crossed the aisle and sat in the other lengthwise seat.

Joe coughed and said, "Pardon me. What's that he said about Chihuahua?"

The man ignored him, but the woman turned and said, "I guess the Villistas have torn up some more track. You'll have to get off at San Isidro and find your way to Chihuahua somehow."

"Ruth," the man said, "if you're still determined to be stubborn, we don't have to go all the way into Chihuahua. We can get mules and a driver in San Isidro."

The woman said, angrily, "You may as well give up, Harry! I'm going! You don't know the country, and you don't speak enough Spanish to make yourself understood."

"Listen!" he yelled in her face, then lowered his voice and said furiously, "We shouldn't go at all! Not till things quiet down. Villa's troops will be scattered all through the sierra, vicious after Agua Prieta, as if they weren't before! This is stupid! Utterly stupid! We'll get off at Nueva Casas Grandes and just wait for a northbound train. Go back to El Paso and wait it out if it takes a year! Villa's beaten! They'll run him to earth one of these days, and then we can go back and start again. Will you, for God's sake, listen to reason, just once!"

"You know very well we can't just sit and wait," the woman said. "What do you expect to *live* on? That three hundred dollars in the bank? You *know* we have to get it! Right now, when the Villistas are beaten, and while there's some semblance of law and order, and the Rurales patroling again."

"Ruth! No! *I* will go on, if you insist. You must get off at Nueva Casas Grandes and . . . "

Joe was sick of their arguing. He went out onto the rear platform, where the wind almost took his hat before he could grab it. The train was rolling through a desert of sand dunes sparsely grown with sage and stunted mesquite and creosote bush. There were no human habitations and no trees.

He tried to plan how he would get Camargo by himself, what he would say to him . . . Maybe friends would meet him, and there'd be no chance to get him alone. Maybe he was aware of Joe's pursuit — although Joe didn't think so — and would jump off just as the train picked up speed leaving some station, or slip away in the dark at San Isidro. There was nothing Joe could do except watch him every time the train stopped. But, by God, he'd make Camargo talk, he'd stick to him like a burr and grab the first chance that came up. He sat on the platform and put his feet on the step and watched the country roll by.

Presently it began to show a little life, and there were ranch buildings, flat-roofed adobes with the vigas sticking out from the parapets, and a few corrals. Dry cornstalks stuck up from bare brown earth, and a few small piñons began to show. Way off in the distance, rugged peaks thrust straight up from the desert floor, and far to the southwest was the flat blue silhouette of a high range — the Sierra Madre Occidental, the backbone of Mexico. The train rattled through a town; a few shacks, a cattle pen and chute, and a sign on a small station shack — MEDANOS — and a little later, CONEJOS. The wind chilled him, and the harsh coal smoke had him coughing, so he went back to his seat.

The bickering was still going on between Ruth and Harry. Harry said, "Ruth, this is final! I will go on, but I refuse to risk the life of my wife. A husband still has some prerogatives even in this age of women's suffrage. I forbid you to go on! You will get a train back from Nueva Casas Grandes, and wait for me in El Paso! And that is *final*!"

Ruth smiled at him and patted him on the head. "Don't be absurd, Harry. Wake me up when we get to Nueva Casas Grandes, so I can buy some lunch. If I leave it to you, you'll get some concoction of ptomaine and dysentery wrapped in a tortilla." Harry swore, got up, and stamped down the aisle and went into the "Caballeros."

Joe stared out the opposite window, watching the country roll by, and presently slept.

The wracking of couplings and the screech of wheezy air brakes woke him. The train was rolling into a sizable town. It pulled up at a station which bore a sign, NUEVA CASA GRANDES, and some of the Mexican passengers were taking down bundles and suitcases from the racks. Camargo got up and stretched, and when the train ground to a stop, followed the others out. Joe hurried out the back door.

He jumped down to the platform and bumped into Ruth Whatever-her-name-was. He apologized and pushed her aside and hurried along the platform. He saw Camargo's back, in a group of Mexican passengers crowded around a little cart where a *paisano* was selling tamales.

A small woman hidden in the folds of a great black rebozo jogged his arm and croaked, *"Enchiladas, patrón! Tacos! Quesadillas."* Joe bought two quesadillas, great round tortillas fried crisp and dripping with melted cheese. He held out a silver peso, and the woman made change. Joe said, *"Cerveza?"*

She screeched at a ragged man, who sold Joe a bottle of beer. Joe pushed beggars aside and kept moving to keep Camargo in sight. Camargo drained a bottle of beer, handed the bottle to the seller, and turned to make his way back to the car. Joe got his first good look at Camargo's face, and doubt began to take root. Troubled, he watched Camargo climb the front steps. Joe made his way to the rear platform and to his seat. Beside her husband, Ruth Whats'ername looked back at him and smiled. She was chewing the last of a bean burro. She said, "*Well!* One male with some sense, anyway! That quesadilla won't hurt you, but my husband persists in buying those enchiladas made of chicken skin and bones and heaven knows what else, and then wonders for two weeks what gave him the diarrhea."

Joe felt like saying, "Lady, don't use me to club your husband!" but he just grinned and shoved the last of his quesadilla into his mouth. Harry ignored his wife's thrust, but his ears reddened as he stared ahead.

The train pulled slowly out of Nueva Casas Grandes, running along a lovely river bordered with cottonwoods and willows, and past a vast acreage of peach and apple trees, bare in the winter sun. Ruth turned to explain to

Joe, "There's a colony of Mormons, here. Even the revolutionists don't bother them. They tend to their own business and grow the best fruit and produce in Mexico."

The train was twisting around sharp curves, with the trucks rattling, and Joe made a polite remark which was lost in the racket. Ruth smiled brightly and looked ahead again. As the train ground its way around the curves, Joe saw timbered foothills to the west and south, and a few far peaks towering into the faultless sky, their upper reaches dotted with snowfields. For a couple of hours there were no towns, just a few sidings where logging cars stood waiting, and loading platforms were stacked with big pine logs. There seemed to be no people at all.

After a while the train fought its way into Madera, and two Mexicans got out. Santos Camargo didn't move. Joe stepped onto the rear platform and looked ahead, watching the hoghead oiling the crossbar with a long-nosed oil can. When they pulled out of Madera the worry came back into his mind. That man up there sure looked like Camargo. He hadn't doubted it until he watched him walk back to the coach, there at Nueva Casas Grandes.

He thought, maybe he'll talk here on the train as well as anywhere else. I sure don't know how I'm going to stop him in some railroad station or on a dark street somewhere, unless I draw down on him or slug him. I better quit pussyfooting around. Right now.

He made his way down the aisle. The train was fighting its way up a grade, lurching around the curves. He had to grab onto the backs of seats, and when he got to the first seat on the left, Camargo was slumped down with his hat over his face. Joe gripped the seat back and said sharply, "Santos!"

The other Mexican, the one by the window, looked up at him sullenly.

Joe said, "Camargo!"

The man mumbled and pushed his hat back and looked up.

Joe stared at him in utter disbelief. He *looked* like Santos Camargo, but he *wasn't* Santos Camargo!

The man said, *"Qué te pasa, hombre?"*

"Sorry," Joe said and turned and stumbled blindly down the aisle. He sat down and stared across at the conductor, not seeing him. After a while he poked Ruth on the shoulder and said, "Lady, excuse me. What's our next stop?"

She and her husband turned around. She said, "It's Guerrero. Isn't that right, Harry?"

"How would I know?" Harry said and turned away.

"Can I get a train there, back to El Paso?"

"Why, I don't know," Ruth said. "Everything's so mixed up. The government people only got back into Chihuahua a week or so ago, and the trains aren't on any schedule. The Villistas are still stopping trains and burning bridges, and you can't be sure when they'll run — the trains, I mean. Aren't you going on to Chihuahua?"

"I just thought of something," Joe said, "and I have to get back to El Paso right away."

"Well, I don't think I'd try it from Guerrero," she said. "You'd better go on to San Isidro and see what you can find out. There's a hotel there, it's pretty awful, but Harry and I will be there a day or two, and if you don't speak Spanish, why maybe I can . . . " she looked at him speculatively and went on. "Are you a miner? I mean, are you trying to get back to your job or your mine or something? Most of us here have been sitting in El Paso or Columbus waiting until things quiet down a little. Nobody knows what's happened at our mines . . . Most of these men are mine foremen or mine owners, and we had to get out when the fighting got bad."

Joe said, "I wanted to see a man in Chihuahua, that's all . . . Now I figure it's a waste of time, and I have to get back."

She said, "Are you . . . I mean . . . now I don't want to insult you, but are you looking for work? I mean, maybe we could use an American to sort of run our pack train and maybe sort of guard us."

"No," Joe said, "I think I better get on back."

Ruth said, "Well, you'd better stick with us in San Isidro, Mr. . . . "

Joe said, "Daly. Joe Daly."

"I'm Ruth Bemis," she said, "and this is Harry, my husband."

Harry wasn't interested enough to acknowledge the introduction. Ruth Bemis said, "I know how to handle Mexicans, and if anyone can get you a hotel room and a return ticket, I can."

The train stopped briefly in Guerrero, and Joe watched Santos Camargo's near-twin get off and be hugged by two small girls, and greeted stiffly by a fat, black-eyed matron.

He managed to go to sleep, and woke only briefly when they stopped at Cuauhtémoc. When they left, he pulled down the window shade against the lowering sun, which was less than an hour above the horizon.

He went back to sleep and was lolling, loose and relaxed, when the air brakes slammed on and stuttered and brought the train to a screeching halt.

Seat backs crashed forward. Ruth Bemis screamed. Suitcases hurtled onto the shaken passengers. Shocked wide awake, Joe saw the conductor get off the floor and jerk the door open and hurry out. The engine coughed and the safety valve blew, and passengers struggled into the aisle and asked each other what the hell happened.

Ruth clung to Harry. There were two shots up ahead and shouting at the front of the coach and people came backing down the aisle.

Joe made for the rear door. It crashed back and the conductor backed in with his hands raised. Joe rammed into him. A big sombrero appeared behind him, shading a brown, whiskered, grinning face. The man bulled his way in, shoving the conductor aside. Joe saw the belts of cartridges crossed on his chest, and the .45 revolver. It was like looking down the bore of a cannon — that six-gun aimed at his head. His hands went up automatically. He backed up and stepped on Ruth's foot, and she yelped in pain. He looked hastily over his shoulder. The aisle was jammed with shouting passengers, all with their hands up. At the front of the car, there was loud talk in Spanish. Behind Ruth, Harry Bemis was whiter than she.

The Mexican rammed the .45 into Joe's belly. Joe grunted and bent over, gagging. The man yelled, *"Todos los gringos, afuera! Todos los hideputa güeros! Afueran!"*

Ruth Bemis said, "Mr. Daly! Outside! All us Americans! Hurry! He'll kill you!"

The Mexican backed out onto the platform and another came up the steps. They searched Joe and took his wallet and the revolver and shoved him down the steps. He stumbled and recovered and looked back.

Ruth Bemis came out, and one of the Mexicans grabbed her and pulled her against himself. *"Los machos, no mas!"* he said. *"Machos, sí. Hembras, no!"*

The other said, grinning at her, "Only the studs, lady! Li'l girls, we don't hurt them!"

He reached past the door and got Harry by the front of his shirt and hauled him out. They robbed him and kicked him off the platform. He lay face down, whimpering, until two Mexicans dragged him to his feet and kicked him aside to make way for the other gringos. They robbed sixteen more Americans and kicked them off the platform.

NINE

The eighteen Americans huddled together, silent and afraid. Behind them was a sign on a post — SANTA YSABEL. There were no buildings. The Mexican boxcar passengers were peering to see what was going on at the passenger coach, some of them laughing. On the flatcar, a dead Federal soldier hung head down over the sandbag parapet which surrounded the machine gun. Joe didn't see the other five. Ahead of the engine, the train crew stood near a pile of crossties stacked on the rails.

Four Mexicans began to shove the Americans into line. A few yards away, several of them held a number of horses, and behind them was a big crowd of mounted men. They wore short jackets and tight, wrinkled charro pants and wide sombreros of felt or straw. Crossed over their chests and buckled around their waists were belts of ammunition. Each of them carried a rifle — Winchester carbine or Mauser bolt-action.

Two riders seemed to be in command, both magnificently mounted, sitting saddles covered with white rawhide, with huge pommels and bull-nosed tapaderos.

One of them called out a string of names — "Valverde . . . Herrera . . . Gómez . . . Camargo . . . Calzadíaz . . ." and about twenty men dismounted and lined up. The officer shouted instructions, and on the platform, Ruth Bemis began to scream. A Mexican jabbed Joe in the kidneys with his carbine and growled an order Joe didn't understand. The other captives raised their hands and Joe followed their example. Harry Bemis broke from the line and ran, and a guard tripped him, hauled him to his feet, and shoved him into line beside Joe.

The guards began to herd them away from the train, forcing them into line abreast. Joe was at the left end. Beside him, Harry Bemis stumbled, and Joe caught his arm and steadied him. Ruth Bemis kept on screaming. Terror mounted in Joe. His mouth was dry and his hands sweating. He barely managed to keep marching.

A hundred yards from the track, an officer shouted, "*Alto!*" and the guards stopped the Americans and turned them around. Coming behind them was the rifle squad, which stopped and stood fidgeting.

The mob of mounted men rode forward for a better view. At the coach, Ruth Bemis stopped screaming, and there was no sound now but the cough of the wheezing locomotive. Harry Bemis clutched Joe's shoulder and tried to speak, but no sound came out. The officer yelled, "*Listo-o-o!*"

There was a rattling of rifle bolts and carbine levers. The officer shouted, "*Apúnten!*"

The rifles lifted and steadied. The officer yelled, "*Fuego!*" – and Joe grabbed Harry Bemis and jerked with all his strength, swung him, and crouched behind him as the volley crashed and the flame lanced out and the smoke rolled, and Joe was down on his back, clutching Harry Bemis. Bemis jerked, arched his back, and collapsed.

The body beside them drew up a leg, kicked out, and went slack. Joe squeezed his eyes tight shut and let his arms flop to the ground. Hot blood was soaking into his coat and running down his right arm. He could hardly believe that he hadn't been hit.

There was a racket of trampling hoofs and men shouting. Joe opened one eye and saw the rifle squad walking to their horses. Two men walked to the line of sprawled bodies. They carried pistols. Joe squeezed his eyes shut and had to fight himself to keep from leaping up and running. Bemis' blood was sticky on his neck and hands.

He heard the footsteps halt about the middle of the line of corpses. One of the Mexicans said, "*Son muertos, todos.*"

The other said, *"Cúmplate el órden!"* and a pistol fired, and another, and Joe heard the booted feet approach. The last mercy shot would be for him. He stopped breathing, and thought that by some effort of will he might stop his heartbeat so they wouldn't hear it. He could hear it himself, the blood pounding in his ears and temples. The footsteps and the shots came closer. There was a shot right over his head, and Bemis' body jerked.

Joe squinted his right eye and looked up. The man bending over him, holding the smoking pistol, was Santos Camargo.

Joe tried to yell, but it came out little more than a whisper – "Camargo!"

Santos Camargo said, "Who you?"

"Joe! Joe Dyer!"

Camargo looked hastily at the other killer, then down at Joe, and said softly, "*Buena suerte*, Joe. Good luck!" He fired into the ground beside Joe's head.

The two executioners walked away.

Joe began to shake. Sweat drenched him. He lay as still as Harry Bemis for . . . a minute? ten minutes? a half hour? He would never know. Flies crawled on his face, and the sick smell of warm blood nauseated him.

There was a great drumming of hoofs which receded over the hill and died away.

Footsteps approached, one person coming haltingly, and Joe didn't dare look. And suddenly there was more weight on him, on top of Harry Bemis, sprawled across him. Ruth Bemis was snuffling and whimpering, lying on her murdered husband, holding his bloody hand to her face. Joe barely breathed.

The locomotive whistled. Ruth didn't get up, just lay there hiccuping and crying silently. Joe didn't move. He was dead, and he had to stay dead until night fell and he could crawl away somewhere and hide. He mustn't move! Mustn't risk Ruth Bemis' scream of horror, and the train crew coming running, and the hundreds of hoofs charging back over that hill.

Someone hurried from the train toward the sprawled line of corpses. A man spoke, and Joe recognized the voice of the conductor saying, "Lady! We leavin'. You can't stay here." The weight shifted on Joe, and he looked through slitted eyes and saw Ruth Bemis struggling silently to free herself from the conductor's grip. The train whistle hooted. The conductor stood for a moment looking at her, shrugged his shoulders, and went away.

The little Mogul and the two boxcars and the flatcar and the coach with only its Mexican passengers went away around the hill. Joe lay there, under Harry's corpse and Harry's whimpering widow, until he could no longer hear the train. He opened his eyes a crack and was dully surprised to see that the sun was down.

He struggled and raised up on his elbows and said, "Mrs. Bemis."

She dropped Harry's hand and jerked her head around and stared down at him. Her mouth was open and there was a look of near-idiocy on her face.

Joe got his hand under Harry's armpit and pushed, heaving himself sideways. Ruth seemed not to be breathing as she stared unblinking into Joe's eyes. He had to shove her aside and heave Harry off. Sand was glued to his hands and coat with Harry's blood. He got to his feet, and Ruth backed away, scrambling on hands and knees, never taking her eyes from his.

He said, "Why didn't you go on the train?"

She didn't answer, and he got his bandanna from his hip pocket and began to scrub at the congealing blood on his hands and on the coat. "Why did they do it?" he asked. "Why would they just shoot us down? Who were they?" He threw the gummed-up bandanna down.

Ruth jumped up and began to run, stumbling over her long skirt, falling, and getting up to run again, not making a sound.

Joe ran after her as she disappeared into the chaparral. The light was going fast as he followed her tracks, zigzagging crazily through the brush.

The breeze sprang up, and the cold came dropping down with the night. In the last light, he found her lying in a little arroyo, scratched and bleeding. She seemed only half conscious, and made no objection when he picked her up.

She was no burden, and the night was clear. He avoided the nopal cactus and the creosote bushes and walked a long time, his one aim to get as far from the railroad as he could, to lose himself and Ruth in the desert, in some hole into which they could crawl like hunted animals.

Suddenly, his strength ran out. He circled in the starlit chaparral until he found a wash with brush overhanging, and carried her down into it and kicked stones aside, and put her down. When he lay beside her and pulled her close and tucked the sheepskin coat around them both as best he could, she was shivering.

His mind kept going in circles — why? why? — until exhaustion drugged him, and he slept, not waking when the night got colder and the bitter wind felt its way into the wash and inside the coat. He roused only a few times, when Ruth Bemis clung tighter and pushed her head into the hollow of his neck. He tucked the coat closer around her. The wind whistled, blowing grit into his face. His feet were numb and the small of his back like ice, because the sheepskin wouldn't cover him unless he pulled it away from her. A brilliant moon rose and flooded the desert with pale light that seemed to make the night colder.

He awoke in the first light. His arm under Ruth was numb, and he tried gently to free it. She mumbled, and her eyes flew open. She stared into his face and her mouth twisted and she began to struggle, silently, desperately, to get away from him. He held her gently.

"Easy, now. You're all right. You're safe."

Little by little she relaxed, and tears flooded down her grimy face. When her sobbing subsided, she put her head on his chest and drew great gasping breaths.

Joe said, "I've got to go back there. Just keep wrapped up and wait for me."

She flung her arms around his neck and said, "No! No! Don't go!"

"I'll come right back," he said. "There might be something in their pockets, a knife or something. We haven't got anything."

"No!" she said. "They'll be there!"

"They went away," Joe said. "Those . . . those Mexicans and the train. It isn't far. I'll be right back."

"No, you mustn't!" she said. "They'll be there! They'll come to rob the bodies, to get the clothes."

"Who?"

"The little people. The farmers, the *campesinos*. We have to go. We have to go right now!"

The light grew stronger, flooding the flat desert. To the east, maybe two miles, buzzards were circling, dropping slowly down.

"You don't know them," she said. "They hate gringos. They'll kill us just for our clothes. They're starving. They're starving from the war. They'll kill you for your boots alone."

"All right," Joe said. "But what do we do for water? Where do we go?"

"West," she said. "And we mustn't be seen!"

"Why don't we go north?" Joe asked. "How far are we from the border?"

"No, we mustn't!" she insisted. "It's too far. It's too far. It's two hundred miles. And we'd be too close to the railroad."

Joe knew they'd never make it to anywhere. This was desert, true desert, like around Tucson, with no water. No water at all. And even if there was water, they couldn't walk two hundred miles unseen. They had to have food and shelter, and the only place to get them was from people — and people would kill them. Ruth was still a little out of her head, he thought, and maybe didn't realize yet what they were up against — but she would. As soon as the shock wore off, she'd know how hopeless it was. But no matter how hopeless, they had to do something. They couln't just sit here till they died of thirst, or some starving *paisano* murdered them for their clothes. Just as well die trying.

"We might as well start," he said and got up and reached his hand to her and pulled her up. Her hair was every which way, and her eyes looked like two holes burnt in a blanket. She handed him the sheepskin coat and saw Harry's dried blood on her hand. She stared at it, and Joe reached for her, because she looked like she was going to be sick. She swayed on her feet and tried to wipe her hands on her shirtwaist. There was blood there, too, and when she saw it she *was* sick. Joe got his arm around her from behind, and she hung bent over, retching and gagging. When the spasm was over, she turned in his arms and clung to him and cried. He held her until it was over, then said, "Well, we better start."

She took his hand and began to climb out of the wash. Looking at her buttoned, pointed-toe shoes, he suddenly felt all gone, finished, and was almost ready to quit and wait right there for whatever was going to happen to them. He didn't know where they were heading, nor how far it was — and those silly shoes wouldn't last five miles.

You might as well have no feet at all as be barefooted in the Chihuahua desert.

She began to walk, hampered by her long wool skirt and God knows how many petticoats and camisoles and corsets, or whatever the hell women burdened themselves with. The only reason Joe didn't say, "We're never going to make it," and quit right there was that it was easier to be doing something than nothing. He took her hand and walked beside her, helping her as best he could.

The desert was a succession of little hills, and gravel that slipped underfoot, and tangles of stunted mesquite that caught at their clothing like fish hooks, and colonies of spiked nopal that forced them into wide detours. Looking back, Joe saw the circling buzzards. That was all there was in the sky, that and the sun — not a cloud from horizon to horizon — and they began to sweat. He was dizzy from the heat of the sun on his bare head, and felt deep compassion for Ruth, struggling along beside him.

She held out for two hours, then suddenly knelt and slid forward to lie prone. She was crying weakly and saying, "I can't. I can't." He knelt and smoothed her hair with his hand and didn't know what to say. What *was* the use of going on, torturing themselves, when it could only end one way — death by thirst and exhaustion, or death at the hands of some miserable, starving *peón*, or by the carbine of some grinning murderer on horseback.

Ruth stopped crying and lay silent for a long time. Then she said, "Did he suffer?"

"He died right away," Joe said. "He never moved."

"And you are the only one left," she said.

For the first time, he had a twinge of conscience. Angrily, he rejected it. That he was alive was a miracle, and if Harry had thought of jumping behind him, Harry might be alive instead of him. He hadn't shot Harry. And if Santos Camargo hadn't spared his life, he'd be lying there, too, bloating and stinking. What twist of fate had put Santos Camargo at that place at that time, what wild streak of luck had steered Camargo to him, instead of that other killer dealing out the mercy shots? Why had Camargo spared him?

Ruth sat up, "I think I can go on now," she said.

He almost said, "What the hell for?" but he got up and pulled her to her feet and they started to walk.

She gave out again when the sun was overhead, beating down like a hammer. Joe found a little shade under a creosote bush and sat and pulled her down so that she lay with her head on his lap. In a few minutes she was asleep, with wisps of tangled, dark hair stuck to her forehead with sweat. Joe gently moved her aside and put the rolled-up sheepskin under her head. Flies buzzed persistently around the bloody coat. Presently, he dropped off to sleep.

When he woke up, Ruth was looking at him, with her head propped on one hand. Her face was swollen, and her lips had started to crack.

He said, "We'd better go back to the railroad. There's bound to be a water tank if we follow the tracks. Maybe we could get to Chihuahua."

"No, we don't dare," she said. "Those were Villa's cavalry. If they're that strong around here, they've probably retaken Chihuahua."

"We haven't got any choice," he said. "We won't last another day. Our only chance is to go back to the railroad and stop a train."

"Joe, no! We don't dare! You don't know! We can get into the mountains. There's water there, and places to hide, and if we can find the Indians . . . "

"Indians! Half of those Mexicans that stopped the train were Indians!"

"No, Joe . . . in the mountains. The Tarahumara. They're friendly. They'll hide us."

"What makes you think so?"

"There are a lot of them up around the mine," she said. "My father's mine, where Harry and I were going. And the Mexicans that worked for us, they're my friends, Joe. If we can get there, we'll be all right."

"How far is it?" Joe asked.

"I don't know. I guess about fifty miles from the railroad to the foothills."

Joe laughed. "And no water, no food, and every Mexican ready to kill us on sight."

Ruth got up and began to walk.

"Now, wait!" Joe said. "People must be there now, where they stopped the train. Somebody'll follow our tracks. We can't get away!"

He looked back and saw two horsemen coming, way back. He looked around, frantic, with the terror rising in him again. There was no place to hide in the waist-high chaparral.

He walked rapidly and overtook Ruth, who was walking determinedly westward. He said, "There's a couple of riders coming."

She looked back, then before he could grab her she began to run, dodging and scuttling among the bushes and clumps of cactus.

Joe ran and caught her and held her still.

"No use to run," he said.

TEN

The two riders approached at a walk — a very small man and a huge bulk of a man, the first on a beautiful claybank, and the big one sitting clumsily on a rangy black, a highbred animal with four white socks and a star.

They were poorly dressed and heavily armed, a paradox of meanness and poverty magnificently equipped. There was a Winchester carbine in each saddle boot on the silver-mounted saddles, and each rider carried a revolver on a belt studded with cartridges, and two bandoliers of rifle cartridges. The saddles had the built-on *cantinas* — big, square saddlebags of carved leather, covered by brilliant Saltillo serapes, folded and tied with the saddle strings. A machete in a leather scabbard hung from the off side of each saddle fork under a rawhide reata, and a large canteen hung from the near side.

The small man had a face like a walnut, under a huge, flop-brimmed sombrero. His jacket was filthy *jorongo*, a sort of long, sleeveless vest. His pants were white cotton *calzones*, gray with dirt, and his footgear, sandals of bullhide with great Chihuahua spurs drooping from the heels. His companion, brute-faced and vacant of expression, also wore a *jorongo* and equally dirty *calzones*. His dirty feet were bare in the elegant *tapaderos* with the silver *conchas*.

They pulled up and stared at Joe and Ruth. The little man said, "*Concepción Osuna, a sús órdenes.*"

He jerked his head toward the lout on the black and said, "*Mi mozo, El Buey.*" He giggled, and his wizened face resumed its lack of expression.

"What did he say?" Joe asked.

Ruth said, "His name is Concepción Osuna. His servant's name is The Ox."

Concepción Osuna listened with great concentration. *"Tenéis sed?"* he inquired.

"*Si mucho,*" Ruth said. And to Joe, "He's offering us water."

El Buey got down and unslung the two-quart canteen from the pommel. Joe began to relax. "I guess we're all right now," he said.

Ruth said, "No! They're bad men!" and Joe saw the panic in her eyes again.

El Buey offered her the canteen. When she hesitated, Joe said, "Take it!"

Her hands were shaking as she raised the canteen and drank. The little man watched, gloating over the swell of her breasts under the filthy shirtwaist as she raised her arms.

Joe was scared now, too. He thought, if I get half a chance, I'll grab a pistol. They've got everything we need. He was almost ready to risk it, to make a grab for the lout's gun and gamble his life and hers for two canteens and two horses.

Ruth offered him the canteen. As he reached for it, El Buey knocked him down with a sweep of his arm. It was like being hit with a length of stove wood. Joe sat up, too groggy to resist, as the big man tied his hands behind him with a length cut from his *mecate*. El Buey hauled him up and shoved him. Joe had to run a few steps to keep from falling on his face. Concepción jabbered a spate of Spanish, and El Buey picked Ruth up and slung her into his saddle. She tried to pull her skirt down to cover her legs.

Concepción laughed and jerked the claybank around and El Buey led the black along behind Joe.

Concepción looked back and made some demand of Ruth. She said, "He wants money."

Joe said, "They robbed me at the train."

El Buey clubbed him with a ponderous fist and knocked him down. Joe shook his head to clear it and got to his feet. He had never wanted to kill a man — not Dutch Hauser or Cal Morgan, and not even that Mexican officer who had given the order for mass execution at Santa Ysabel. Now he knew he would kill, and kill again, if the chance should come. The dark urge rose in him like a tide, from the murky depths of his ancestry of a million years — something that, yesterday, would have been incomprehensible to Joe Dyer.

El Buey pushed him to get him started. Concepción jabbed the claybank with both spurs and hauled it in savagely when it lunged ahead. Its mouth was bloody from the ring bit. Joe plodded along ahead of El Buey, who led the black on which Ruth rode, hunched over and silent. The late afternoon sun lost strength and the wind rose, lifting curtains of dust, blowing Ruth's heavy skirt flapping around her knees, sifting into Joe's sheepskin coat. Far ahead were a few trees, a straggly line of cottonwoods. It seemed to Joe that he was walking endlessly on an uphill treadmill.

At last, Concepción pulled up on the edge of a steepsided arroyo. A gnarled old cottonwood hung over it, and there was a thin screen of young trees on both banks. Concepción led his horse down into the arroyo. He yelled at El Buey, and the brute hauled Ruth out of the saddle. Concepción yelled at her, too, and she said, "He wants us down there," and walked uncertainly down into the wash. Joe followed. El Buey mounted the black, took the reata from its strap, and rode away.

Concepción unsaddled, carelessly dropping the ornate saddle sheepskin-side down. He untied the brilliant serape from behind the cantle, spread out the saddle blanket, and laid the serape on it.

"*Siéntate, consentida,*" he said to Ruth. Joe understood that much – "Sit down, sweetheart." Ruth looked at him pleadingly and sank down onto the serape.

Joe's knees were trembling with fatigue. He sat down. Concepción took off his crossed belts of rifle cartridges, and began to gather twigs and shreds of bark and pile them in a little heap. He got a piece of flint and a scrap of an old file from his saddlebag and struck sparks and got a little blaze started.

El Buey rode into the arroyo dragging a bundle of sticks at the end of his reata – sage roots and dead branches and twisted roots of mesquite. He dismounted and dumped the roots beside the fire, and Concepción said, "*Más! Mucho más!*"

El Buey mounted and rode away. Concepción built up the fire, and El Buey dragged in three more bundles of fuel. Joe moved to the other side of the narrow wash, to sit in the last of the sun.

El Buey unsaddled the black and removed the bridle, and he, too, removed the heavy belts of rifle ammunition and took off his jorongo. He led the two horses a few yards up the arroyo and tied them to thin cottonwoods. He dragged his saddle to the fire and sat on it and pulled the Winchester carbine from the boot and leaned it against the attached saddlebags. Concepción spoke to him, and he took the serape from his saddle and tossed it to the small man, who put it around Ruth's shoulders and tucked it in around her.

Shadows filled the arroyo, and the heat of the fire was welcome. The mesquite roots were now glowing coals. El Buey piled on the rest of the fuel and watched it blaze up.

Concepción grunted orders, and El Buey took some hunks of meat from his saddlebags. He got his machete and hacked the meat into pieces against the trunk of the old cottonwood and split a branch into crooked skewers. He drove the machete upright into the ground beside the fire, then impaled gobs of meat on the skewers and planted them so they slanted over the fire. When the meat was hot, but not thoroughly cooked, he handed a piece to Concepción and took one himself, and began to worry at it with his strong teeth. Concepción offered a skewer with a lump of meat on it to Ruth. She looked as if she were about to throw up, and Joe said sharply, "Eat it!"

She tried to eat, chewing at the tough meat, but gagged and dropped it. For a long time, while Concepción and El Buey grunted and haggled at the meat, spitting and cleaning their gums with dirty fingers, nothing was said. Joe thought he might faint with hunger. El Buey asked a question of Concepción, and the little man replied. Joe sat trying to loosen the rope around his wrists without attracting attention.

Ruth said, "They say they'll get a reward for us. Those Mexicans that stopped the train . . . I think they've put up a reward."

Concepción snarled, *"Puta!"* and slapped her face. "*No habla! Calla la boca!*"

Joe said, "Tell him to take us to Chihuahua and we'll pay him there." She spoke to Concepción, who laughed and didn't answer.

Concepción grunted an order, and El Buey jerked the machete from the ground and cut another length from his *mecate*, then walked over to Joe and bent down to tie his ankles. Joe kicked at him, and he shoved Joe's face with the heel of his hand, slamming Joe's head against the bank. Joe slid down, dizzy and shaken, and El Buey wrapped the pieces of hair rope around his ankles and tied it. Again he thrust the machete upright into the ground.

Joe rolled onto his side and began to wrench at the bonds on his wrists as El Buey resumed his seat on the saddle and stared vacantly into the fire, which was now a glowing bed of incandescence.

Joe watched in horror as Concepción began to murmur insistently to Ruth. She moved aside in response to some demand, and Concepción got the saddle blankets and the other serape and spread them out on top of the first one. Ruth's face was expressionless — but Joe could see the whites showing all around the irises of her eyes and the pulse beating in her throat.

Concepción said to El Buey, "*Guarde ese hideputa!*" and pointed at Joe with his outthrust lower lip. El Buey, sitting on the saddle near Joe's bound feet, picked up his Winchester carbine and laid it across his thighs, pointing it at Joe.

Concepción took off his hat and his jorongo and unbuckled his shellbelt and laid the holstered pistol on the ground.

He said, "*Vente, chamaca! Vente, linda!*" and grinned at Ruth and patted the serapes spread beside him.

Ruth's eyes flashed hysterically in the firelight. She looked quickly at Joe and back to Concepción and said softly, almost whispering, "Joe!"

She'll go off her head, Joe thought. He said. "Do what he wants! He'll kill you!" and thought, he will anyway. He'll kill her after! Unless he wants the reward . . . Joe jerked at the rope around his wrists and tried to force his bound ankles apart. The ankle rope slipped a little, but the one around his wrists didn't give a quarter inch.

El Buey stared across the fire at Concepción, hypnotized, paying no attention to Joe.

Concepción snarled something, and Joe said "Ruth! If you fight him, it'll be worse!" She whimpered and lay on her side on the serapes. Concepción turned her onto her back and hunched over her, his mouth slobbering on hers as she turned her head frantically from side to side.

"Don't fight him!" Joe said.

Ruth lay still, then, with her eyes closed. Concepción began to paw at her skirt. El Buey stared at them, his slack mouth dribbling spit. Joe rolled onto his back, ignored the pain of his bound hands, and arched his back. He dug in his shoulders and straightened out, moving his feet three inches closer to El Buey.

Concepción ripped open the front of Ruth's shirtwaist and pawed at her breasts. With his left hand, he pulled her skirts up above her knees. She moaned and clamped her knees together. Concepción slapped her – and Joe moved another three inches toward El Buey, humping painfully along on his heels and his butt and shoulders. El Buey moved the carbine from across his thighs and stood it on its butt plate, leaning it against the saddle. He leaned forward, staring across the fire. Joe inched nearer.

Concepción forced his hand between Ruth's knees, and Joe slid another four inches and got his feet around the stock of the carbine, one on each side. Suddenly Ruth clawed at the little man's face, and he cursed savagely and struck with his fist. She rolled her head and the blow glanced from her cheekbone, and Joe twisted his legs sharply, wrenching them over, and flipped the carbine into the middle of the glowing coals.

For a moment, a second or two, El Buey didn't realize what Joe had done. Then a cartridge in the carbine exploded, a racketing blast in the narrow arroyo. El Buey yelled and lunged forward, bent over, trying to reach and pluck the carbine from its sparkling bed of fire. The ten remaining cartridges in the magazine went off like a string of giant firecrackers. Glowing coals scattered and sparks flew. Concepción, shocked out of his wits, clawed his way up the side of the arroyo, with his pants down around his knees and his skinny buttocks bare.

Joe shoved El Buey's rump with both feet and catapulted him face down onto the coals, on top of the exploding rifle. El Buey's shrieks drowned out Joe's shout to Ruth – "Get the machete!"

Ruth stared at him, immobile. He glanced at where Concepción had scrambled up the bank. Concepción had fled into the night. El Buey's screams rose higher as the cartridges in his belt began to explode. He rolled out the fire and thrashed about, howling.

Joe twisted around, sitting, and pushed backward, feeling for the machete. His fingers found it, and he moved his hands up and down against the blade, sawing at the rope. His hands came free. He rolled to his knees, chafing his numb hands, and saw Concepción up on the bank, staring down at him from behind the cottonwood.

Concepción looked at his holstered pistol beside Ruth, and back at Joe. He dived down the bank, hands outstretched, and grabbed the pistol, tugging at it to free it from the holster.

Joe snatched the machete from the ground, lunged past the fire on his knees, and struck. He didn't aim the blow, and didn't know where it struck — but Concepción shrieked and dropped the pistol and writhed on the ground like a beheaded snake.

Joe got the pistol and shot him in the head. El Buey, smoldering, rolled around moaning. There wasn't much life in him, terribly burned as he was, and torn about the waist where his belt cartridges had exploded. Joe's shot, truly a mercy shot, killed him.

Ruth sat braced on her arms, legs sprawled, mouth open, eyes wide. She looked as if she were screaming, but no sound came out.

Joe cut the rope around his ankles with the machete. He moved her off the serapes, picked one of them up and wrapped her in it, then carried her a few yards along the arroyo and laid her down. He brought the other serape and the horse blankets to make a bed for her.

He heard a horse moving, and went to where the two mounts had been tied. The black had broken loose and was gone. The claybank shied and blew at him through fluttering nostrils. He talked to it and got it quieted down before he got the *mecate* from Concepción's saddle and tied it securely.

At the fire, he found a piece of roast meat on a skewer and brushed it off carelessly and gulped it down. He had a long drink from one of the canteens, and was trying to muster the strength to drag the bodies out of the arroyo, when suddenly he was too tired to stand. He stumbled to where Ruth lay and dropped down beside her.

The night was very cold, now, and the icy wind right on schedule, sifting bitterly along the arroyo. Joe was so drugged with exhaustion that he couldn't make the small effort to pull a corner of a serape around his shoulders. He lay a long time between sleeping and waking, wondering if Ruth had been driven out of her mind.

Then she reached from under the covers and took his hand. He turned to her and she unwrapped the serapes and pulled herself close to him. She managed to get the covers tucked around them both, and got her arms around him. The warmth of her small body comforted him. His last thought was that he must get her up before daylight. They mustn't linger here.

The moon rose, fuller than last night, and even colder.

ELEVEN

In the bitter chill of dawn, Ruth woke him, struggling to get her arm from under his neck. She sat up, turning her back, and tried to pull her torn blouse and camisole top across her bare breasts. He saw the flush of shame suffusing her grimy cheek and felt very sorry for her. He got up, shivering, and said, "Get some more sleep. I'll get things straightened out and we'll leave."

She glanced past him and drew a sharp breath and got that funny look in her eyes again.

The stink of blood and death and burned meat hung in the arroyo like fog. She was staring at the hulk of El Buey, with the burned skin peeling from his face and the side of his head painted red with blood. Joe thought he had made the bed far enough around the bend in the arroyo to be out of sight.

"Don't look!" he said.

He walked around El Buey and Concepción Osuna, lying crumpled with his right arm almost hacked off and a bullet hole through his head.

He picked up Concepción's sombrero, a heavy hat of tightly woven straw, and filled the crown with water from a canteen, then walked to where the claybank stood tied. It took the hatful of water with one long suck, and Joe filled the sombrero twice more for it.

He tied a reata around the horse's neck and put the loop around one foot of each body. He took off Concepción's sandals and whacked the horse on the rump, dragging the bodies out into the chaparral. When he led the claybank back into the arroyo, buzzards were already quarreling over the corpses, and a skeletal coyote cringed past, heading for the fight.

Joe kicked dirt over the bloodstains, had a drink and took the canteen to Ruth, who was sitting up on the serapes. She tore a strip from her underskirt and poured water on it. Joe snatched the canteen from her.

"Don't waste it! We need every drop!"

"But . . . " She hesitated. "The blood . . . on my hands. Harry's blood!" Her voice rose hysterically.

Joe said, "All right! All right!" He took the wet rag and sponged her hand and said, "Now the other one." It made him think of his three-year-old sister, twenty years ago. "No more, now. We mustn't waste it."

He brought her Concepción's jorongo and sandals and said, "Put these on. The hat, too. And throw your corset away."

"Oh, no! I couldn't!" she said.

"You do it," he said. "You'll be more comfortable, riding. Don't worry, I won't watch."

She said, "All right."

He put on El Buey's jorongo, which was much too large for him, and picked up the serapes and saddle blankets and went to take inventory of what they had inherited from the Mexicans: two Winchester carbines and four bandoliers of cartridges; two ornate saddles and bridles; two long rawhide reatas and two horsehair *mecates*, one shortened where El Buey had cut off pieces to tie Joe's hands and feet; two Colt's revolvers and one good belt and holster.

El Buey's shellbelt had been wrecked by the exploding shells and the hard rubber grips of the pistol partly burned away. He threw that pistol aside. There were two half-gallon canteens. He shook them and judged they were each half full. He poured one into the other, and there was a cupful left, which he drank. He threw the empty canteen away.

He led the claybank out of the arroyo and found a few sparse clumps of grass and tied him to a sage bush where he could reach it.

The contents of Concepción's saddlebags were a surprise. Wrapped in what might be an altar cloth — a long embroidered cloth with gold fringes — was quite a lot of money — copper twenty-centavo pieces, thirty-four silver pesos, and four fifty-peso gold pieces. Wrapped in a silk scarf was a long rosary, its beads carved ivory and gold, its crucifix a solid gold figure of Christ, on an ebony cross. The four arms of the cross had precious stones embedded in them, two diamonds and two big rubies. Certainly these were the profit of robbery, and probably murder. Joe put everything back. In El Buey's saddlebags were only a big clasp knife and a few scraps of rancid meat.

He chose one of the machetes, an ornate tool with an inscription etched on the blade. It was not the tool of a *peón*, but rather of some wealthy *patrón*, as were the saddles, with their embossed silver pommels and cantles, and the skirts embroidered half an inch deep with rosettes of silver wire thread.

Ruth came slowly down the arroyo. Concepción's jorongo fit her loosely, and she had it fastened to the neck, over her torn shirtwaist. The sombrero fit her well, but the sandals were too big, and Joe had her take them off. He trimmed their soles and tied them on again.

He threw the blood-stiffened sheepskin coat away, and put on El Buey's dirty jorongo. The undamaged carbine in Concepción's saddle boot was in good condition and fully loaded. He shucked the cartridges out of three of the bandoliers and put them in the saddlebag and hung the fourth over his shoulder.

He led the claybank into the arroyo and put both saddle blankets on it and cinched the saddle on. Then he rolled the two big serapes up and tied them across the saddlebags.

The gelding's mouth was cut and its chin lacerated from Concepción's brutal use of the ring bit. Joe discarded both ornate bridles because he wouldn't subject the horse to more torture. He figured he could tie a hackamore with a reata when he needed reins.

As he adjusted the hang of the saddle boot and the canteen, a train whistled, far back to the east and south. He walked out of the arroyo and took a long look, all around the horizon. A flapping mass of buzzards showed where El Buey and Concepción Osuna lay, and ravens were sailing in, but he saw nothing else moving, not even a flag of dust anywhere.

He said, "Well, where are we going? You said something about your mine."

She said, "I don't know where we are. The train . . . well, they stopped at Santa Ysabel, and I know where that is, but I don't know where we are now."

"We haven't come ten miles from there," Joe said, "and we've traveled generally west."

She pointed to the west and said, "There's the sierra. That's where we've got to go. Once we get into the foothills, the Tarahumara will find us, or we'll find them, and I'll find out how far it is to the mine. If we can get there we'll be safe. Our people live there, and they go and hide when there's any trouble; they aren't guerrillas or anything. I've known them for six years, now, and Papa was good to them."

"What's between here and there?" Joe asked.

"Well, at least one big hacienda, and a few little ranches. Sometimes the Yaquis come and camp when the pitahaya are ripe — but they wouldn't be here now."

"Any towns?" Joe asked. "We went through some on the train."

"We're west of them, now. But there are a lot of little places — Tosamachic and Pahuirachic and Tutuaca and some others."

"We've got to stay away from the towns and the ranches as much as we can," Joe said. "But we've got to have food and water. I don't talk much Spanish so it'll be up to you, if it comes to that."

She looked away from him, her eyes wandering, and said, "I . . . I don't know if I could . . . "

Joe said, "Well, maybe we'll be lucky. If we can find water, I can knock something down with the carbine, a steer or something."

Then, cupping his hands for her foot, he said, "Come on, time to go." She started to climb up and swayed off balance. As she fell against him she began to cry.

He hugged her gently and pushed her hat back and smoothed her dirty, tangled hair and felt like crying himself. Not for himself — he felt pretty good, now, with a horse and water and a pistol and carbine. But compassion flooded him, and he knew he couldn't understand, really, how terrible it had been for her, how terrible it still was, and how brave she had been in spite of her grief and terror.

He put his hands around her waist and said, "Now, jump! There's a good girl!" and swung her up into the saddle, then took the end of the *mecate* and led the claybank out of the arroyo, heading for the far blue of the Sierra Madre Occidental.

He said, "Look back once in a while. Tell me if you see anything moving, even dust anywhere."

He plodded west. The ground was rising, and a few stunted trees appeared, and there were a lot of washes that forced them off course. He had to keep swinging around clumps of sage and great branching colonies of nopal and small hillocks. The claybank was willing and eager, almost stepping on his heels. Every time he looked back at Ruth, she had her head turned, looking back.

After a couple of hours, she said she would get down and he could ride. He said he'd keep going, but if she wanted to, she could walk a while and give the horse a little rest.

She walked beside him for maybe two miles, but made hard going of it, so he put her back on the horse. After another hour, he called a halt, and they sat in the thin shade of a paloverde. The mountains didn't look any closer. He gave the claybank another hatful of water and let Ruth have a drink and drank sparingly himself. When they started again, the ground seemed rougher and steeper, and he was getting pretty tired.

By midafternoon, he was beginning to stagger and the claybank was hanging back on the *mecate*, but there were three or four hours of daylight left. He didn't want to lose them, but he thought they'd better rest a while. He said, "Get down, we'll stop a few minutes," and she stared at him with her mouth working and no sound coming out.

"What's the matter?" he demanded.

She kept staring at him, but pointed over her shoulder. He looked back and couldn't see anything, and stepped up onto a little hummock. Way back, there was dust rising, and at the bottom of it, four little dots.

He watched for a while and was sure it was horses, ridden horses. Cattle or horses alone wouldn't bunch up like that, and wouldn't keep coming so steadily.

He said, "Hang on," and began to trot, cutting away from their line of travel. The claybank was raising dust, too. He trotted a hundred yards, then stopped the horse and handed the *mecate* to Ruth. He walked partway up a little hill and got down and crawled to the top and looked back. The dust cloud seemed closer. He swore and slid down and pulled the carbine from the boot.

He said, "I don't think they're after us, but we'll find out. Get off!"

When she got down he said, "Sit here and keep down. Hold the rope. Don't let the horse get away, no matter what happens." He climbed again to the top of the little hillock.

They kept coming, and he could begin to see detail. They looked a lot like Concepción Osuna and El Buey, except that they were poorly mounted. More of those murdering bastards from the site of the massacre, Joe supposed; human vultures hunting for anything crippled or defenseless.

He thumbed back the hammer of the carbine, got his left elbow securely planted, and laid the sights on the chest of the leader. Another ten yards and he'd cut *that* one down at least, before they got him.

The leader raised his hand and the four pulled up. They talked a few minutes, then one of them pointed north, and they reined around and went away. Either they were bad trackers, or they weren't interested in stray footprints. Maybe, too, they had followed to that bloodstained arroyo and beyond and had seen a glint of sun on Joe's carbine, and had decided four to one was not advantage enough. Joe watched them a long time as they diminished in size.

He slid down the hillock. Ruth ran to him. He put his arm around her and said, "They're gone. They weren't after us." He was weak and sweating, and so tired he could hardly put one foot before the other, but he took the rope and started to walk, plodding mechanically, moving west. Toward dusk, the wind came up, cold, seeking and prying. Ruth rode like a doll, clutching the claybank's mane, lurching back and forth with her head lolling. She must be very cold. He stopped and untied the two serapes and gave them to her. She draped them over her shoulders, and he tucked them in around her legs and behind, and started to walk again.

When the sun went down, he found a hollow under a tangled clump of paloverde that offered some shelter.

He lifted Ruth down. She watched listlessly as he spread the saddle blankets on the ground and said, "Lie down, Ruth." When she was settled, he lay close beside her and managed to get the two serapes tucked in around them.

They were out of the wind, and the sun had warmed the sand under the paloverdes. Joe sighed and stretched out. He said, "Get some sleep. We'll make it. We'll make it to the sierra."

She didn't answer, and he thought she was asleep already, but she found his hand and held it. She sighed, long and deep, and in only a moment she was snoring.

Coyotes, squalling like maniacs, woke him before daylight, and he struggled to his hands and knees, confused and scared, and felt indescribable relief when he realized what the racket was. Ruth still slept, despite the noise.

Joe thought they had better get as far as they could before the temperature climbed forty or fifty degrees in mid-morning. He got up and walked a few yards away and relieved himself.

He had to shake Ruth before she came dazedly out of her sleep of exhaustion. In the east, the sky was a fan of rosy light, and the peaks of the sierra caught fire in the first shafts of sunlight. Ruth wandered off drunkenly into the chaparral, and by the time she came back, he had given the horse a hatful of water, almost the last in the canteen. He shook the canteen, took one mouthful, and handed the canteen to Ruth. "Finish it," he said. He tied the empty canteen to the saddle.

When he boosted her onto the horse, the light was strong enough to show her puffed face and cracked lips and the mare's nest of her hair under the sombrero. She smiled and said, "I feel a lot better." He grinned at her, and said, "You're a good girl," and didn't believe her. He said, "Don't forget to take a look around once in a while," and lifted his sore feet and plodded ahead.

They climbed steadily all morning. Whenever she saw smoke ahead, indicating a ranch or perhaps a village, they swung wide to miss it. About eleven o'clock, they scared up a steer, a gaunt wreck with no meat on its bones. It scrambled away before Joe could get the carbine from the boot.

He began to see cow chips, but they were as dry as so many slabs of bark, and he couldn't tell if the cow tracks he saw were fresh or old, because the wind had blurred them.

He was plodding along, hauling on the *mecate* now, because the claybank seemed to be giving out, when Ruth said, "Joe!" He stopped and the horse blundered into him.

"There's some buildings. A ranch or something." She pointed off to the right, but he couldn't see anything because the chaparral was thick and high.

"Get down," he said. "You stick up too high."

He helped her down and got the carbine, then led the claybank into a clump of brush that was high enough to conceal it.

He said, "Stay here and hold the horse while I have a look."

Immediately she was scared and started to protest. He said, "I'll go just far enough so I can see what's there."

"No!" she said.

"Don't make me holler at you," he said. "You want someone to hear me?"

She took the *mecate* and stood watching him as he slipped into the brush. He had gone about fifty yards, and something ahead made a sound, a sort of "blat," and he jumped and came down with the carbine cocked at his hip. A small goat came mincing around a clump of brush and blatted at him again.

He almost shot it, right there, but caught himself in time. It would scare the hell out of Ruth, even if no one else heard it – and God knew who else might hear it. He walked ahead and came near the top of a rise, where he got down and crawled on his elbows and knees, peering through a screen of brush.

The sprawling adobe ranch house was enclosed by a rotting adobe wall about seven feet high, with a big gateway, and a gate hanging by one hinge. Outbuildings were built against the inside of the wall, and a great circular, stonewalled corral just outside. There was a well and a well sweep.

Nothing moved. Then gravel rattled behind him, and he turned carefully and slowly. The goat had followed him.

He stared again at the ranch. A few narrow windows were all broken. There was a *carreta* in the yard – a huge, wooden-wheeled ox cart – and miscellaneous junk strewn around. A buggy with its wheels gone lay on its side in front of a shed that had a forge and an anvil. Against the far wall of the huge patio was a great stack of corn shucks, undercut where stock had chewed it away. There was a deserted feel about the whole place. He knew no one was there.

When he got up, the goat backed off a few steps, and again he refrained from shooting it. He went back to Ruth and said, "We've found a home."

They went in, with the goat following. Joe stripped the claybank and turned it loose. It went at once to the stack of cornstalks and began to jerk at the base of it. There was a *ramada* against the back of the ranch house – a framework of crooked poles thatched with cornstalks – and he left Ruth in its shade while he went to the well. There was water there, about twenty feet down, but some slimy bulk was floating in it, and the stink almost made him throw up.

Inside the ranch house he found nothing but chaos – overturned furniture and smashed china and broken chairs, and a few scraps of torn-up clothing. There was not a usable pot or pan in the kitchen, nothing but shards of clay pottery and a couple of iron kettles with the bottoms deliberately broken out. Rat droppings were everywhere, the dust and sand drifted into corners.

He got onto the roof through a trap door, hoping to find gutters that would indicate a reserve cistern inside somewhere. From the roof he made the big discovery. On a hill behind the corral was a streak of greenery — coarse grass and rank plants along a ditch that led to an open tank for watering stock. Hastily he climbed down and ran across the patio and found a gate into the corral. He climbed the far corral wall and trotted to the tank. There was water, but it was blanketed with green slime. The mud in the ditch was dry, crazed like bad pottery, but at its head end the mud was damp, imprinted with myriad tracks — javelina, roadrunner, cow, horse, and goat. A trickle of water ran from a crack in a cement spring box in the shade of a rock. In the box was a big toad, in an inch of water. Joe threw it out and knelt and put his mouth to the crack and sucked at the seepage.

He packed the crack below the spout with stones and mud, and hurried to get the canteen.

TWELVE

It was midnight, and they were full of roast goat — leg of goat smoked on the spit Joe had made from a steel rod. The blacksmith shed had been a treasure trove, from which came the rod, a battered bucket, and charcoal from the forge for their fire, which Joe started with Concepción's flint and steel. The bucket had served to heat the water with which they washed the dried blood and the ground-in grime from their bodies, and some of the dirt from their clothes. They rested now, under the *ramada*, wrapped in the two Saltillo serapes while the laundry dried.

The wall and the ranch house blocked out the wind, and the *ramada* cast a broad moon shadow.

Ruth tucked her legs under her and sat gazing into the fire. Without looking at Joe she said, "Did you say that Mexican spared you, there where they stopped the train? I think you said so, but I was so . . . well, so scared, I guess I was a little out of my mind."

"Yes, he did," Joe said. "It sounds like something out of a dime novel . . . but I know him. Matter of fact, I thought he was on the train. That's why I took the train. I was trying to find him, and when I found out it wasn't him — "

"What?" Ruth said. "I'm confused."

He told her the whole story — the murder of Dutch Hauser; the accusation against himself and against Santos

Camargo, and how he knew the only way to clear it up was to find Camargo; and how he tried to find him in El Paso, and had to leave Brownie with Florencio Vidal. He didn't leave anything out. And when he was through, she said, "Why, how incredible! I mean, that he was one of those that shot Harry and all those others! And that he would spare your life! That he would happen to be right there, right at that time!"

"Well," Joe said, "I guess it sounds that way. But he went from El Paso on purpose to join Villa's División del Norte. He had a cousin, a colonel, commanding a squadron of cavalry for Villa, and he was going to find him. So if those murderers were Pancho Villa's men, why maybe . . . "

"Oh, they were," she said. "No doubt of that. I've seen Villa's cavalry many times. There's no mistaking them."

Joe said, "What I can't understand is why! Why would they just pull a bunch of men off a train and murder them? They didn't rob the train, did they? Didn't attack if for any reason except to kill the Americans?"

"It wouldn't make sense to you," she said, "but I guess it does to Mexicans. They hate the gringos. I mean in Chihuahua they do, because Pancho Villa is a god here. They leave their little farms and die for him. He says he will give them all a piece of ground, get the big *hacendados* off their backs and divide up the big ranches."

"Well, I can see that," Joe said. "But why do they have to kill Americans? How does that help them get their land back, and their freedom?"

"It goes a long way back," she said. "You know, the American navy bombarded Vera Cruz and occupied it just last year, when Mexico was helpless to defend itself and had been bled white by a succession of dictators. They all loved Francisco Madero when he won the revolution and chased Porfirio Díaz out of the country and made the same promises Pancho Villa made. And then, when Huerta, that cynical, drunken assassin, imprisoned

Madero, the legal president, and the vice president, Pino Suárez, he was helped by the American ambassador, who had no business in it at all, but plotted against Madero. Well he, the ambassador, could have saved Madero's life and got him safely out of the country, but he wouldn't lift a hand, even when Madero's wife pleaded with him. And he let Huerta go ahead and murder both of them. They've got some reason to hate us. Americans are the ones that make money in Mexico, not the Mexicans. Actually, my father shouldn't have had any right to a rich gold mine here."

"Well, maybe so," Joe said, "but none of that's any reason for senseless murder of people that never did them any harm."

"There's a lot more than that," she said. "Specially here in Chihuahua, because he broke up the big ranches of wealthy Mexicans and gave them back to the farmers. When he and Madero and Orozco and Obregón were all fighting Huerta, our government backed them up in a lot of ways that weren't legal. And they let all those weapons go across the border to Villa and the other rebels and just winked at it. Then, when Villa fought Carranza, President Wilson suddenly shut off all the guns for Villa."

"That's what Santos Camargo told me, too," Joe said.

"But the worst," Ruth said, "was when Villa attacked Agua Prieta, where Carranza's troops were. And President Wilson let General Calles bring troops from Eagle Pass, Texas, American territory, and into Douglas across the line, and attack Villa's troops. And they say the Americans turned searchlights on Villa's troops and blinded them when they attacked and actually turned machine guns on them from across the line."

"Well, I saw them kill your own husband, and a lot of other Americans," Joe said. "They almost got me, too. And you're defending them."

"No, not defending," she said, "but I can understand it, even when I know it's wrong."

"Well, are they *all* killers?" Joe asked. "All the little people, too? You were just as afraid that some farmers would catch us as those cavalrymen."

She said, "How many men have you killed before those two night before last?"

"Why, not any!" he said, affronted and angry. "I'm no killer."

"No?" she demanded. "But you killed! Twice!"

"But that was our lives or theirs! It saved *your* life, didn't it?" Joe was pretty angry.

"Exactly," she said. "So if years of war had taken your home, and maybe your sons, and you were always hungry, and your wife and kids starving, and you couldn't raise a crop, and your cattle and horses were confiscated . . . well then, suppose you heard about someone passing by that had enough money in his pocket to feed you for half a year, to buy clothes for your kids, someone whose country had invaded yours and had deprived your soldiers of guns and helped your enemy defeat your own troops by treachery . . . well, what would you do?"

"Well, I wouldn't kill for food and clothing," Joe said.

"You don't know that," she said.

"You're pretty much on the side of the people that killed your husband," Joe said.

"No, not on their side, Joe. But I know them, and how desperate they are. Do you know they could sell that pistol for say thirty dollars? Do you know a man can live six months on thirty dollars, if he's a Mexican *paisano*? No, Joe, I don't defend them . . . but I'm sorry for them! So very sorry for them!"

"Maybe so," Joe said, "but they better keep out of range of my gun!"

"Or *you'll* kill *them*, is that it?" she said. "I'm afraid of them, but I don't hate them. They're starving, and they're slaughtered like cattle by both sides, and they don't really understand what it's all about."

"Well, what about those two, that Concepción and El Buey?" Joe demanded. "They were going to rape you, and turn us in for a reward. Blood money."

"That's different," she said. "There's always the jungle beasts feeding on the misery and helplessness of others. And I'm not sure about Villa offering any reward for Americans. The rumor is around, and maybe it's true. But speaking of rewards, do you know that an American woman, with a ranch in Chihuahua, thousands of acres and thousands of cattle, in a foreign country where she has no right to be, offered fifty thousand dollars for Pancho Villa's head? Why doesn't she help them? Or her son, her millionaire son, why doesn't he help them, instead of trying to stir up a war between Mexico and the United States with his newspapers? Which is worse, her or Pancho Villa, when it comes to blood money?"

She sighed and gazed into the fire, and Joe said, "Well, I don't know the right or wrong of it. I just know that I didn't do them any harm, and Harry didn't . . . and here's you and me running for our lives and not daring to be seen by any Mexican, including those poor little downtrodden people of yours, who will kill you for the clothes you wear."

She reached and took his hand. "Let's not quarrel," she said. "We've got enough trouble. I think you're the finest man I ever knew."

Embarrassed, Joe squeezed her hand, and looked away. "Come on," he said. "Let's make up the beds. You don't have to sleep with me tonight."

She flushed and pulled her hand away.

The looted ranch had been a real haven, and Joe had a queer feeling that when they left at dawn, they were abandoning their only safety. The claybank was revived with a bellyful of corn husks and all the water he could hold. Ruth sacrificed an underskirt to wrap what was left of the roast leg of goat, which Joe crammed into a saddlebag.

She had combed some of the tangles out of her hair with her fingers. She said, "Ugh! It's crawling! I'd sell my soul for a piece of soap."

Joe helped her to mount and tied the bucket to the saddle. He jerked the lead rope, and the claybank began to walk.

By midmorning, Joe could see the pattern of clumps of trees on the upper slopes of the foothills, and the dark blue-green of pine woods on the shoulders of the mountain above. He stopped and helped Ruth dismount so she could stretch her legs.

"We'll be well up in the hills by dark," he said. "There'll be water up there. Here, have a drink. A big one!" He gave her the canteen and she drank deep, the line of her small body and the swell of her breasts lovely as she raised her arms and tilted the canteen. Joe looked away and thought, I better not start thinking like that. He was a little shocked at himself. She was a "good woman," he knew that, and she'd been a widow only four days.

She wiped her mouth with the back of her hand. Joe grinned at her and took the canteen, and his gaze swept idly up to the nearest hills. He lowered the canteen and stood staring, not sure that he had seen anything.

Ruth said, "What? What is it?"

"Maybe nothing," he said and saw it again, a line of movement, something coming out of the belt of pines way up on a shoulder of the mountains, where a wide, timbered canyon mouth opened out. The dark line moved slowly onto a foothill slope, and a thin banner of dust rose behind it.

Joe said, "Something moving up there. Come on, we'll get out of sight."

Her eyes went wide, and she raised her hand to her mouth.

"Now don't panic," he said. "It's only steers or horses . . . But we won't take any chances." He took her hand and pulled the claybank's head up and began to walk down a small, twisting valley. The long spikes of ocotillo were thick on the nearby slopes, and yucca and Spanish bayonet were profuse. The valley deepened and ran between steep cutbanks, and he stopped there.

"Now, don't argue!" he said sharply. "I've got to know what those are. You stay right here. Hold the horse. Keep one hand on his nose. If he looks like he's going to whinny, clamp down on him."

She gulped and nodded.

He got the carbine and walked back up the draw and climbed the north bank under a clump of nopal.

It was half an hour before they came into view, filing slowly out of the canyon – cavalry and a string of pack mules and straggling infantry. Astounded, Joe went back to Ruth. She had tied the horse and climbed the bank and was gazing at the column passing a mile or more away.

"My God!" Joe said. "Do you see that?"

Her voice quavered as she said, "The remnants of Villa's army, coming back from Hermosillo."

"Hell, that was weeks ago," Joe said.

"Yes. But you don't know the sierra. Little twisting trails that a burro can hardly climb, and no roads at all, except in a few high passes. How they got across at all . . ."

They watched the horde move past and away through the foothills.

Creosote and sage gave way to clumps of coarse grass and islands of heavy brush and stands of aspen and oak. The first fingers of the vast pine forest reached down into the foothills, but nopal cactus and yucca were still as plentiful as on the desert below. They crossed a little stream and followed it up until a great cliff of rock intervened, down which water foamed and sparkled. They drank and rested, then went on until the cliff ran out. For the past hour, Joe had been searching out ground that would show the least marks of their passing, and he had been sticking to grass and outcroppings of scab rock. He found a series of rock benches — giant, irregular steps that climbed steeply. With a little persuasion, the horse managed to climb the steep three hundred yards of declivity. Above the great stairway was wide, flat, plateau rich with grass. On the far side, the pines and oaks came down, with sunny glades and little parks dividing them. The stream meandered down through the pines and widened into shallow pools across the plateau. There were many tracks of deer and goat and sheep and coyote, and the prints of a big lion like five-petaled flowers in the mud.

"We'll rest a while," Joe said.

"Can't we stay tonight?" Ruth pleaded. "Please? I'm . . . well, I guess the word is saddle-galled." She made a grimace, and rubbed her behind.

"Sure," he said. "I said we'll rest. Two or three days, if I can knock over a deer."

The camp was well hidden among the pines. Two poles stuck in the ground and a cross-pole connecting them formed the front of a lean-to thatched with pine branches over the two beds — heaps of the soft tips of pine branches. A reflector formed of a stack of short lengths of branches propped by two sticks threw the heat from the fire pit back into the lean-to. The remains of the leg of goat hung over the coals, skewered on the steel rod, supported by two forked sticks. A length of log, a windfall, made a seat back, where Ruth sat beside Joe, in an unladylike sprawl, wriggling her bare toes in the heat.

Night deepened slowly, and the claybank ranged around his picket pin, cropping the grass, his eyes reflecting the glare of the fire. Joe pulled the serape around his shoulders, and glanced sideways at Ruth. Tears were sliding down her cheeks.

She said, "He used to be scared all the time, at the mine. He didn't trust our Mexicans, and he was scared to death of the meek little Tarahumaras that came in sometimes. And he never learned any Spanish, just a few words, and he was overbearing and kind of nasty to our people. You couldn't blame him for being scared really. . . . There was always the danger from the Villistas. They robbed a lot of big mines, and burned some of the little mountain towns anywhere they even suspected there were Federal sympathizers. And there was always the danger of bandits, they really infest the mountains and raid the towns. They aren't on anyone's side, they just loot and murder like beasts . . . like those two awful creatures that found us."

She had stopped crying, now.

"He never liked the primitive conditions at the mine. You'd hardly think it was the twentieth century. We crush the ore with an arrastra, Joe. An old Spanish-style arrastra, with a burro going round and round the pole, dragging that big stone wheel. We sack the high-grade ore and pack it on burros down to the railroad, and the mint pays gold coin. We've got a pile of lower-grade ore, and some day we'll have a stamp mill." Suddenly she stopped, and her face went still. "But I'm forgetting, aren't I. Papa's dead and Harry's dead. And I haven't got anybody. I didn't tell you, did I? Papa died on the trail when we had to leave. It was such a hard trip, and I think his heart just gave out. We had to bury him there in the mountains."

Tears came again and she choked them back and went on: "Poor Harry, scared all the time. But his greed was greater than his fear. He loved the gold for itself, like a woman. Like an opium eater. But he wasn't a bad man, Joe. He wasn't!"

Joe wanted to say, "Who the hell said he was? I don't know a damn thing about him, except I used him for a shield, or I wouldn't be here. . . . I'd have been picked clean by the buzzards, like him." What he said was, "Maybe you better try not to think about it, not till you're home again."

"I haven't got any home," she said. "Only the mine. And if we get there, we'll stay just until it's safe to travel, and I'll never go back. I never want to see it again."

Joe said, "We've got to concentrate on just one thing — staying alive. How do we find those Indians you talked about?"

"We just keep climbing higher into the mountains," she said. "They'll find us, if they want to show themselves. They know everything that goes on in the sierra. They're very shy, very suspicious; but they're gentle people, not killers like the Yaquis. They'll know all about me because some of them worked for us, cutting mine timbers, and we gave them food in bad times and used to bring things back for them when we packed the ore out — cartridges and needles and things like that. And Papa and I went to visit them in one of the villages."

She got up and went to the stream to wash her face and hands. When she came back, Joe washed, too, careful not to get his beard wet, so it wouldn't turn to ice in the night. When he got the carbine and crawled under the lean-to, she had already made up the two beds, with a saddle blanket and a serape apiece. He wrapped himself in the serape and was almost instantly asleep.

It was much later — the moon was low on the horizon — when Ruth brought her serape and crawled in with him. "I'm freezing," she said. "I thought I'd build up the fire and sit up all night, but I told myself I'd already slept with you two nights, and you're like a big base burner, and it isn't as if we were in a bed in a nice house somewhere, is it? Do you think I'm awful?"

He didn't think she was awful. He just felt very sorry for her and wanted nothing at all but to warm her and comfort her. He said, "Don't talk foolishness," and she sighed and relaxed, backed into the curve of his body.

Something woke Joe when it was barely light — nothing frightening, although he didn't know at first what it was. Then he saw the deer browsing on the brush out of the plateau, within seventy or eighty yards. He propped himself on one elbow and gently put his hand over Ruth's mouth. She came awake with a start and tried to pull his hand away..

Joe whispered, "Don't make any noise. There's deer out there." She relaxed, and he got hold of the carbine and held it under the serape as he cocked the hammer and sat up. He waited five anxious minutes, seeing only the silhouettes against the gray of the eastern sky; then his vision adjusted, and the light kept increasing, and he picked the nearest deer and shot it. The others fled in great bouncing jumps and were out of sight between two heartbeats.

Joe said, "We're going to get pretty sick of meat. I don't doubt there's a dozen things we could eat, roots and greens, right at hand, that an Indian would know about, but at least we'll eat."

The clasp knife he had found in El Buey's saddlebags was a real tool — two good cutting blades, a flat hook on the back for prying stones from horses' hoofs, and a leather punch. Joe soon had the carcass bled, gutted, and skinned. He took time to water the horse and stake it out on fresh grass, then wrapped the venison saddle and the hams in a piece of the hide. He wrapped the guts in the rest of it and hauled them back into the trees where coyotes, ravens, and buzzards would clean it up.

Ruth said, "What about the liver? Papa used to say the liver is the real nourishment."

"Haven't got anything to fry it in," Joe said. "And I don't want to get the bucket greasy. It'll just have to be the same old roast."

"Well, at least," she said, "no pots and dishes to scrub."

"You going to take a bath today?" he asked.

"Yes. If I don't freeze."

Joe hung the meat on a branch and dug into the ashes with the machete to uncover the live coals. He chopped up dead branches and got the fire going, then handed her the knife and said, "Get breakfast, will you?"

She got the venison saddle and began to cut it up. Joe took the machete and followed the creek up-stream around a clump of oak trees to where a windfall dammed the creek. He dug a hole a few feet from the pool, loosening the earth with the machete, and scooping it out with his hands. When he had a basin about a foot deep and three feet square, he tramped it down, and dug a shallow channel to the creek. Water began to flow into his makeshift tub.

He could smell the meat cooking and thought of how much he would give for a pot of coffee. He went back to the fire. The meat on its skewers was done, and he cut two long splinters for forks, and they ate to repletion.

After breakfast, Joe dug up a quantity of yucca roots and pounded them with the handle of the machete and set them to soak in the bucket.

"What in the world?" Ruth asked.

"Soap suds," he said. "Wonderful stuff. The only Indian lore I know. Wait till the sun's overhead. I made a bathtub around the bend there. The water won't run out, and the sun ought to take the chill off. You can take the suds and wash our clothes, and have your bath."

"It sounds like heaven," she said, "But I don't think I'll ever be clean again. And I'll never get the tangles out as long as I live." She ran her fingers through the great mass of her matted hair, which hung below her shoulders. "And I don't think I'll ever get rested again. I think I'll go back to bed, Joe. Wake me up when it's time for my bath."

She crawled under the lean-to and wrapped both serapes around herself, and lay on her bed. Joe took the carbine and made a circuit of the camp, careful about leaving tracks. There were game trails converging on the little plateau, and burro tracks mixed in with the wild ones. Birds were noisy in the trees, and buzzards circled overhead. He walked slowly down the creek, reading the night's messages — bobcat and deer tracks, and the flat-footed prints of a racoon — and lay for a half hour at the cliff top, looking out across the foothills and the far, hazy desert and saw nothing, not even a hint of dust.

When he went back to the lean-to, Ruth didn't wake up, but her eyelids were fluttering and she was muttering words to mumbled for him to understand.

He lay a long time thinking about Dutch Hauser and Cal Morgan and Frank Pritchard and Santos Camargo . . . and the grinding stop of a train, and crashing of shots, and Harry Bemis slamming back into him, coughing blood. And of Ruth Bemis lying there muttering in her sleep, small and dirty and scared, with not a soul in the world that belonged to her, and her survival depending on luck . . . and on Joe Dyer.

THIRTEEN

Some time after noon, Joe got up. Ruth didn't stir, but lay on her back breathing slowly and deeply. Her face was drawn and pale.

Joe went to the little pool he had dug beside the creek. The water was quite warm. He went back to the camp and got the bucket in which the crushed yucca root had been soaking, and woke Ruth. He said, "Your bath is drawn, madame, and here's your scented soap. The water's as warm as it's going to get."

She got up and took the bucket, and a serape, and disappeared around the clump of trees.

He heard her splashing, and to his surprise, she began to sing — a high sweet soprano. She's not much for size, he thought, but she sure doesn't lack for guts!

He puttered around, hanging the other serape and the saddle blankets up to air, and collecting firewood. Slapping sounds came from upstream — the laundry was in operation, Mexican style, Ruth beating the soaped clothing on a rock. She called his name, and her voice was calm, nothing scared about it, and he took his time walking to the bath place.

She was sitting on the bank, wrapped in the serape, wringing out her mop hair. Her clothes were spread out to dry.

She said, "I'm a new woman. It's pure heaven! I only used half the soap, and if you had something you could carry it in, you could go down the creek and have your bath while I wash your clothes in the bucket."

"I'll get the sombrero," he said, and walked back to the lean-to. He was picking up the other serape and the sombrero, when he heard a great splashing upstream. He turned and saw Ruth come down the creek at a full run, throwing sheets of spray, and out onto the bank stumbling toward him – and she didn't have a stitch on. She threw herself into his arms, and slick and wet and shivering and yelled in his ear, "There's something there!"

"What are you talking about?"

"Somebody's there! Where I was!"

Joe pulled her arms away and got the serape around her and held her off when she tried to grab him again.

"What did you see?"

She threw a frantic glance over her shoulder.

"I . . . I decided to give my things another rinse, and I took my underwear to the pool, and it was nice and clear water and all of a sudden it got muddy. I mean, muddy water ran into it! And it would have stayed clear, wouldn't it, unless something stirred it, above the pool?"

"You're damn right it would!" Joe said, and jerked the revolver out and started to trot away. He stopped and handed her the revolver and said, "Get down behind the log!" He snatched up the carbine. "Stay there, no matter what happens!"

He gave her a push, and she hurried to the log and dropped down behind it. He looked around and couldn't see anything, and instead of running, he walked casually away on a wide circuit that would bring him to the creek upstream of the bath place.

Only a deer, he thought. But she had kept her head and hadn't yelled . . . and recognizing what that muddy water meant was pretty damn sharp. He slipped in among the trees and circled quietly to the creek. Slowly, he followed it down and found footprints — the marks of flat-soled sandals — across the creek, where they had come out dripping water. They led under a scatter of oak trees, and he was able to follow them by the whitish sides of dead leaves that had been turned over.

He walked carefully around the leaves so they wouldn't rattle underfoot, and cut back to intercept the trail and saw the Indian who carried a rifle and was crouched, peering through the brush. The Indian turned his head and saw him and was gone like a ghost.

Joe broke into a run and yelled, "Ruth! Look out!" He crashed through the bushes and broke out into the open below the camp. The Indian was cutting between the lean-to and the firepit, for the nearest timber. Joe yelled again, and swung the carbine up and came within a heartbeat of shooting him down — but he couldn't make himself do it, and yelled again, "Ruth!"

She rose from behind the log, and the serape fell away from her. She stood crouched, her small, rounded body white in the sun, and held the pistol shaking in both hands. She yelled, "*Alto! Alto!*"

The Indian slid to a halt and turned to look at Joe, who trotted toward him with the carbine cocked and poised. The little brown man dropped his rifle and seemed to wilt, and went to his knees with hands outstretched, silently begging for his life.

Ruth screamed, "Don't hurt him!" Suddenly she squawked and dropped the pistol, to snatch up the serape and fling it around her nakedness.

The Indian stared fearfully at Joe. He was a little brown man in a loincloth like a big diaper, and rawhide sandals and a full-cut shirt with big sleeves, tied around the middle with a woven belt. His shoulder-length hair was bound with a red head-band, and he wore a rosary of the whitish seeds of Job's tears that ended in a wooden crucifix.

Joe picked up the rifle, a Mauser bolt-action.

Ruth said, "Well! I might as well forget about clothes and just walk around naked! I hope you enjoyed it!"

Joe saw with astonishment that she was mad at *him*, in some complicated reaction to her fright. He began to laugh.

"Well, *I* didn't tear your clothes off!" he said, and she muttered angrily, then began to grin, and in a moment they were both howling with laughter. The Indian stared at them as if they were crazy.

Ruth, still grinning, said, "*Quién eres? Qué quieres*?"

The little man stood up, and Joe got a look at his legs — brown, trim and neat, with the thighs and calves of a circus strongman in miniature.

Ruth sat on the log and pulled the serape around herself, and said "*Siéntate*," and patted the log beside her. He glanced at Joe, and went to sit beside her.

"He was prowling around in the brush, trying to get a look at you," Joe said. "Now what the hell do we do with him? We can't let him go."

"We need him," Ruth said. "He's a Tarahumara."

She asked questions in Spanish. The Indian didn't answer, but it seemed clear that he understood.

Ruth said, "Well, I know a little Tarahumara," and spoke haltingly. When she stopped, he answered in guttural, queerly intoned Spanish that Joe couldn't understand.

"He's got two names," Ruth said, "Julio for Spanish and Kosimowa for Tarahumara, and he's been to Bavícora trading apples and some kind of dried fruit . . . I think apricots . . . for an ax and needles."

"I don't see any ax or needles," Joe said, and when Ruth translated, the Indian opened a leather bag he carried slung under his arm, and took out two packets of darning needles and a spool of carpet thread. He spoke to Ruth and she said, "He's got some burros tied up somewhere near. He saw our smoke, and I guess he heard me splashing, and came to find out what it was about."

"Has he got anything to eat?" Joe asked, and Ruth asked questions, and said, "He's got pinole and a few tamales. Joe, maybe if we feed him. . . ."

Joe said, "Get the venison. I'll watch him."

"Honestly, Joe," she said, "he's harmless. And he's dying of curiosity. I don't think he'll run away."

"I'll watch him," Joe said. "Give me the pistol."

She gave it to him and he holstered it. He unloaded the Indian's Mauser and pumped the cartridges out of the carbine and put them in his pocket.

Ruth got the meat down from a tree branch and unwrapped it, and the Indian put on a grin that threatened to split his handsome face. He gathered chips and splinters and had the fire blazing up before Joe had brought more firewood. Ruth spoke to him at length, and he made a long reply. She told Joe, "He hasn't heard of anyone after us. I told him we were running from Villa's soldiers and that they murdered Harry and a lot of others. He heard about it in Bavícora."

The Tarahumara jabbered at her, and she said, "He wants to get his burros. He says he'll give us some tamales and pinole."

"We don't dare let him go," Joe said. "He'll lead somebody right to us, for the reward."

"No, he won't!" she said. "They're deathly afraid of the Mexicans. They've been enslaved, robbed, and murdered for centuries. He won't betray us."

"Well, he sure won't come back," Joe said.

"Yes, he will, Joe. He isn't afraid of us, now. He knows you could have killed him. Anyway, you've got his rifle . . . and he can't resist the venison."

Ruth explained to the Tarahumara and he went loping off across the flat as lithe and graceful as any deer.

Joe said, "You'd better get some clothes on. They're likely dry by now."

She blushed and walked with dignity around the trees guarding the bathtub. When she came back, with her clothes on, she sat on the log and began to work at the knots in her hair.

The Tarahumara rode in, kicking the ribs of a big jenny. Five burros followed. They had small, boxlike panniers made of flat pine sticks lashed together with rawhide. The panniers were hung from crude wooden saddles. Two white wool blankets, very dirty, were stuffed into one of the panniers on the jenny the Indian was riding, and clay *ollas* and yucca-fiber bottles, waterproofed with pitch, rattled in the other.

Julio yelled at the burros and stopped them by the firepit and took off the pack saddles. He picketed the jenny and turned the others loose. He wandered around pulling up herbs and bulbs, washed the dirt off in the creek, and brought them to Ruth, and gabbled Spanish at her. She said to Joe, "Wild onions and some kind of mustard greens. We're going to have a banquet!"

Joe cut up the meat and hung it on skewers over the fire, and Julio got a clay jar from a pannier and poured a white flour from it into another jar. "*Pinole*," he said. "*Sabroso!*"

He went to the creek and dipped water into the bowl and stirred it with a dirty finger and brought it to Ruth.

She drank and offered it to Joe.

"What is it?" he asked.

"Corn flour, ground fine. It's their staple food and it's very nourishing."

Joe tasted it and found it delicious.

Ruth said, "We'll need the bucket to boil the onions and the greens, so I'll go use the lather that's in it and wash your clothes now. And you can have your bath."

Julio mixed more pinole, and Joe said, "I'm not going to have you out of sight up there, and me naked in the creek, and him running loose with all our gear to tempt him."

"Joe, please believe me! He's a nice person, and he won't steal from us or hurt us. You'll have the rifle beside you. He couldn't load his burros and get away, could he!" She handed him the serape and said, "Give me those awful clothes of yours."

She turned her back while he got out of the dirty Levi's and sweat-stained shirt and socks and the stinking longjohns and wrapped himself in the serape. She picked them up and went around the trees to the bath place.

The Indian didn't need the bucket after all. He got a brass pot from a pannier, filled it with water, dumped in the onions and greens, and set it on the fire.

Joe hung the pistol belt around his naked hips, and picked up the sombrero and walked to where Ruth was soaping his clothes. He dumped the cartridges on the grass and said "Pour some of the lather in the hat, will you? I'll go down to one of the pools on the flat."

Her skirts were hiked up, exposing her legs as she knelt on a rock, soaping his clothes. He tried not to look at them, She pushed damp hair our of her eyes, and said, "That's kind of silly, after I've been running around naked. Why don't you just get into the tub? It's warmer, and full of soapy water. I won't look . . . and I guess it wouldn't kill you if I did."

He had never in his life been naked in the presence of any woman except Aggie, who sang in the Kentucky Bar, and a little Mexican whore in Tucson one time. He hesitated, then dropped the serape and sat in the little pool. He looked hastily around at Ruth, but she had her back turned. He was a little disappointed.

The soapy water in the little pond was not frigid, like the creek water. He soaped himself and washed his hair and beard, then got out and trotted across the sand and flung himself into the stream, shuddering and gasping. He rolled over twice, and got out and sprinted for the serape. Ruth still had her back turned, but her shoulders were shaking with laughter. He sputtered in anger, and wrapped himself in the serape, and began to rub his congealed hide.

When he went back to the fire, Julio was sitting beside it, chewing a lump of half-cooked venison. He pointed to a not-too-clean cloth on the ground, on which were a half dozen big tamales. At least he called them tamales — but they looked more like oversized bean burros, wrapped as they were in tortillas. Joe ate two of them. The inside was a boiled bean paste encased in corn meal.

Ruth came back with his clothes and spread them on bushes. They gorged themselves on venison and tamales and wild onions and mustard greens, and no banquet was ever more delicious.

As dusk settled, they sat around the fire. Ruth began to work at the tangles in her hair. Julio got up and found a big pine cone. He beat it on the log until it was only flexible stems around the core. He combed his hair with it and gave it to Ruth. She patted his cheek and said, "You're a genius Julio!" Soon she had the tangles combed out, and her black hair, clean and soft and shining, hung like a cloud around her face and below her shoulders. Joe thought she was beautiful.

Julio examined the saddle lying on the log. He fingered the deep embroidery of silver thread, and the silver-mounted pommel and cantle, and said, "*Qué bonito!*" and talked about the saddle to Ruth.

She said, "He thinks it's the most beautiful thing he ever saw. A man would have to be great chief to own a saddle like that."

"Will he take us to his village?" Joe asked.

Ruth engaged Julio in a long conversation, his part of it only shakes of the head and emphatic negatives.

"I've appealed to his humanity and generosity," she said, "but those words aren't his vocabulary."

"Did you tell him we'll pay him? There's a lot of Mexican money in the saddlebags."

"I'll try," she said. "But money means very little to them. They trade for the things they need, and they don't do any mining. Gold brings Mexicans, and they want nothing to do with it. They're careful not to own anything that will tempt the Mexicans. They're always encroaching on Tarahumara territory, taking the good farming areas, and the Tarahumara keep retreating higher into the mountains."

She asked more questions, but got only negative replies, and Joe finally said, "Try him with the saddle. Tell him when we get to his village, it's his."

She asked, and Julio grinned and said, "*Sí! Sí! Por la silla!*" and went on talking.

When he stopped, Ruth said, "He'll do it for the saddle. We'll go first thing in the morning."

Julio spoke again, and Ruth translated: "He says it will be a hard trip by the back trails, because Villa's cavalry is still coming back to Chihuahua through the passes, and the Tarahumara are very much afraid of them."

Joe took Ruth's hand and led her to the lean-to. She said, "I guess it will save time if I crawl in with you now instead of later when it really gets cold. That is, if you don't mind."

"Well, we have to be sensible," he said.

But tonight, he wasn't exhausted. And when she lay beside him, and they got the serapes well tucked around them, he was careful not to put his arm around her.

But in the middle of the night, when the air was as cold as the creek water, he woke with his arm numb under her, and her small body curled tight against him, as relaxed as a kitten. Gently, he pulled his arm free, and she muttered and hugged him and snuggled her face against his neck. He wasn't sure whether he was glad or sorry that there was all that clothing between them.

FOURTEEN

The morning was very cold. Frost crackled underfoot when Joe reluctantly untangled himself from Ruth and they got up.

While what was left of the venison cooked in the brass pot, they drank pinole. Joe packed their gear on one of Julio's burros. When he saddled the claybank, Julio, already mounted on the jenny, jabbered at Ruth, and she told Joe, "He says we can't take the horse. The trail is too rough. And he wants his rifle."

"He can have it," Joe said, "but we're taking the horse." He gave Julio the Mauser. Julio stuck it in a pannier and shrugged, riding into the trees, followed by his five burros. Joe held the stirrup, and Ruth mounted and spent several minutes arranging the awkward bulk of her clothing. Joe took the lead rope and followed the Tarahumara.

The burros were trotting. Joe dragged the horse along with its neck stretched out, and Julio and his train disappeared around a stand of pine. The way wound among trees and boulders, and soon Joe was blowing and swearing at the claybank, which was struggling up very steep stretches, with stones rolling underfoot. Joe stopped and sat on a rock. Ruth looked anxiously down at him and asked, "What are we going to do?"

"Well, one thing I'm *not* going to do is ignore that Indian's advice," Joe said. "We've got to leave the horse. Get off, will you?"

Julio came riding down to them, with a self-satisfied look on his face. His burros followed the jenny as though tied to her. He had already transferred the panniers to another burro, to make room for the Mexican saddle. Ruth dismounted, and Julio helped Joe strip the saddle from the claybank and put it on the jenny. Joe smiled at him and said pleasantly, "You goddamn smug little son of a bitch!" Ruth gasped, and Joe grinned blandly at her.

He turned the horse around and untied the *mecate*, and said, "Thanks for all you've done, friend. Keep clear of Mexicans." He slapped it on the rump and it went down the hill and turned to look at them.

Julio indicated that the biggest burro was for Joe, and another for Ruth, and went into a long dissertation. Ruth translated: "We can ride when it isn't too steep. If it's very steep, we hold a tail and let ourselves be pulled."

The day was an agony for Joe, and he tried not to think about how hard it was on Ruth. She didn't complain, although she was limping and fighting for breath. There were no stretches at all where they could ride, and she hung onto the burro's tail and let it haul her along. What trail there was wound deviously around deep ravines, snaked through clusters of huge boulders, clung to the edges of rockfalls, scraped through timber that dragged at the *alforjas* and hung dizzily to the rims of gorges that scared Joe when he looked down. And always they climbed, turning and twisting until Joe lost all reckoning of direction and distance.

They stopped on a narrow shelf and ate venison and drank from a spring. But Julio allowed no rest. In ten minutes, he started up the trail again, and Joe had to help Ruth to stand. He was near exhaustion and he knew that it was pure courage that kept her going.

The cold increased. Ruth was stumbling, and Julio stopped occasionally to let her recover a little strength. At last he led them into a vast cave in the face of a cliff. Its slanting floor was covered with a black deposit that had an acrid odor. There was a ring of stones for a fireplace, and a stack of firewood. Joe spread one of the serapes, and Ruth collapsed onto it. He took her feet into his lap and took off her sandals and began to rub her feet and calves.

She managed to grin, and said, "This must be the first time you ever camped on a pile of goat manure. They corral their goats and sheep in these caves, and hoard the manure for their corn fields."

The heat of Julio's fire released the stink of goat manure, but didn't decrease anyone's appetite nor, after they had eaten, did it keep them awake.

When Julio prodded him awake in the first light of dawn, Joe had a hard time crowding his swollen feet into his boots. Ruth got up groaning and moved around working the stiffness out of her muscles. They drank pinole and got the *alforjas* on the burros and started out.

The trail became easier, and by the time the sun came slanting through the timber, they were crossing a succession of beautiful mountain parks, alternating with steep climbs through piñon and tall, big-cone pines.

Then there was a great, broad bench and neatly fenced cornfields, with the dead stalks sticking up like spikes. There were cows and oxen in some of the fields and in fenced corrals. A woman and a little girl fled into the trees, abandoning a dozen cows, as the burro train came out of the timber. Julio yelled at them. and they came out shyly. They were dressed identically, the woman not five feet tall, wearing many ankle-length skirts and a sort of three-cornered shawl, and a scarf tied around her head. Julio talked to them, and the little girl went trotting away and disappeared among the trees.

"We're getting close, I think," Ruth said.

Julio mounted his jenny, sitting proudly in the fancy saddle, and Ruth said to Joe, "Will you help me up?"

Joe boosted her onto the rump of her burro and it followed the others, indifferent to the extra weight. There was a big peeled pine log by the trail, with two great planks neatly split off, and a third started with wedges. Julio called out, and two Indians came out of the trees. One had a Mauser military rifle and the other a Winchester carbine. They stared at Ruth and Joe but said nothing until Julio showed them the Mexican saddle, which they exclaimed over. They were dressed exactly like Julio. When he whacked the jenny, Joe got onto his burro, and the two Tarahumaras walked along with them.

They began to pass corncribs on stilts, neatly built of hewn planks, each with a notched log for a ladder. Soon they smelled burning pine and oak and heard shouting ahead, and a crowd of people came around a bend in the trail.

Only the countless emaciated dogs objected to the strangers, charging and retreating, and snarling and barking. Small boys drove them off with stones. Julio kept up a running commentary, and the crowd, seventy or eighty people, parted to let the burros through. The women covered their faces with scarves and turned shyly away. It seemed to Joe that every woman had a baby tied to her back with a shawl.

The village was scattered down a valley, with houses and corncribs and corrals in no planned order. More people came out of the neat cabins, accompanied by sheep and goats and chickens.

There was a central plaza with an altar — a plank table with a few crude clay bowls on it. Behind the table were three small wooden crosses set in the ground. The skinned head and part of the carcass of a cow hung from a pole by the crosses.

At the moment, the Tarahumara were not interested in Joe and Ruth, but in the saddle on Julio's jenny. They crowded around, exclaiming, and reaching to touch it.

Julio stopped at a cabin and motioned for Ruth and Joe to dismount. He spoke to Ruth. She said, "This is the *gobernador*'s house. Julio has to report to him."

A man emerged from the cabin. He looked like any of the others, and he was equally impressed by the wonderful saddle. Julio talked and the *gobernador* replied, then spoke to Ruth in good Spanish. He was glad to welcome her and her husband to the village. Anyone who had fought the Mexicans, as they had, was welcome. He spoke again in Tarahumara to Julio, who then led his burros to the center of the village.

Joe and Ruth walked behind him, with the people trailing along. Julio stopped in front of a new cabin. He took their things from the panniers and dropped them on the ground and turned to walk away.

Joe said, "Stop him! The horse blankets and the things from the saddlebags don't go with the saddle!"

Ruth explained to Julio, and Joe began to take the things from the saddle and the saddlebags — the canteen, the two reatas and the *mecates*, the extra rifle cartridges, the gold-embroidered altar cloth, which drew a murmur of admiration from the onlookers, the silver and gold coins, and last, the ivory and gold rosary with its gem-studded crucifix. As it hung sparkling from his hand, the Indians knelt and made the sign of the cross.

Julio led the burros away, and Ruth said, "Well, we're home. This is our house, courtesy of the *gobernador*."

"*Our* house! Why, they can't . . . I mean there is only one room in there!"

"I tried to tell Julio," she said, "but it doesn't make sense to him, or to any of them. I'm your woman, that's all there is to it. I hope you won't mind too much, but we've got to do it. The more normal we appear, the less likely that stories about us will circulate through the sierra. There are Mexican communities in the foothills and we've to be inconspicuous."

The prospect was not displeasing to Joe, but he wasn't going to say so. "I'm thinking of you," he said.

"Of my reputation?" she laughed. "If I refused to live with you, my reputation would be bad with the

Tarahumara, and that's what matters now. Joe, we're here, and we're alive, and that's a miracle. And whatever it takes to stay alive, we'll do."

Joe said, "Well, he can't just leave us to starve! Put this stuff inside, will you? I'll go find him."

"He's going to bring food," Ruth said. "It's a sort of down payment."

"Down payment? For what?"

"A down payment on the *tesgüinada* you're giving tomorrow."

"What's that?"

"Everybody get drunk on tesguino. That's corn beer. When anyone wants some work done, like building a house or a corral, he gives a *tesgüinada*. The host furnishes the tesguino, and everybody works, men and women, and gets drunk and falls in the fire, but somehow the work gets done."

Joe asked, "Why am I giving one?"

"This *tesguinada* will be a little different," she said. "Not community work, but they're going to give us pots and fuel and food. You know, sort of a bridal shower." She smiled and looked ruefully away.

"How do we pay for it, if they won't take money?" Joe asked.

"Well, the *gobernador* has been out to civilization. *He's* not indifferent to money."

She moved the upright planks from the end of the cabin and began to take the things in. The cabin was about eight feet by ten, entirely ax work, and the thick planks looked as though they had been planed. The sides were horizontal planks, joined with V-notched tongues and grooves. The four-foot corner pots and the seven-foot pots at the gables were forked poles supporting plates and the ridge pole. The roof planks were concave, fitted together like roof tiles. The vertical planks closing the gable ends were movable, for access.

Ruth piled their gear on a platform extending the width of the room, at the rear. In a front corner was a fireplace of mud and stones, with a plank chimney. Opposite the fireplace were two wall shelves.

Ruth sat on the platform and said, "This is the bed. I can't say much for the springs."

Joe was trying to think of something to say, when Julio came in, followed by a small, pretty woman bent under a load of firewood. She dumped it down and Julio spoke to Ruth. Ruth said, "Meet Mrs. Julio. Her name is Tilalia."

Three more diminutive women struggled in and put their loads down – a big *olla* of water, four crude pottery bowls, a big jar of pinole, a stack of tortillas and tamales, and a wooden platter with a pile of cooked meat on it. They backed out, and Joe heard them giggling outside.

Ruth said, "Julio wants to know how much tesguino you want for tomorrow."

"Hell, how do I know? How many're coming?"

"Every adult in town will be here," Ruth said, "and all the babies, too, slung on their mothers' backs."

"Tell him to bring all he can get," Joe said. "Fifty pesos worth."

Julio jabbered at Ruth again, and she said, "He wants that rosary. Don't give it to him. You can pay the *gobernador* with a gold piece. Okay?"

"Whatever you say," Joe said, and she spoke sharply to Julio. He grinned and went out, not discomfited by the refusal. Tilalia came in with a stack of goatskins for bedding, and quickly built a fire with flint and steel, and when she left, she closed the door opening.

The pine knots blazed up sending a fragrant black smoke billowing up the chimney. Somewhere in the dusk an ax was working. A burro went through the coughing preliminaries of getting ready to bray before the raucous bellowing reached a crescendo and faded out in dying grunts.

Ruth smiled up at Joe from her seat on the platform, and her eyes filled and tears spilled down her cheeks. Joe wanted to take her in his arms and comfort her.

She said, "I don't know what's the matter with me. We're safe now."

Joe said, "You're exhausted. No woman I ever knew could have stood what you've been through. Get up for a minute, and I'll get the bed fixed."

She got up and leaned against the wall, and he spread the goatskins on the platform and put the saddle blankets and the serapes over them. She lay down and pulled a serape over herself.

Joe said, "Take it easy. I'll fix something to eat."

He almost gagged at the food on the wooden platter. There were four field mice and a ground squirrel, already cooked — but they hadn't been gutted or skinned. He pushed aside a door plank and threw them out. It was almost dark, and there was light showing in the cracks of the planking of nearby cabins.

There was goat meat, and he set it to cooking in a clay bowl. Then he mixed a bowlful of pinole and took it to Ruth. She drank, and he tended the cooking meat and heated two bean tamales on a flat clay platter.

When they had eaten, and washed their hands and faces, Joe said, "I'll build the fire up. You can sleep out of your clothes, tonight. I'll make Julio give me a bunk somewhere."

She lay back on the bed and said, "No, Joe. We've got to behave as they expect us to. And I know we're safe now, but I'd be scared to death to be alone. Anyway, what does it matter, after the last few nights?"

He thought it did matter, because tonight they'd be by themselves, and fed and safe and comfortable, and no need to wear everything they had to keep from freezing. He went out into soft moonlight and ice-like air, and found some bushes where he could relieve himself.

When he returned, Ruth went out. By the time she returned, he had debated keeping his clothes on for modesty's sake and rejected the idea as foolish. He had stripped to his longjohns and was rolled up in one of the serapes, against the wall, leaving a good five feet of bed space for her.

She said, "Don't look, Joe," and he heard her undressing, then the creak of the planks as she got settled, wrapped in the other serape.

After a while, she said, "This is pure luxury. Are you comfortable?"

"It's a feather bed," he said.

There was a long silence and he thought she was asleep, until she said, "I owe you my life, Joe. I never believed we'd make it, not until this very moment."

"I didn't either," he said. "Hadn't been for you, I'd have quit a dozen times. We wouldn't have made it without each other, Ruth. And if you hadn't had all the guts in the world, we'd never have made it. There can't be two like you in the world."

"There wasn't any choice," she said. "Nothing else to do but keep going."

"Well," he said, "we're safe for a while. There was no point in planning anything except to get here. But now we've got to find a way to get back. Word will get around that we're here."

"I know about where we are," she said. "The mine isn't more than thirty miles. We've got a cabin there, and there's canned goods cached and our Mexicans are trustworthy. Maybe we can get Julio to take us there."

"I don't know," Joe said. "I think we've got to start north just as soon as we can."

There was another long silence before she said, "I suppose you've been wondering why I'm not more broken up over Harry."

He said, "Look, you've been fighting for your life. You couldn't just sit around and cry for him. And you don't have to tell me anything. Go to sleep."

Ruth said, “After what we’ve been through, I want you to know. Joe, Harry loved the gold mine, not me.”

She waited for his answer, but he couldn’t think of anything to say.

“You know, we didn’t get married until we got to Columbus.”

Joe said, “Why, I thought you were an old married couple.”

“No, she said. “We had only been married six weeks. Papa had a bad heart, and he just collapsed and died when we were trying to get to New Mexico. It was a very hard trip. . . . We took burros, but we had to do a lot of walking, and when we got down onto the desert, we couldn’t find any horses to buy. And we had some bad scares, hiding from bandits . . . at least they could have been . . . and we never got enough rest and, well, one day he just died. And we had to bury him out there.”

Her voice choked up, and Joe thought she had said all she was going to, but she went on: “And Harry and I got to a ranch and bought two horses and a mule, and let our Mexicans go back. They had been good to us, but by helping us they were risking their lives. And we had an awful time, because Harry didn’t know how to pack the mule. But we finally made it.”

“If Harry wasn’t your husband, what was he doing at the mine?” Joe asked.

“Papa hired him six months agao, in El Paso. Harry was a pretty good mining engineer and we had got into some really rich rock, and were going to mill our own ore and extract it with mercury, and Harry knew all about that. He kept our books, too, because Papa just wasn’t interested in that part of it. And then it got bad . . . I mean the fighting between Villa and Carranza’s troops, and a lot of mines were robbed by both sides, the bandits robbing and killing, and we knew we had to get out.”

Joe got up and piled wood on the fire. Ruth was sitting up, now, with the serape around her. When he was settled again, she went on:

"And then when we got to Columbus, it was pretty bad, because Papa'd had only about five hundred dollars in an account there, and I had a hard time getting it because we couldn't even prove he was dead. But we finally got it, and that's all we had to live on. I have an assignment of Papa's lease from the Mexican government. . . . He made it out a long time ago, in case anything happened to him.

"And Harry started asking me to marry him. He was a lot older than me and, well, I never liked him very much. He never smiled, only when we got a lot of good ore out and packed to the railroad, and got paid in gold pesos. But then, he was really good to me in Columbus, and I didn't have anyone else. And he said I couldn't ever run the mine by myself, a woman alone in the sierra, and it was just plain common sense to get married. So I did, Joe."

"Can't blame you," Joe mumbled, for lack of anything else to say. Harry Bemis was dead, and what was the use of hashing it all over? He wished she'd stop talking and go to sleep.

She said, "Then, after Villa got beaten so badly at Agua Prieta and his garrisons surrendered, I said we ought to go back while we had the chance, and get the money. Harry didn't like the idea at all! He said it was too dangerous and we'd got out with our lives once and shouldn't risk it again. But I went to El Paso and talked to other Americans who had mining interests in Chihuahua, and a lot of them were going back. Harry didn't want us to go, and really fought me about it. but we needed the money badly, and I said I'd go alone, because I knew the country, and the people and could talk Spanish . . . and he didn't have to come with me. Well, he finally gave in, but even after we went to El Paso and took the train, he still tried to get me to turn back."

"What money was that?" Joe asked.

"The payment for three ore shipments, all in gold hundred-peso coins, in a safe at the mine. When we left, Papa was going to bring it with us, but Harry said there was too much danger of being robbed on the way. He said to send our Mexicans back into the mountains for their own safety, and that would get them out of the way, and then we'd bury the gold. And that's what we did. We buried the whole safe."

"You think it's still there?" Joe asked.

"Yes," she said, "because the morning we left after we got started with our pack burros and our three Mexican *arrieros*, Harry said he wanted to make sure we had done a good job in the dark, hiding the safe, and he rode back to make sure. We waited for him, and after while he came back and said it was covered up very well, and no one would find it."

"How much is there?" Joe asked.

She said, "Eight thousand in gold pesos. More than four thousand dollars."

Joe said, "My God!"

Ruth said, "So I'm sorry, Joe, and it nearly killed me seeing him shot down right in front of me . . . and I wouldn't ever want him dead. But I, well, I just . . . " her voice trailed off into silence.

She crawled to him across the smelly goatskins and found his hand and held it. In a small voice, she said, "Do you think I'm awful?"

Joe said, "No! Course not!" which wasn't at all what he wanted to say. And what he had to do wasn't at all what he wanted to do. He pulled his hand away and said, "Now, go on back to your side and go to sleep."

"All right, Joe," she said meekly and crawled away in the dark.

FIFTEEN

In the morning, Ruth got breakfast, as a good housewife should — four eggs and tortillas fried crisp in fat on the "comal," a large flat disk of baked clay supported on three stones over the fire. She went out, later, and brought back a large *olla* of water and a piece of soap she had begged, which looked like a lump of brown sugar. She said, "I'll give you half an hour to clean up, then you have to get out for a while."

Joe heated water and had a bath. His beard was growing and no longer itched his throat. Dressed again, he went out and found her talking with women who had taken their *metates* out into the sun and were grinding corn. They were smiling, and replying to her Spanish with Tarahumara, and there was mutual misunderstanding which nobody minded. Joe said, "*Buenos días, señoras*," and they giggled and wouldn't look at him.

"I suppose you left a ring in the tub," Ruth said. "Don't come in without knocking." She went into the cabin and closed the door panels. Joe took a stroll through the village.

Preparations were being made for the tesguino party. Two men set a huge bowl on the table in the plaza, and others filled it from jars and gourds of the corn beer. Burros, chickens, and dogs scattered as Julio came clattering up, proudly riding the Mexican saddle on a rawboned mule. He spoke to Joe, and all Joe understood was "dinero" and "gobernador," but he guessed that Julio had come for the money for the chief, to pay for the tesguino.

He went to the cabin. Julio rode beside him. Joe knocked and said, "Hey, are you dressed?"

"No, Keep out!" Ruth yelled.

Joe said, "They want their money. How much should we give them? Fifty pesos?"

"Oh, no, Joe! That's a fortune! Wait a minute."

She slid a door panel back and handed him ten silver pesos. Joe caught a glimpse of a bare shouler and a round breast, and hastily looked away. He paid Julio, who clattered off to the *gobernador*'s house.

The villagers began to gather, and the music arrived — four drummers, two woodwinds in the form of cane flutes, and the string section, two violins and two guitars. Joe asked to see a violin, and the musician handed it to him. It was beautifully made, whittled from pine and ash, and strung with wire guitar strings. Joe said, "*Muy bueno! Muy bueno!*" and patted the musician's shoulder.

Julio and his Tilalia came with the *gobernador* and a haughty man who looked like all the others, except that he had a skirt of fox tails over his diaper. The *gobernador*, with great ceremony, offered the fox-tailed man the first drink of tesguino from a gourd dipper. Julio pointed to the arrogant man with his chin, and said, "*Oorúgame*," and when Joe didn't respond, said, "*Curandero!*" Joe didn't understand that, either, but figured he must be some kind of witch doctor. The chief led the *curandero* to a seat on a goatskin.

Ruth came from the cabin, took Joe's arm, and said, "Admire me!" and stepped back and made a pirouette. Her hair was in two braids and she wore a red scarf around her head, and a full Tarahumara skirt, and a triangular shawl over her shoulders. Her face shone with cleanliness and she was smiling.

"Tilalia brought them," she said. "How do you like your Tarahumara girl?"

"I'm going to join the tribe," Joe said. "You're beautiful!"

Julio brought him a bowl of tesguino.

"You're the guest of honor," Ruth said. "But watch that stuff!"

He drank and almost spat it out. It was sour and smelled bad. "Don't worry!" he said. "It's God awful!"

"Drink it down," she ordered. "Don't offend them!"

The party started decorously, with the people filing up to the table and serving each other. The musicians drank copiously and began to play, and didn't stop except to drop out and slug down a bowlful of the tesguino at frequent intervals. The music went on and on, repetitious and monotonous, a quick beat like a *paso doble*, wailing and minor, with the drums pounding steadily. The dancing began, and went on and on, the women gyrating with their four or five skirts swirling, the men bent over and stamping. Joe and Ruth joined in, imitating the steps until they were quite proficient. The trouble was that Joe, as host, was given a gourdful of tesguino by everyone who drank and the stuff began to taste not bad.

He woke up in his underwear, under the serape. sweating, with his stomcah writhing and his head as big as the tesguino bowl. He got up and staggered out into the sunlight and heaved until he thought his stomach would come up. He stumbled back inside and fell on the goatskins, barely noticing Ruth squatted by the fire as he passed.

He groaned and rolled over and mumbled, "My God! My head's gonna break open!"

"I hope it does!" Ruth said viciously.

Joe said, "Huh?"

"Well, you joined the tribe, all right!" she said. "I hope you're satisfied! And I tell you one thing, I'm moving out!"

Joe sat up too suddenly, and his head swelled and diminished in three distinct waves. He lay back and said, "What the hell's the matter with you?"

"Oh, nothing! Nothing at all! Only I don't appreciate being raped when all I did was undress you so you'd be comfortable!"

"Oh, God!" Joe said. "I didn't . . ."

"Well, the only reason you didn't was because you were too drunk to stand up!" she snarled. "You know I wasn't . . . well, I wasn't inviting anything, just because I had to help you get your own clothes off. Pawing me and slobbering kisses, and trying to pull me down on the bed!"

"Christ!" Joe said. "I don't remember anything like that!"

"Well, you *did*!" she said. "And if you ever touch me again, I'll . . . I'll *kill* you!" She stopped, shocked, and said, "Oh, no! I don't mean that!" She began to cry, and sat on the bed platform, and put her face in her hands. "I should have known you're *all* beasts, drunken beasts! Only Harry! He never even took a drink!"

Joe mumbled, "Ruth, please! I don't even remember it. I don't know what got into me!"

"Well, *I* know what got into you!" she said. "Ten gallons of that stinking beer!"

Joe was almost sicker with the thought of what he had done than he was from the tesguino. She snuffled and blew her nose on something, and held his hand in both of hers.

"I guess I shouldn't be so mad," she said. "But you've been so good to me, and I wasn't expecting . . . and you were laughing like it was a big joke."

"Well, Jesus," Joe said. "I couldn't have *done* anything, anyway!" and was startled to hear her giggle. He risked looking at her, and she was grinning with the tears glistening on her face. She said, "Well, actually, sometimes I used to wish he would."

"What? What's that?" Joe asked, more confused than ever.

"Sometimes I used to wish Harry *would* get a little drunk. He might have shown a little affection." Swiftly, she sobered.

"The rape part, too?" Joe asked sarcastically.

She looked at him steadily. "Maybe," she said. "That's an awful thing to say, isn't it?"

Joe said, "Let's not talk about Harry any more."

The tesguino brawl seemed to break the barriers, and the village accepted the two foreigners. Joe went with the woodcutters, just to get exercise, and helped split planks from a log. He used to pride himself on his skill with an ax, but he didn't know a thing compared to them, and couldn't keep up physically. He was further humiliated when he saw an example of the national pastime, so to speak, which was a foot race. Ruth had told him that the young Tarahumaras lived to run, and this accounted for their wonderfully developed bodies.

The race started in the morning, between two teams of three each, and the betting was unbelievable. Each team's backers bet blankets and pots and rifles and cows. Julio bet his mule against the *gobernador*'s, the only mules in the village. Each team kicked a wooden ball with their bare feet, and didn't touch the ball with their hands unless it got hung up in a cactus or a crack in the ground. They went at a steady lope, and Joe couldn't even keep up with the backers. Ruth told him she had seen such a race at the village farther south, and she and her father checked it out, and it was three circuits of a 40-mile course, without stopping — one man running, and the others dropping out only to have their legs rubbed and to drink a little pinole, before relieving the front runner.

The next morning, when the runners hadn't yet returned, a middle-aged Tarahumara came in carrying a deer. Its hoofs were completely worn away, and Ruth told Joe the man had run the deer to earth in two days, never letting it rest, and when it finally dropped from exhaustion, he had choked it to death.

Julio's team came staggering in that afternoon an hour ahead of the other, and now Julio owned the only two mules in the village.

Joe had lost track of time, and began figuring back. The massacre had been on January 10th, he remembered that, and he figured how many days they had been getting to the village and the time they had been here, and it came to January 20th.

He and Ruth settled into domestic routine, and time passed rapidly, with so much of interest in the village. It was inconvenient to keep modestly under a serape when they dressed and undressed and bathed, and too hot with the fire going all night to wear clothes to bed, and Ruth got careless about keeping covered up — never naked, but not caring much whether he saw her bare above the waist. It was pretty hard on him.

The nights were very bad in that little eight by ten world of their own, with the fire flickering and him knowing that she was sleeping naked under the serape. When it got too bad, he would get up and fix the fire and, if she were awake, talk with her about the years she had spent with her father at the mine. He was very careful not to show how she bothered him, because she wasn't aware of how careless she was getting about dressing and bathing, and she would be ashamed if she realized.

Then, one night as they lay awake in the firelight, each wrapped in his serape on the goatskins, he said, "We ought to get your money from the mine."

She said, "It's too dangerous. We're safe here. We've just got to wait until we can go home."

"Maybe things have quieted down," he said. "Maybe the fighting has stopped and the Villa troops aren't crossing the passes any more. You said it's only thirty miles. We can get Julio and his two mules and be back in two days."

She thought about it a long time, finally she said, "I do need it. There's only about three hundred dollars in the account in Columbus. If you think it's safe to try . . . "

"No, it isn't safe," he said. "But we aren't safe here, either. Not because of the Tarahumaras; I know that now. But if any Mexicans stumbled onto us here, or heard we were here. . . . We might as well try it as lay around here. Look, we'll get your money and then get out of here. If you and Harry could make it two months ago, you and I can sure do it."

"Well, Joe, if we get back all right, what about you? There's that murder charge."

"I'm better off back in the States than hiding in Mexico," he said. "I've got to clear it up, sometime. I'll go back to Prescott and get Mike Burnham to hire me a lawyer. If I'd just had a chance to talk to Santos Camargo, I could have found out what was going on at that ranch. There has to be a way to prove I didn't kill Hauser."

She sat up and forgot to keep hold of the serape, and didn't realize that it slid down and left her naked from the waist up.

Joe tried to look away, but then looked back at her, and scarcely heard what she said — "I'll hire a lawyer, Joe. You can have half the money. We'll clear you!" She reached her hand to him, and he couldn't help himself, but pulled her to him. She gasped and pushed against his chest, then suddenly relaxed and let him pull her close.

She was sweet and passionate and eager, and when it was over and she lay with her whole length molded to him, he was a little shocked. He knew that "good women" didn't enjoy sex, but got married and endured their husband's attentions because that was the way marriage was. You expected cooperation with girls like Aggie at the Kentucky bar, who thought of fornication between friends as just a friendly gesture, like shaking hands, and frankly enjoyed it, even though she had so many good friends it cut deeply into her earnings. But not Ruth! He had the feeling that she ought to be ashamed.

She sighed and ran her hand down his hard belly, and said, "My goodness! That's the most fun I ever had!" and Joe had to laugh, knowing she meant it. She kissed him and said, "Ugh! I hate beards!" and went to sleep.

But in the light of day, she woke up and was ashamed. When he turned to her, her face flamed and she twisted away and scuttled to her side of the platform and wrapped the serape around herself.

Joe crawled over to her and got his arms around her and said, "Now, now! What's this!"

She wouldn't look at him or respond to his caress. She said, "I've been a widow only a couple of weeks, and I let you . . . I never let anyone, before, not until I was married. And even that wasn't right, because I didn't love him."

"Don't you know it had to happen?" Joe demanded. "With us together day and night?"

She said, "I should have been able to control myself. You don't expect it of a man, but . . . the worst thing is, I'll probably do it again tonight!"

She began to cry, choking and coughing, with her shoulders shaking. All Joe could do was hold her close and make soothing noises. She pushed him away and got up, skillfully wrapping herself in the serape so that he caught no glimpse of her. She put wood on the coals. "I'm hungry," she said. "Get up and get some water, will you?"

Julio came to the cabin that afternoon, and Ruth fed him and made much of him, then asked him if he knew where her father's mine was.

"*Tu padre muerto*," he said – "Your father is dead."

He said all the Tarahumara knew about her, and the flight from Mexico, and how she and her father had befriended the Tarahumara and not cheated them.

With Ruth translating for Joe, the bargaining began.

"We want to go to the mine. Will you take us there?"

"Oh, no. It's too dangerous. Too many soldiers. Too many bandits. Very dangerous."

"We will pay you."

"I need nothing. I have my house and my saddle and my woman, and two mules."

Joe reached under the bed platform and brought out the marvelous rosary. Julio made the sign of the cross. Joe began passing the rosary from hand to hand, letting the beads cascade through his fingers.

Joe said, "Tell him the bargain includes food, use of the mules, and everything we need for the trip, and he is to guide us all the way to the border."

Ruth said, "One thing at a time." She talked to Julio again, and then said to Joe, "He'll take us to the mine if he's convinced it is safe. He won't go until he talks to the woodcutters and sheepherders and finds out if no more troops are making their way back from Sonora."

"That's the way we want it," Joe said. "Tell him about the mules and saddles."

Ruth put the question, and Julio assented readily, but when she added the demand that he guide them to the border after stopping at the mine, he refused.

Joe said, "Okay, pardner. No guide, no rosary," and he coiled up the rosary and put it in his shirt pocket, letting the ebony crucifix and the golden figure of the tortured Christ dangle outside. He held out his hand to shake goodbye, and Julio's face twisted. Joe thought he was going to cry.

Julio wrung his hands and started to leave and came back and sat down. Finally he said, angrily, "*Stá bueno*."

Ruth said, "Well, he agreed."

"Tell him," Joe said, "that he doesn't get it till we're within sight of the border."

She told him, and he said again, "*Stá bueno*!" and went out.

Joe said, "You think we can trust him?"

"He trusts you to give him the rosary, doesn't he?" Ruth asked.

SIXTEEN

Julio disappeared for two days. When he returned, he told Ruth he had been watching the passes and talking to Tarahumara goatherders and loggers, and the migration of Villa's defeated army had stopped. He said they would start for the mine the next morning.

He refused to include blankets and a saddle for Ruth in the bargain for the rosary, until Joe showed him El Buey's clasp knife. A compulsive swapper, he couldn't resist. The two blankets he provided stunk of goat manure, having been dragged on the ground and over cabin floors, and never washed. Ruth worked on them with the last of her soap.

Tarahumara saddles, carved out of cedar in imitation of Mexican saddles, were never ridden, but used only as pack saddles. They had no stirrups. The Tarahumara had no horses, and rarely rode their few mules because they, themselves, were faster afoot on the almost impossible mountain trails. Joe improvised stirrups for Ruth by boiling flat strips of ash and bending them to shape. He made rawhide stirrup leathers to hang from the sidebars. He got two sheepskins for the saddle pads, and made two crude headstalls with twisted rawhide bars for bits. Julio provided four big sacks woven out of yucca fiber for saddlebags.

It was snowing lightly when they started at daylight. Ruth wrapped pieces of goatskin over her sandals.

Joe had the revolver at his hip and the Winchester in its scabbard slung on his back. The saddlebags bulged with all their possessions — blankets, food, canteen, extra cartridges, Mexican money, and the escrowed rosary.

Julio was barelegged, with only sandals on his feet. His rifle and bandolier of cartridges, a folded blanket slung over his shoulder, and the little leather pouch under his arm constituted his entire equipment. He went at a steady lope, the mules following in a bone-jarring trot as they threaded their way along hogbacks, between deep chasms, and around vast rockfalls. Julio frequently stopped them to scout ahead. They took two days to reach the vicinity of the mine, camping two nights in caves, each of which had its manure-piled goat pen and fuel supply.

Joe was unable to recognize any kind of trail, but Julio never hesitated and always found a route the mules could negotiate.

On the morning of the third day, Ruth said she knew where they were, and that the mine was not far ahead. Julio would go no farther, for fear of the Mexican employees who lived at the mine.

Joe was worried that Julio would leave them, but Ruth assured him that the Indian was too obsessed with the costly rosary. They left him squatting under a tree. Ruth took the lead, and soon struck a well-defined trail, and a little after noon pointed out the mine dump on a far shoulder of mountain.

An hour later, they rode into a yard in front of what was left of the log cabin that had served as home for Jack Harmon and his daughter. The cabin was burned to the ground. Behind it was a smaller cabin, where Harry Bemis had lived. It, too, was nothing but a charred wreck beside the road that wound up a long slope to the dump and the opening of a mine shaft.

Papers and debris were scattered about, and there were the carcasses of two dogs and a burro, stripped by vultures and dried by the sun.

Ruth said, "My people! My friends!" and thumped the mule with her heels, reining it toward the road to the dump. Joe caught up and said, "Wait! Where you going?"

"Over the hill."

Joe said, "Better let me," and left her, and went up the road. A path cut into the road and dipped into a valley. There were three burned cabins by a stream. A corral, a corncrib and a hog pen were intact.

Joe rode down and looked around. There were a few pieces of scattered clothing, but nothing else. He went back to Ruth.

"The cabins are burned," he said, "but that's all. There's no bodies and no sign of any fighting."

"Oh, thank God!" she said. "We paid them and sent them away into the mountains for their own safety when we left, but when I saw our house . . . I was so afraid they had come back!"

"I'm glad," Joe said. "Let's dig up that money and go."

"It's buried in the dump, up there," she said. "Maybe we can find a shovel."

They went up the road to the mine, and Joe found a pick and a shovel by the arrastra, the stone-paved circle like a giant millstone, where patient burros had circled endlessly, dragging the stone wheel that crushed the ore. They tied the mules and went down to the tail of the dump.

Ruth pointed out a stake driven into the broken rock. "Under there," she said. "It isn't deep."

Joe began to dig and struck metal with the shovel, and soon had the small iron safe uncovered. Ruth knelt and brushed dirt away, and worked the combination lock and swung the door back. There were canvas bound account books and a sheaf of papers, but nothing else. Joe started to say something, and she said, "It's in the little locked drawer, and I haven't got the key."

"We'll fix that," Joe said, and drew his gun and shot into the flimsy lock. He opened the door and pulled out the tin drawer with its hinged lid and handed it to her. From the lack of weight, he knew the drawer was empty.

She opened it, and stared uncomprehendingly, and said, "Why . . . why . . . but we put it in there, and he said . . . "

Joe said, "Your fine little people, your Mexicans that kill people for their boots, those friends of yours that are so loyal."

She said, "Be quiet! It wasn't them! They never knew the combination, and they couldn't work it if they did. They can't count. And they'd have taken the safe, wouldn't they, if they couldn't open it?"

"Well, who else?" Joe asked.

They said nothing as they backtracked their incoming trail, until Joe said, "If Harry went back and got it after you got started, why wouldn't he have told you?"

"Maybe he decided after all it would be better to take it, and didn't want us to have the extra worry about having it with us."

"Even so," Joe said, "why wouldn't he tell you after you got to Columbus? And what did he do with it?"

"Joe! Don't keep asking me! I don't know! Maybe he just forgot!" she was almost crying. She wiped her nose on her sleeve and rode in silence for a while, then said, "But it explains one thing . . . why he was so set against me going back for it, because he knew it wasn't there. And when I insisted, he tried to get me to let him go alone. Even on the train, he tried to get me to go back."

"Yeah, I heard him," Joe said. "What do you suppose he was going to do when you got back to the mine and found it gone?"

They rode another mile, and the trail gave out, but the mules knew the way. They cut around a cluster of boulders, and Julio was there, waiting for them. Without a word, he led off at a trot.

Joe, riding behind Ruth, said, "How far do you figure, to the border?"

"I don't know," she said. "We called it sixty miles to Madera when we packed out the ore to the railroad, and from there to Nueva Casas Grandes about eighty. There's a very rough road from there through Janos and Ascensión and Las Palomas to Columbus. It must be another eighty or ninety miles. But we don't dare use the roads."

"Something over two hundred miles, then," Joe said. "And a lot more, winding around through the mountains."

He marveled at the nonchalant readiness readiness of Julio to start on foot for a round trip of perhaps five hundred miles, through mountains as rugged as were to be found. Julio was either a near-imbecile, or the toughest human Joe had ever seen.

"How long will it take?" Ruth asked.

"I haven't any idea. Depends on the trail, the weather, whether we have to spend any time hiding out."

She looked very small and helpless, hunched on that miserable saddle on that rack of bones encased in mule hide, contemplating a ride of more than two hundred miles across trackless mountains in the dead of winter. Joe said, "We better go back to the village and be sure the danger is past. Wait till spring. I guess this is pretty foolish. You want to go back?"

She didn't hesitate. "No. We'll go, now. It can't be any worse than what we've been through. When we cross the border, I'll get down and kiss the ground. And never cross it again."

The month-long journey seemed almost a pleasure jaunt for the Tarahumara, who ignored cold and driving snow and hunger and seemed not to suffer fatigue, while Joe grew gaunt and taciturn and was never without hunger and a dragging weariness, even while his muscles hardened and his hide toughened. Ruth, growing progressively skinnier, rode in dull apathy, or stumbled doggedly along holding to the mule's tail when riding was impossible. She spoke little, complained not at all, and traveled the last week on sheer nerve. In the bitter nights, they lay blanket-wrapped around a fire in the caves with the goat pens, or merely in some hollow behind a rock for shelter from the wind. Their faces and hands were chapped and scaling and shiny with dirt, their bodies aching and dirty, their feet chilblained. Their food was gone in the first four days, but Julio never failed to get game with one shot — deer or turkey or squirrel, and sometimes coyote and badger.

He led them down the spine of the sierra where there was no trail of any kind, and they made wide digressions from their northerly course to pass around vast canyons and tremendous cliffs and harsh ridges of frosty rock. They saw no one, not even an occasional Tarahumara herder. They were now out of the Tarahumara area, and getting into Apache country, which made Julio doubly cautious. They saw the smoke from Colonia Juárez and Nueva Casas Grandes, and heard the faint whistle of a train. Twice they hid all day when Julio said there was danger, although Joe could see no evidence of it — but he made no objection, having learned that the Indian saw and heard things invisible and inaudible to him.

At last they began to descend, and got out of the timber and into brush-choked foothills, and could see the flat desert spreading endlessly beyond. Julio became very nervous and didn't want to go on, but Joe wouldn't give him the rosary, and they moved on. They saw dust to the east, and Ruth said it was the road from Ascención through Las Bajadas and Vado de Piedra to Ciudad Juárez and El Paso. It branched to go through Las Palomas and the New Mexico border, only seven miles from Columbus. They stayed a couple of miles west of the road and came down onto the desert, skirting the town of San Carlos.

Ruth said that Las Palomas was only twenty kilometers ahead, about twelve miles.

When they came upon a rough, cart track, Julio refused to go farther. Joe argued, but Ruth took Julio's part. She said he had kept his bargain and Joe should give him the rosary. Joe said, "Well, maybe. I'll ride along this road a little, and see what I can see. If I can see Las Palomas, we know where we are, and I'll let him go."

Ruth argued, but he rode on. Coming around a bend, he saw a wagon ahead, with its rear axle propped up on a pole and a man working on the wheel. There was a woman and a bunch of kids squatting by the wagon.

Joe rode back. Julio wasn't there and Ruth said, "Julio says there are people ahead. He's scared to death. He just disappeared. He won't come out of the brush."

"There a wagon up there, and a Mexican family," Joe said.

A pebble struck his leg, and he spun around with his hand on the Colt's, and saw Julio's head poking up from the brush. Julio made motions, as though hanging something around his neck.

Ruth said, "Joe! Give it to him!"

Joe got down and took the rosary from the saddlebag and held it out. Julio came cautiously through the brush, glanced fearfully up the cart track, and snatched the rosary. He backed into the brush and was gone. There was no sound of his sandals, and not a leaf or twig moved.

Ruth called, "*Julio! Las mulas! Tus mulas!*" but there was no answer.

Joe said, "Well, I guess we inherited the mules."

"All right," Ruth said. "He really got a bargain. With the rosary and that saddle, he'll be a big man. We'd better get off the road and ride around that wagon."

"I don't think they're dangerous," Joe said. "It's only one man and his family. Come on."

He mounted and made sure the gun was loose in the holster, and they rode to the wagon.

The man was almost as frightened as Julio, and the woman and children darted into the chaparral. Ruth reassured him, and asked if there was any trouble, any Villistas around. He told her that nobody had seen any, but that Villa's forces had gathered at Namiquipa, down by Chihuahua, and there had been some battles and some towns burned, and that a week or so ago, Villa himself had led four or five hundred troopers into the sierra and disappeared. Nobody had seen them or heard of them since, and it was said that he had a big attack planned for some place, maybe even Columbus, some people said.

When Ruth translated, Joe said, "Attack an American town? He's smarter than that!"

Ruth said, "Well, the Mexicans don't think so. This man is the last one to leave Las Palomas. Everybody else has gone into the mountains or across the border for fear Villa will burn it on the way to raid Columbus."

"He's not that stupid!" Joe said. "He'd have the U.S. Army on his tail in no time!"

Ruth asked more questions of the Mexican, and told Joe, "He says there's a gunrunner in Columbus, a hardware man, that took a lot of money from Villa for rifles, and now the man won't give him the guns or return the money, and Villa's going to burn the town."

"He wouldn't dare!"

"He dared to take eighteen Americans off a train and murder them," she said.

"He wasn't there," Joe said. "It was some of his men."

"It's the same thing," Ruth said.

SEVENTEEN

They rode northeast through the chaparral until they came to the road that ran through Las Palomas. Nothing moved on the road, and they continued on it until they saw the dome of the church. Joe said they'd be foolish to take any risks at all, now that they were so close to safety, so they reined into the brush again and rode wide around Las Palomas.

Ruth said, "We have to go in through the gate at the army post. There's a fence along the border."

Dusk was thickening, and they could see lights two or three miles ahead, the goal that for a month had seemed as remote as the stars. Joe didn't feel any particular elation — he was too worn down by hunger, and miserable freezing nights, and exhausting days on the ridgepole of that mule, and the never-ending pressure of anxiety. His admiration and respect for Ruth — who had endured as well as he, without his physical resources, without complaint or self-pity — was very strong, as strong as his growing affection. He wanted to tell her so, but the time and place didn't seem right and the words wouldn't come. He kicked his mule up beside hers and reached out and squeezed her shoulder and said, "We made it, pardner."

"It will be a while before I realize it," she said. "All I can think of now is a bath. It's safe to go back to the road now, isn't it? It's only a couple of miles to the line."

"Sure," Joe said, and pulled the mule around.

A sergeant stopped them at the guard post of the Thirteenth Cavalry, a few hundred yards south of the El Paso Southwestern depot. He said, "Who the hell are you?" When he got a good look at them, he said, softly, "My God!"

Ruth said, "I'm Mrs. Bemis. Mrs. Harry Bemis."

"The one . . . the one that . . . ?" He gaped at her, then spun on his heel and bellowed, "Elmer! Git the lieutenant!"

A private shuffled out of the shack and through down a cigarette. The sergeant said, "On the double!" and the private looked at Ruth and Joe in the light streaming from the door of the guard shack and said, "What the hell?" He trotted off in the dusk.

Joe said, "Any reason we shouldn't get down Sergeant?"

"No! No! Here, lemme help!" He held his arms out and Ruth slid into them and got down. She clung to the sergeant's arm and said, "I don't think I can get up there again, Joe."

Joe dismounted, and soon a young lieutenant hurried out of the dark, with the private trotting at his heels. He said, "You're Mrs. Harry Bemis? Have you got any identification?" Then he got a full look at her, and said, "Sergeant, what are you standing around for? Why didn't you take these people to the hospital? Or the mess hall? Why didn't you send for a wagon? Can't you see they need help?"

Ruth said, "Lieutenant, I don't think we . . . "

"Lieutenant Castleman, ma'am. Officer of the Day. Now don't you worry!" He turned on the gaping private. "Elmer, get an ambulance. And I'm sure if you concentrate, you can dream up a pint of whiskey."

"Lieutenant," Ruth said, "thanks, but we're so close, now. I think I'd rather go to the hotel. I need a bath and clean clothes more than anything else. So if you don't mind . . . "

"But, Mrs. Bemis! Ladies on the post will be glad to . . ."

Joe said, "We'd better do it her way, Lieutenant."

"Who are you, sir?" the lieutenant asked courteously. "They couldn't find Mrs. Bemis after the killing, but I thought all the men were accounted for."

"I'm Joe Dyer . . . that is, Joe Daly." Inwardly, Joe cursed the slip, but Lieutenant Castleman seemed not to have noticed it. "Somehow the firing squad missed me, and Mrs. Bemis and I got away. Now, if you don't mind, we'll go on into town."

"Yes, sir. But in the ambulance, sir. I warrant that Mrs. Bemis has ridden that mule a lot longer than she would have liked. I'll take care of your mules here in the stables, sir."

"You're very kind, Lieutenant," Joe said. "Riding that jughead even on that goatskin is like being ridden on a rail."

Soon a Dougherty spring wagon rattled up, pulled by four mules. Beside the driver, the private said, "Sir, we have the coffee, and I concentrated like you ordered, but the whiskey didn't appear. Sarge, take it, will you?" He handed down a two-gallon coffee pot and several china mugs. The lieutenant did the honors, and Joe burned his mouth, but didn't care when he felt that wonderful coffee spreading through his capillaries and warming his soul. Lieutenant Castleman said, "We'll provide something more fitting to toast your escape, next time we meet."

He helped Ruth to a seat beside the driver. Joe got up beside her, and the private put all their possessions except the mules on the floor in front of the middle seat.

The wagon pulled up in front of the Commercial hotel at about seven, and the driver carried in Joe's carbine and the four sacks that had served as saddlebags. As they crossed the lobby, people turned to stare. No one recognized Ruth until they stood in front of the desk, where the clerk stared at her in growing astonishment. He said, "Is it . . . is it Mrs. Bemis?"

An uproar broke out, and they crowded around her, reaching for her hands, patting her shoulders, loudly and sincerely proclaiming relief and gladness. Nobody paid attention to Joe, and he watched Ruth with concern. The long tension, the bitter ordeal, was over, and the reaction was bound to set in, he thought. She looked dazed and frightened by the boisterous welcome.

Joe grabbed the arm of the desk man. "She's had a bad time. I'm afraid she'll break down. She ought to be in bed."

"She can have her old room, Mr. . . . ?"

"Joe Daly."

"Were you with her, Mr. Daly? Were you on that train?"

"Yes," Joe said. "Been with her ever since. You got a room for me, near hers?"

"Adjoining, if you like. I'm Will Ritchie, Mr. Daly, I manage the hotel for Sam Ravel. That was awful about Harry Bemis. Nobody ever expected to see *her* again, either. You want to sign the register?"

Joe signed "Mrs. H. Bemis," and below it, "Joseph Daly." Startled, he looked at the top of the page. "Is that the right date?"

"It is, Mr. Daly. March sixth."

Where had it gone to! Two months since he had grabbed Harry Bemis and pulled him into the path of those slugs!

Ritchie said, "Rooms ten and twelve, upstairs," and wrote the numbers in the register and gave Joe two keys. "There's a connecting door, but we keep it locked."

There was a commotion at the door, and a man came pushing through the noise and people in the lobby. "Where is she?" he demanded importantly. "Mrs. Bemis?"

On sight, Joe didn't like him, with his pressed city suit and his nose and blond wisp of mustache. Joe said, "Come on, Ruth," but the blond man shoved him aside and confronted her. "George Seese, Associated Press! You're news, Mrs. Bemis! Now, we'll get away from this mob and tell me the story. I'll bring a photographer in the morning. You're going to be famous, little lady!"

Joe took his arm and turned him around and said, "Not now, mister. She's exhausted."

Seese said, "You come with us. You were with her, weren't you?"

Joe shoved in between him and Ruth. "Seese, get the hell out of here!"

Seese glared at him. "Now just a minute! She's national news! She has certain obligations to the public, Mr. Whatever-your-name-is!"

Joe elbowed him aside roughly and led Ruth to the stairway going up to the second floor. Ritchie came down the stairs and said, "I carried your things up. Mrs. Bemis, we're very glad to have you back, all of us! Now, shall I bring up the suitcases you left here?"

"Not tonight, Mr. Ritchie. I'm ready to drop. Thanks so much!"

At the door of Room 10, Joe said, "Don't you need a nightgown or something, out of those suitcases?"

"I've got out of the habit," she said. "Joe, I'm just too gone. Give me one of the blankets, so I can get to the bathroom."

He got one of the Tarahumara blankets, stiff with dirt and pine pitch, from the sack. Ruth pulled his head down and put her cheek against his whiskers for a moment. Joe hugged her and said, "Good night, Ruth," and went into Room 12 and closed the door. He pulled off his boots and El Buey's torn and filthy jorongo, and stretched out on the bed. He heard Ruth go down the hall.

Someone knocked, and he woke, startled, and realized he had fallen asleep. Through the door, Ruth said, "Bathroom's empty. It's at the end of the hall."

He woke again to a knocking on his door and, half stupefied with sleep, wrapped a blanket around himself and went to the door.

"Who is it?"

"It's me," Ruth said. "How long are you going to sleep?"

He opened the door, and she came in. She was smiling and looked rested. "It's ten o'clock," she said. She was neatly dressed in a long skirt and frilly white shirtwaist and a jacket with padded shoulders, broad lapels and a pinched-in waist. She even wore a hat, some kind of straw thing with artificial red cherries on it. "Mr. Ritchie brought our things from the storeroom," she said. "Try this on." She held up a man's coat.

"That's Harry's?"

"Yes."

"I don't want any of his things," Joe said. "And it doesn't look good, you running in and out of my room."

She looked hurt, and said meekly, "All right, but please wear the coat, just till you can buy some clothes. There's some shirts and things, too, but I don't suppose . . ."

Joe said, "If it will make you feel better. Go on out for a minute, will you?"

She went out and he dropped the blanket and tried the coat on. It was tight across the shoulders and the sleeves were too long, but it looked well enough. And it would cover his filthy, grease-stained shirt. He said to the door, "It fits all right. I'll be out in a minute."

Ruth opened the door and came in. He snatched up the blanket and flung it around himself and said, "For God's sake, watch it, will you?"

She giggled, and said, "You don't look very dignified. That reporter's down in the lobby with a photographer. There's a lot of other people, too."

"Well, go on down and talk to him," Joe said. "They're not interested in me . . . and anyway, I can't afford to be seen any more than I can help. I've got to be careful."

Oh, I forgot!" she said. She looked frightened and uncertain. "I can't talk to them alone. Everybody's asking about the massacre, and what we did, and how we escaped."

"Goddmamn it, why can't they leave us alone!" Joe said. "Have you had any breakfast?"

"No. I was in the lobby, waiting for you, and they came in."

"Is there a back door?" Joe asked.

"Why, yes. Down the stairs at the back of the hall."

"Give me a chance to get dressed and washed. We'll eat, then I'll buy some clothes. Maybe they'll get tired of waiting."

She went out. Joe dressed hurriedly in the stinking, baggy longjohns and the worn out Levi's and ripped shirt and the broken boots. He put on the coat, the legacy from Harry Bemis, and washed his face and hands. When Ruth answered his knock and came out, they could hear the talk down in the lobby. He took her hand, and they went down the rear stairs and into the alley.

Ruth said, "Can't we get you some clothes before we eat? We can go to Ravel's Mercantile."

They turned onto Taft Street and passed the Lemmon and Payne store and the Hotel Hoover and Ravel Bros. Hardware, and went into Ravel Bros. Mercantile.

Louis Ravel waited on them. Joe walked along the aisle of the men's department, selecting underwear, a hickory shirt, Levi's, and a cheap gray hat that looked like a Stetson but wasn't. He spent more for new boots than for all the rest, and changed from the skin out, in a narrow dressing room. He paid Ravel with one of the Mexican gold pieces and got a lot of change, and told him to burn the castoff clothes.

They had breakfast in a small restaurant sandwiched in between Walker's Hardware store and Dean's Grocery. As they lingered over coffee, Ruth asked, "What are we going to do, Joe? I mean, there was no use thinking about the future when it looked like we'd never have one, but now . . . it's like being born again."

That "we" startled him. Whatever he was going to do, it couldn't include Ruth Bemis. He had deep affection for her, and they probably knew each other more intimately than a lot of married couples ever did. She was now starkly alone, and he was very sorry for her, but he didn't know how he could help her, now. Her problems were her own. God knew he had some good ones himself!

He said, "You'd better go to the bank and find out if Harry did bring that gold out. That will give you a new start, time to think about what you want to do."

Her eyes filled with tears. "I wouldn't even be here if it wasn't for you. That money is ours, Joe, not mine."

"Ruth, be sensible! You know I couldn't do that! I mean . . . I'm not your husband, or anything like that."

She looked away, and he knew he had hurt her, but didn't know why she was hurt. Did she think they were bound together now, that there was a responsibility to each other because they'd had to fight desperately for their lives together? Or did she think that because she had slept with him . . . ? Surely she wouldn't try to hold *that* over his head. Just because they'd both given in to their desires and the weight of loneliness and desperation in a situation a pair of saints couldn't have resisted. But, then, that was assuming that she wanted to tie him to her. There was no reason to think that. She was just grateful, that was all.

He said, "I'm a wanted man, Ruth. Towns are dangerous to me. I've got to get a horse and some gear and ride the owl hoot. I've got enough left out of those pesos."

"What then?" she asked, and still wouldn't look at him.

"Well, I guess take the back trails and get back to Prescott. Mike Burnham'll help. He's already lined up a good lawyer. I can't do anything till that's settled. Then I guess, work that gold strike I made. It's a good one."

"You'll need money to pay Burnham back, and to work the claim," she said.

"If I have to, I'll sell the ranch," Joe said. "But Mike's grubstaking me. He doesn't put any more of his own money in than he can help.If it's as big as I think it is, we'll incorporate and sell stock. And all I want is a stake big enough to stock my ranch, and maybe make a few improvements. I'd sell my share to Mike for that, and glad to do it. I'm a cowman, not a miner."

"Four thousand dollars would buy a lot of cows," she said.

He was a little angry, now, and a little frightened. "That's *your* money! You'll need every cent of it. That is, if you've even got it!"

She got up and Joe paid for the breakfast. As they turned down Taft Street, she said, "I'm going up the back stairs. I don't want to talk to that reporter."

"He'll hound you till you do," Joe said. "You might as well get it over with."

"Then you have to be there, too," she said.

"No, I better not, Ruth. I don't want any pictures of me in the papers."

"Joe, I can't do it alone! All those people and all the questions, and I don't want to talk about it . . . that time at the train, and Harry, and how hungry and scared we were . . . I just want to forget it!" She tucked her hand under his arm, and squeezed. "Only, not all of it," she said. "Some of it I never want to forget."

He looked down at her, and was surprised to see that she was blushing.

He said, "Well, all right, I guess there's not muoh risk, with the beard and the different clothes, and the time that's passed."

George Seese, the Associated Press reporter, was angry with them for having sneaked out. The hotel lobby was crowded with townspeople come to welcome Ruth Bemis back. Joe was introduced to many of them — Doctor

Hart and Mrs. Ritchie; Lee Riggs, Deputy Collector of Customs; Mr. Burkhead, the Postmaster; Doctor Dabney; Edwin Dean, and others, so many that he couldn't match up names with faces.

George Seese rapped on a chair for quiet. He was very annoyed that Ruth and Joe were not wearing the frayed and dirty clothing of their travels. He said, "You should have thought of it! Real color for dramatic story. Don't you realize you'll be in the papers from coast to coast?"

He told the photographer to hurry to Ravel's Mercantile and see if he could get Joe's old clothes.

The photographer said, "Yes, sir, Mr. Seese!" and turned to go.

Joe grabbed his arm and swung him around. "Just stay put!" he said. The man gulped, and looked for directions from Seese.

Seese glared at Joe and said, "Now look here, Mr. Bailey . . ."

Joe said, "We'll give you ten minutes. Photographs and interview."

Seese sputtered, and Joe said, "And ten minutes is all. Don't bother Mrs. Bemis after that. If you do, I'll have to have a talk with you."

They posed for two pictures and answered questions, then Joe said, "Time's up. Come on, Mrs. Bemis."

"How do you presume to speak for her?" Seese demanded. "You go, if you want, but I've got a lot more to ask her."

Joe said, "I just presume, that's all. Interview's over," and took Ruth's arm and headed for the stairs.

They sat in Joe's room, talking. Joe found it hard to say that he was going to leave in the morning . . . buy a horse and gear and start riding the back trails to Prescott. He had about a hundred and seventy dollars in Mexican and American money. He pondered taking the train to El Paso to get Brownie, his tough little buckskin, and his saddle from Florencio Vidal, supposing Florencio hadn't sold them for the feed bill; but that would be risking arrest, and would add a hundred miles onto his long ride back to Prescott. No reason why he shouldn't just pick up and go, but it wasn't going to be easy, saying goodbye to her. She was pretty lost – not a soul in the world, and not fitted for any of the few jobs open to women. And that wasn't all. For a moment, he pictured her on that little ranch in the valley under Mingus Mountain, and the picture was pretty attractive. He had never in his twenty-eight years been close to marriage, but now . . . He had a sudden thrill of excitement as that night in the Tarahumara cabin came vividly back to him . . . her loving eagerness, her small naked body against him, her kisses – and her miserable shame when daylight came.

She broke into his revery. "I'd better go to the bank. There isn't much in our account, about three hundred dollars. Do you think they'll let me have it? Harry didn't make a will."

"Don't see why not," Joe said. "They know he's dead. But it ought to be over four thousand dollars, shouldn't it?"

"Joe, I don't know! If he brought it out with us, he certainly didn't deposit it in our account."

"Well, find out at the bank," Joe said. "Unless he buried it in a tin can."

Ruth said, "Well, shall we go now?"

"Look!" he said in exasperation. "I can't go with you! It's none of my business! The bank will tell you it's none of my business. You have to handle things yourself! I'm leaving tomorrow."

She got up and came to him and grabbed his shoulders. "Oh, Joe! Not tomorrow! I . . . I'm not ready to, to . . . Oh, please! You can't!" She looked almost as panicky as she had when those two stinking Mexicans caught them on the desert.

She crawled onto his lap and put her arms around his neck, and began to cry. He patted her head and said, "All right, Ruth. I'll stay a day or two. But it's dangerous for me, don't you see? That picture'll be in the papers. Somebody'll recognize me."

She caught her breath. "Oh, Joe! I didn't think! I don't want to be selfish! I'll get the money, and we'll go together. I can ride through the mountains. That will be easy, after riding through the sierra. We'll hire a lawyer and get it all straightened out!"

"No," Joe said. "I can't take money from you, and you can't come with me."

"Then where can I go?" she wailed. "Who have I got?"

Joe gently set her on her feet. "Go to the bank. I'll be here, or down in the lobby, and we'll have lunch someplace when you get back."

Meekly she said, "All right. I'll go wash my face."

When she left, Joe put Harry Bemis' coat on, and went down to the lobby. Dr. Dabney was there, talking with Ritchie, the hotel manager. They greeted Joe warmly, and he asked Ritchie if he could borrow a ramrod and oil to clean his carbine.

Ritchie said, "Sure. Let's have a drink first." He got a bottle and glasses from behind the desk, and set them on a table, and pulled three chairs up.

They talked for a while about the ordeal Joe and Ruth had come through, then Joe said, "A Mexican near Las Palomas told us Pancho Villa's going to attack Columbus."

"You hear a lot of wild rumors," Dr. Dabney said. "But the Mexicans believe it . . . They all took to the hills. There's another rumor, even crazier, something about the U.S. Government paying Villa $80,000 to do it! You ever hear anything crazier?"

"Maybe it's not so crazy," Ritchie said. "President Wilson knows we're going into the European war and we aren't ready. He wants to really stir folks up so they'll demand mobilization of the National Guard and drafting civilians into the army. Well, an attack on an American town would sure do it, the way people feel about Villa, especially after that massacre at the train. Some people say George Seese is here with the payoff money for Villa. I don't figure that . . . but it's kind of funny he'd show up here in this backwater all of a sudden, big-time reporter like him. What's Columbus going to produce in the way of news?"

"Well," the doctor said, "there's reason to believe, too, that Wilson offered to back Villa for President, in exchange for ceding Baja California to the U.S. . . . and Villa turned him down. Those two don't love each other! But what makes me think old Pancho might really hit Columbus is something else. You hear that Sam Ravel quit furnishing guns to Villa? Took a lot of money and wouldn't give it back?"

"Hell," Ritchie said, "I was right there! Three tough Mexicans came into his store. It was quite a row. They were hollering for him to either deliver a lot of rifles or give the money back. Said something about twenty thousand dollars. Sam tried to hush them up, because there were two or three of us there . . . but they were sore, and kept yelling at him. Then he got sore and said he didn't have any guns for them and hadn't been paid any money and didn't want anything to do with dirty bandits. Said if they didn't go, he'd have 'em thrown out. Man, if he's running something on Pancho Villa, he better look out!"

"What do you think we ought to do?" Dabney asked. "Doesn't the army know anything about it?"

"Why, sure. They must have heard all the talk that's going on. If Villa's stupid enough to try it, there's the whole Thirteenth Cavalry, right across the tracks. But believe me, he's not stupid!"

He broke off and smiled at someone behind Joe. "Why, hello there, Mrs. Bemis!"

Ruth hurried across the lobby, threw Joe a stricken glance and hurried up the stairs.

Joe said, "Excuse me," and got up and followed her.

She was fumbling with her key, and Joe took it and opened the door. She walked into the room and turned to face him. He shut the door.

"What's the matter, Ruth?"

"He *had* it!" she said. "He deposited it, right after we got here from the mine!"

"Why, that's great!" Joe said.

"It isn't in the joint account," she said. "He put the four thousand dollars in a private account and never told me!"

"Why, that bastard!" Joe growled.

"Why would he do that?" she asked. "I'm his wife! I *was* his wife, then. Do you think he didn't want me to know about it? Was he keeping it for himself?"

"Well, what do *you* think?" he demanded.

She sat on the bed and stared at him, then slowly turned and lay down with her face in her hands. Her shoulders began to shake. Joe stepped toward her, hesitated, and went out, closing the door quietly. He went into his room.

That son of a bitch! Joe wouldn't ever have any more twinges of conscience about pulling Harry Bemis in front of him when that fusillade went off.

He took Harry Bemis' coat off to hang it in the closet, and felt something under the fabric on the right breast. He shoved his hand into the inside breast pocket, and found a safety pin. The lining had been slit and clumsily pinned together, and there was a crackle of paper under it. Joe pulled it out and unfolded it — an official looking document in Spanish, dated "18 noviembre, 1915." Harry Bemis' name appeared in the text. At the bottom were two florid signatures, Mexican names, and another — "Ruth Bemis."

Joe could read a little of it, but not enough to understand it. He took it to Ruth's door and knocked. She said, "Come in."

She was staring out the window, quite composed and turned to him, still-faced. He said, "This was in the lining of his coat."

"What is it, Joe?"

"You ought to know," he said. "You signed it."

She took it and said at once, "That's isn't my signature!"

She read it slowly, and said, "It's an assignment of the lease to the mine. It says I assign the lease and all interest to Harry."

"Well, by God, he was thorough!" Joe said. "How could he think he'd get away with it, forging your signature?"

And suddenly, he knew. Harry had tried desperately to get Ruth to abandon her trip back to the mine. And when she wouldn't, he had gone with her, still trying. What was he going to do when they got to the mine, when they opened that safe? Claim it had been robbed by the Mexican help? But that wouldn't have explained an assignment of lease to him, with Ruth's signature forged on it. Supposing the theft of the gold had never been uncovered . . . he still would have had to something about the forgery. But what?

Ruth Bemis never would have returned from that expedition to recover the gold.

Joe was about to explain to her, but found that he couldn't, not after all she'd been through, not now. It wouldn't bring Harry Bemis back where Joe could get his hands on him, and she'd better off if she never figured it out.

Then she said softly, "I'd never have come back, would I, Joe?"

She looked so lost, so stricken and forlorn — and before he realized it, he had her in his arms and she was hugging him fiercely, and he was saying, with his face smothered in her hair, "Never mind! Never mind! It's all over!"

She cried for a long time. The collar of his new shirt was soaked with tears. Joe petted her and said things that neither of them heard, and at last, she quieted. She said, "You aren't going tomorrow, are you? You aren't going to leave me?"

EIGHTEEN

A knock on his door woke him, and he said, "Wait a minute!" and got up and wrapped the blanket around himself and went to the door. Ruth pushed past him. He closed the door and said, "You've got to quit running in and out of my room!"

"Well," she said, "it's ten o'clock, and I can't wait any longer." She had a funny look on her face, constrained and hesitant.

He said, "What's the rush? I've got a lot of sleep to make up. Now get out of here so I can get dressed."

"Hurry, will you? I've got to go to El Paso. The train leaves in twenty minutes."

"El Paso? What for?"

"It's about the money – Harry's account. There's no time to tell you now."

She went out. Joe threw his clothes on and found her in the lobby.

The station was diagonally across the street, the train already there. By the coach steps, waiting until the last minute, was a small bearded man, neatly dressed.

The side of his face was swollen. He looked at Ruth and said, "You're Mrs. Bemis, aren't you? I'm Sam Ravel. We are all sad about your husband, Mrs. Bemis, but greatly relieved that you got back. Is this Mr. . . . Daly, is it? You're my guests, in a way. I own the Commercial Hotel. Live there myself."

Joe shook his proffered hand and said, "You're going to El Paso? Will you sort of keep an eye on her?"

"Gladly, sir. One of my molars is killing me. I've got to have it out. You're coming back tonight on the Drunks' Special, Mrs. Bemis?"

Ruth laughed. "Is that what they call it? Yes, I expect to."

The conductor yelled, "All aboard!"

She squeezed Joe's hand and said, "Will you meet the train tonight?" It's midnight, I think."

"I'll be here."

Ravel helped her aboard. The train pulled out, and Joe bought a copy of the El Paso Herald, had breakfast, and went back to the hotel. He stayed in his room most of the day, sleeping, reading the paper, cleaning the carbine and revolver, and sleeping again. The paper said Pancho Villa and a large detachment of his División del Norte had gone into the mountains. Carranzista cavalry had followed, but nothing had been heard of the rebels since.

When the midnight train whistled, Joe put on Bemis' jacket and went out and was waiting on the platform when the train pulled in. The nightly contingent of shaky celebrants from El Paso got off, and Ruth came last, smiling radiantly, and caught his hand and hugged it under her arm. She seemed almost effervescent with good spirits, and Joe said, "It looks like everything went all right."

She said, "Everything's just fine! Come on!" and began to pull him along the train, past the two passenger coaches and a gondola, to where a boxcar had stopped opposite the chute of a cattle pen. A brakeman came out of the boxcar carrying a saddle, walked down the chute and put it on the rail of the pen, and went back up the ramp. He said, "Easy, now! Easy there, boy!" and led out a nervous horse which cautiously made its way down the chute.

Joe yelled, "Brownie!" and vaulted the fence and grabbed the halter rope. The buckskin, its eyes rolling, reared and pulled on the rope. Joe said, "It's me, you damn fool!"

Brownie stretched his neck and sniffed at him, and stood quiet.

Joe looked across the fence at Ruth, her face shining in the glare of the light over the freight platform. She said, "I tried to think of the nicest thing I could do for you, and I remembered you left him with Florencio Vidal, and I remembered the name of the saloon – El Centauro del Norte – so I just went and got him."

Joe said, "I'll tend to you, later." He threw the saddle on Brownie and led him through the gate. Once outside, he grabbed Ruth and kissed her.

She said, "I guessed right, didn't I! You are glad!"

Joe said, "I'd've married that horse a long time ago, if he'd been a mare!"

"Florencio Vidal was so nice to me," she said. "He's a real friend of yours. He only charged fifty cents a day. And, Joe, he said he'll talk to Santos Camargo whenever Camargo comes back to see his wife."

"Camargo's got no reason to help me," Joe said. "I'll never see him again." "Well, he spared your life," she said. "And if he hadn't, I wouldn't be alive, either."

She knew of a livery barn at the west end of Lima Street, and as they walked the deserted streets, Joe said, "So you lied to me. You didn't have any business in El Paso at all. Didn't even go to the bank this morning."

"Yes, I did," she said. "I got the three hundred from my account, because we'll be leaving pretty soon, won't we?"

They woke the hostler at the livery barn, and saw Brownie put into a stall, with good sweet hay in the manger and a bait of barley.

Ruth clung to Joe's arm as they walked slowly back. She said, "They told me I'll get the four thousand dollars eventually, but there's a lot of red tape to untangle. And we'll have the money to fight that murder charge, then."

"I can't take money from you," Joe said.

She said, "You're awful stubborn," and was silent for a while. Presently she went on: "You said Mike Burnham would sell stock to develop your gold strike, and I've got to invest the money somewhere. And I do know about hard-rock mining. Joe, if you won't use the money because it's ours, you've got your ranch for your share. It must be worth quite a lot, if it's as good as you say."

"You never saw such grass," Joe said. "You can dally it on your saddle horn. All it needs is stock."

"It sounds like a good investment, to me," she said. "If you have to quibble over words."

"Well, maybe," Joe said. "But I'm *not* Joe Dyer. I don't exist. I'm a nobody with a fake name, on the dodge from a murder charge. When that's cleared up, we'll see."

They entered the hotel, crossed the deserted lobby, and climbed the stairs. She unlocked her door, and Joe said, "I don't know how I can thank you for Brownie."

It was one A.M., March 9, 1916, when he locked his door and began to undress.

At two-thirty, four hundred and three of Pancho Villa's cavalry smashed into Columbus, New Mexico, yelling, "*Viva Méjico! Viva Villa!*"

Joe, his heart pounding, was standing naked in the middle of the room before he was fully awake. There was a sudden great clatter of pounding hoofs in the street, three staccato shots, and a long yell, "*Vi-i-iva Vi-i-illa!*" He jumped to the window and put his head out. Horsemen charged past, weird in the dim light of a corner lamp. Something was going on at the railroad station, a dozen big-hatted men moving around inside and on the platform. There was burst of firing on Taft Street, rifles and pistols, and a bullet whacked into the window frame beside his head. He jerked back and ran to pound on the connecting door, yelling, "Ruth! Get up! Get up!" South, at the army post, a machine gun stitched a long seam of sound.

Not wasting a motion, Joe pulled on pants, shirt, and boots. He belted the pistol on, stepped to the connecting door, and kicked it open with one smash of his heel.

Ruth, white-faced, was pulling her drawers on, with her underskirt bunched around her waist. They could hear people running in the hallway, and there was a lot of yelling in the lobby, and four spaced pistol shots.

Joe turned the light out, and jumped to the window. The racket in the lobby was increasing. A woman screamed. A wash of ruddy light flickered over the opposite building — something afire, probably over on Broadway.

Ruth said, "I'm ready!" Her clothes were twisted and bunched up, but she was fully dressed, all but her stockings. Joe held the pistol in his right hand, he said, "Stay right behind me. Hang onto my belt. You got the key?"

"It's on the dresser," she said. She was very scared, but pretty steady. Joe unlocked the door. The room was alight with the glare of fire spilling in the window. He swung the door in and looked down the hall. The shooting and screaming in the lobby continued. He pulled Ruth into the hall and went slowly until he could see into the lobby. He watched as the pile of furniture that was barricading the street door tumbled inward and three Mexicans plunged over it. One of them didn't get up. The others shot down two half-dressed Americans, and more Mexicans came in, yelling, "*Ravel! Sahm Ravel! Donde 'stá el hideputa?*"

Mr. Ritchie, fully dressed, faced them. They yelled in his face, demanding Sam Ravel. Ritchie answered in Spanish, telling them that Ravel had gone to El Paso.

Three or four women ran out of the second floor rooms behind Joe and Ruth, screamed, and ran back.

The Mexican obviously in charge yelled, "*Vargas! Órtiz! Busca! Piso primero!*"

Ruth said something urgently, but he couldn't hear over a sudden crash of shots out on the street. "What?" he shouted in her ear.

"They're coming upstairs!" she yelled, and he pulled her down the hall intending to go down the back stairs, but there was a glare of fire in the stairwell, and a billow of smoke. He pulled her into her room and locked the door. She stood wide-eyed, with the old look of near-hysteria that he had seen before.

He holstered the pistol, grabbed a chair, and smashed out the double-hung window. He jerked the blankets off the bed, grabbed the mattress and doubled it, and staggered to the window and forced the mattress through and let it drop. He leaned out and saw that it lay flat on the ground.

"Over here, Ruth!"

She came to the window, and he said, "Stand here. Don't show yourself!"

He ran across the room and unlocked the door, opened it a crack and looked out. Three shouting Mexicans were battering at doors. One of them shot into the lock on a door. Another dragged a terrified youth down the hall. Joe heard pounding at the door of his adjoining room, and two Mexicans herded five women and three girls toward the stairway. He recognized Mrs. Ritchie and her daughters. The hall was full of smoke.

He slammed the door and locked it. Someone was hammering at the connecting door. He ran across the room to Ruth.

"Get out the window. Kneel on the sill, facing in!" He boosted her onto the sill, and got her wrists, and said, "Hang down and drop." Her skirt caught on glass in the sash, and he saw blood on her knee. When she was hanging outside, he let her drop.

They were shouting outside the door. He heard a shot, and hoped Ruth was not directly below. The door burst inward, and he hung onto the sill with one hand and had trouble getting the revolver out of the holster.

In the doorway, two Mexicans momentarily jammed together. He shot four times as fast as he could. They both fell, one into the room, and one back into the hall. Flame crackled in the hallway, and smoke rolled into the room. He shoved the pistol into the holster, grabbed the sill, flung himself outward, and dropped, his knees smashing against the brick. He landed on his feet and fell face down.

He rolled against the wall, blinking in the glare of firelight. Ruth had her back to the wall. There was a clatter of galloping hoofs, and the firing was now all around. Slugs were ricocheting off the walls.

He got up, grabbed Ruth's hand, got the pistol in his right fist, and sprinted for the alley behind the Columbus Theater. In the alley, they leaned against the wall, gasping.

Taft Street seemed to be burning from end to end. A mob of Mexicans milled around the bank. Ravel's Mercantile and his hardware store were towering masses of flame. Walker's Hardware was afire, and Moore's Warehouse. In front of the Hotel Hoover, whose roof suddenly bloomed in a vast billow of flame, Mexicans were herding women and children into the street.

There was shouting and rifle fire and a long rip of machine-gun fire at the cavalry post, south of the station. The raiders weren't having it all their own way, now. Flame lanced from windows and doorways. There were Mexican bodies in the street, and riderless horses stampeding aimlessly.

Joe said, "Come on! We'll get out of town!" He reloaded the revolver, and they trotted along the dark alley to North Main.

Joe looked both ways. Figures were flitting around in the murk and smoke, farther up the street, but no one was near. He grabbed Ruth's hand and was starting to run across the street, when four figures came around the corner from Broadway — three Mexicans dragging along the kid they had pulled from the room in the hotel. One of them fired at Joe.

He threw Ruth down and dropped down in front of her and aimed carefully at the one who had fired. They were quite clear, the man dropped, kicking. Someone else, or a stray shot, had nailed him. The other two, holding the kid, shot at Joe. The bullets whined off the ground and grit stung his face. He shot, and one of them staggered back and sat down. Joe took a deliberate bead on the other, afraid he might hit the kid. The Mexican was coolly doing the same, taking his time. Joe shot first. The Mexican stumbled and fell, and lay writhing, clutching his left leg.

The kid ran into the alley across the street. The sitting man slowly slid down full length. The one Joe had shot in the leg dragged himself around the corner. Joe fired at him again, but missed. He hauled Ruth to her feet, and they ran across into the opposite alley.

They went cautiously and came out of the alley, and got across the railroad tracks and into a drainage ditch. On hands and knees, they crawled two hundred yards in the ditch into an open field. The fighting was behind them, now, in the town and south at the army post. It was slacking off in the town, although there was still a lot of shooting and yelling and men charging around on horses. At the army post, it flared up and died down, and burst out again.

They lay in each other's arms, straining together. Joe kept telling her, "It's all right! We're safe here!" She said nothing, but clung tighter. Joe wondered what time it was.

At last the sky lightened in the east. Only an occasional shot sounded. The fires were dying down. The fighting at the cavalry post had stopped altogether, and in the eerie silence Joe heard wagons moving on the road. Certainly the Thirteenth Cavalry hadn't won any quick victory. He hadn't seen any soldiers in town, backing up the civilians. They must have been pinned down, and if they'd been as completely surprised as the town, they might have taken a beating.

The first shafts of sunlight caught the pall of smoke over Columbus. A train came from the east, from El Paso, slowed down, stopped, then slowly backed half a mile and stopped again. Joe got up and stood on the edge of the ditch, and saw a long line of riders and wagons heading east along the international fence. Pancho Villa's cavalry was pulling out.

Joe got down into the ditch and knelt beside Ruth and said, "Are you all right?"

She nodded.

"Let's see that knee. You cut it going out the window, didn't you?" She nodded again, and pulled her skirt up. The cut had dirt ground into it, but wasn't serious.

The train pulled into the station. Joe said, "Come on! We'll see if we've got anything but the clothes on our backs. And I've got to see about Brownie."

He helped her out of the ditch, and she stood swaying, with her eyes closed. He put his arm around her and couldn't think of anything cheerful to say. She clung to him and burst out crying. He held her until the spasm subsided.

"We'll find something to eat. Get some hot coffee into you."

They walked across the field and crossed the tracks. People were coming and going from the station, and a man called to Joe, "They telegraphed from the train. Troops coming from Fort Bliss. They'll show those greaser sonsabitches!"

They passed people picking up a body. Joe recognized it as Ritchie, manager of the Commercial Hotel. Walking slowly along Taft Street, they passed a number of bodies, Mexican and American, among them Edwin Dean, near the smoking shell of his store, and Walker not far from his burned-out hardware store.

Residents were converging on the business district. Men were picking up American bodies and dragging the Mexican dead to a place by the tracks, and piling them in a heap. A couple of mounted men dragged two of them with lariats.

Four automobiles came chugging down Sierra Madre Street, crowded with passengers and packages and boxes — probably help from Deming, thirty miles north.

Loose horses wandered around. A good-looking roan, a small horse wearing a Mexican saddle, shied away as Joe and Ruth turned into Lima Street. Joe jumped and caught the reins. The horse fought for a moment, then surrendered. There was a bullet-plowed furrow across the cantle, and blood on a fender. The roan followed quietly when Joe pulled on the reins.

"Guess we've got as good a claim as anybody," Joe said.

They passed through the smoking shambles of the business district. There was no damage in the residential areas. People were coming out of the houses to see the damage and help where they could.

The Mexican hostler was not at the livery barn, but Brownie was all right, hungry and thirsty. He let Joe know it, emphatically. Joe unsaddled the Mexican roan and put it in the stall next to Brownie. He fed and watered them, and took a half hour to tend to four others.

"Now," he said, "it's our turn, if there's still a restaurant in town."

Ruth was recovering from her terror, but she clung to his arm as they walked.

Suddenly, Joe said, "My God! Your money!"

Ruth patted her chest. "I have it. I had it pinned to my nightgown."

Joe whistled in relief.

As they walked slowly back to the business section, Joe said, "Who was that kid they took out of the hotel?"

"I didn't see him," she said. "But Sam Ravel's brother lives there with him. Arthur, I think it is."

"You saw him when they started shooting at us," Joe said. "They were dragging him down the street."

"I was too scared to look," she said. "I just lay there with my eyes shut."

"Well, anyway, he got away," Joe said. "You didn't see those Mexicans I shot?"

"No, I didn't."

"Well," Joe said, "the one I hit in the leg looked a lot like Santos Camargo."

NINETEEN

Ruth was drawn and pale, very dirty, and very tired. Joe said, "We've got to find some place where you can rest. Then I'll see if there's anything we can salvage from the hotel, and find out what happened at the bank."

"I'm going with you," she said. "I'll be all right, really."

"Well then, we'll see if we can find some breakfast."

There was a pervading stink of smoke and wet ashes, and a thin column of black smoke rising from beyond the depot. The center of Columbus was a shambles, hotels and stores and the bank and the drug store gutted by fire that still smoldered. Four men carried a blanket-covered body from the ruins of the Hotel Hoover. Women had set up tables and were serving coffee and sandwiches.

Ruth and Joe sat with other exhausted, smoke-grimed people, eating and listening to the talk. Dr. Hart and DeWitt Miller had been killed in the Commercial Hotel, but Mrs. Burchfield and Mrs. Ritchie and her daughters had been spared. Lee Riggs had saved his family in that holocaust by putting a mattress over them, on the floor. Ed Dean and Mr. Elliott, on Boundary Street, had run to the army post in their underwear, where Lieutenant Castleman couldn't fire at the attacking Mexicans because they kept behind Dr. Dabney's house, which was full of wounded soldiers. A lot of soldiers had been killed around the stables. Nobody knew quite what had happened at the camp, but somebody said that Colonel Slocum hadn't showed up till the fighting was over. Major Frank Tompkins had chased the Mexicans across the border, but couldn't follow because he didn't have enough men. Troops were on the way from Fort Bliss, and they'd get that son of a bitch Pancho Villa if they had to chase him to Mexico City!

Help was coming from Deming, and a relief train from El Paso. Eleven dead civilians had been found. The bank officials didn't know how much had been taken by the raiders and lost in the fire. Louis Ravel had saved his life in the Ravel Mercantile by hiding under a pile of hides while the Mexicans searched for him and Sam as they plied the torches. And fourteen-year-old Arthur Ravel had got away when somebody shot the three Mexicans who were dragging him away to show them where his brothers were hiding. There were a lot of dead Mexicans and several wounded had been captured — someone said two important officers, a Colonel Carmen Órtiz and Colonel José Rodriguez. Citizens had tried to take them from their captors and throw them on the heap of dead Mexicans they were burning, down by the depot, but an army guard had taken them to the military hospital, and Doc Dabney had treated their wounds, just like they were human. Some of the Mexicans they were pouring oil on and burning weren't dead yet, and a good thing, too!

Hearing that, Ruth put her cup down and walked away. Joe got up and followed her. She said, "They're as bad as the Mexicans." There didn't seem to be any answer, so Joe said nothing. You couldn't change human nature, even if it sickened you.

They turned south on Wisconsin Street, just walking aimlessly. She looked about ready to drop in her tracks, and Joe said, "Isn't there someone you know, some place where you can lie down a while?"

There were people milling around south of the station, and black smoke rising, and a stink of burning meat. Joe saw four men drag a body across the road and swing it, yelling, "A-one! A-two! A-three!" and heave it onto the fire.

He swore and turned Ruth around. She said, "What's the matter?" Just then a buckboard swung around the corner of Boulevard Street with one man driving and two sitting behind the seat with their feet dangling over the back.

The driver grinned at Joe and Ruth and yelled, Got a live one! C'mon an' watch him wiggle!"

Joe stepped in front of the team and help up his hand. The driver swore and hauled on the reins. The team slid to a halt.

"What the hell's the matter with you?" the driver said. The matter was the haggard, gray-faced Mexican with the bloody leg, in the back of the buckboard. The man beside him jumped down and growled, "Git the hell out of the way!"

Joe said, "Let me take him, will you? It's personal between me and him."

The driver said, "Mister, I'll run right over you!" and the other said. "You'll take a slug in the guts! Now move!"

Joe pulled his gun. He said, "I'm the one put the slug in him last night. I got something special in mind for him."

Ruth grabbed his arm and said, "Don't let them take him!"

He said, "They won't! That's Santos Camargo!"

The man in the street was on the verge of gambling for his gun. Joe said, "Let's trade. There's another in the alley behind the theater, still alive. Now dump him out!"

Ruth said, "Joe! No!" and he shoved her away with his elbow and said, "Shut up!"

"Another one, eh? Okay, this one's yours!" He hauled Camargo off the buckboard. Camargo groaned and fell down.

The American jumped up beside the driver and said, "Swing 'em around, Morris!" The buckboard turned, grinding a wheel on the floorboards, and rattled away.

Ruth said, "Joe! You can't . . ."

He said, "There's nobody behind the theater, far as I know. Let's get him into the alley."

He helped Camargo to stand, and they got his arms over their shoulders and took him into the alley, half-carrying him. He tried to walk, but his left foot dragged. They sat him down against an adobe wall.

He said, "You Joe Dyer. I didn't know you. The whiskers fool me, like when I almost shoot you, at the train."

"I guess we're even," Joe said. "You know what they were going to do? Pour oil on you and burn you."

Camargo said, "I was tryin' to get to Paul Contreras, but I can't move so good, an' they caught me."

"Paul Contreras? Who's that?"

"Before we come into town last night," Camargo said, "my cousin tell us if we get hurt or get separated, there's some Mexicans will help us. One of them name' Paul Contreras, he live on Wisconsin Street."

"You know the house?" Joe asked.

"No . . . I don't know." Camargo's face was gray, and he was about to faint. The blood on his leg was wet and bright.

Joe said, "Ruth, go over to that house. Ask somebody where Paul Contreras lives."

She hurried across the street. Joe ripped Camargo's pants leg and exposed the wound — a small, blue hole in the front of the thigh, and a big bleeding hole in the back. The bone hadn't been hit. He tore a strip from the pants and twisted it into a rope, and tied it above the wound with a figure-eight knot that could be pulled tight and wouldn't slip. He tightened it and was looking for a stick to twist it tighter, when Ruth came back.

"I could hardly find anyone home," she said. "The Mexicans have almost all left. But a woman told me . . . it's at the corner. I found Contreras. He'll be here in a minute."

A small, middle-aged man walked rapidly into the alley. He didn't waste words, but helped Joe lift Camargo. They carried him to the corner house and down a dark hall to a bedroom and laid him on the bed.

"My wife's getting bandages and hot water," Contreras said. "Can we get his clothes off?"

Joe wasn't sure that Camargo was conscious when he undressed him. He had lost a lot of blood.

A young, pretty Mexican woman came in with a worn sheet and court plaster and a bottle of carbolic acid. She said, "Hot water, *pronto*," and went out and came back with a basin and a steaming teakettle.

Contreras said, "This is my wife, Concha."

Ruth tore the sheet into strips and went to work. Camargo drew in his breath sharply through clenched teeth, but said nothing, even in the intervals when it didn't look as if he were fainting. The bite of the carbolic acid made him grunt. Joe admired his guts.

Ruth said, "Do you think we can risk a doctor?"

"No," Joe said, "not the way people feel."

Concha came in with a pint of whiskey and a jug of water. "Very good medicine," she said, grinning with a flash of white teeth. She handed the bottle to Joe. "Look like *you* need, too."

Joe had a drink and poured one for Camargo, helping him to sit up with an arm around his shoulder.

"How you feel, Santos?" he asked. "You want to talk now?"

"I guess I sleep li'l while. Then maybe I talk, if I feel like it."

"You'll feel like it," Joe said. "Because if you don't, I'm going to hand you to those boys burning the Mexicans down by the depot."

Ruth gasped. Paul Contreras swore. Camargo's eyes flew open and he stared into Joe's eyes. He said,

"You not foolin', are you? Give me li'l sleep. We gonna talk!"

Contreras said, "Mister, I don't like that kind of talk!"

"Then don't listen," Joe said. "Just keep your nose out."

Camargo seemed already asleep when they left him. Ruth asked where the bathroom was, and Concha led her down the hall.

In the kitchen, Contreras sat at the table and poured two drinks and said, "Who are you?"

"Joe Daly. My friend is Ruth Bemis."

"You mean Mrs. Bemis that was on that train?"

"Yes," Joe said. "I was there, too."

Contreras' eyebrows went up. "I heard about you. I don't understand how you can save a man's life, then threaten to burn him. You know, I could get some help here, real quick."

Joe said, "He's got information that's very important to me. You might say a matter of life and death. *My* life, maybe. Now, he said he'll talk, so there'll be no trouble. Or, if there is, you're right in the middle. How'd you like people to find out you've got him here?'

"That cuts two ways, Daly. You brought him here."

"Then you keep out of my business, and I won't tell anybody you're a traitor, sheltering a man that helped burn their town and murder their friends."

"All right," Contreras said. "I'll get him over the line to Las Palomas as soon as he can ride and I can get hold of a couple of horses. There's people there will take care of him."

"You need transportation?" Joe asked. "Get me a pencil and paper."

Contreras brought them, and Joe wrote a note to Lieutenant Castleman at the Thirteenth Cavalry post: *This will introduce Paul Contreras. Please turn my two mules over to him, as he bought them. He will pay any charges for their keep. I am much obliged. Joe Daly.*

He gave it to Contreras, who read it and said, "You're an odd kind of man, Daly. Thanks."

"Hell," Joe said, "I didn't know what to do with the damn jugheads, anyway. I didn't tell you, Santos Camargo saved my life."

Ruth and Concha came into the kitchen. Ruth was clean now, but still very tired. She said, "I looked in on him. He's sleeping."

Concha said, "That's what you oughta do. I gonna feed you, then put you in my bed."

Concha cooked ham and eggs and hotcakes. Ravenous as he was, Joe nearly fell at the table. When they finished, Concha said, "Come on, Mrs. Bemis. Rockabye for you."

Ruth got up and said, "You get some rest, too, Joe. He isn't going to run away."

Joe said, "Ruth, did you take care of that cut on your knee?"

She said, "Yes, it's just a scratch," and went down the hall with Concha.

Contreras said, "I think I'll go get those mules, if Villa didn't get 'em. I hear he got a lot of stock and wagons." He went out, then appeared in the hall wearing a hat and jacket.

"Wait a minute," Joe said. "I've got to see if there's anything salvaged at the hotel."

They went out together. The morning was gray and very cold. Joe put his hands in his pockets and hunched his shoulders, shivering. They walked to East Boundary Street, and Contreras turned south toward the army post.

On Broadway, townspeople and volunteers from Deming had set up a relief station and were handing out soup and sandwiches and clothing. Joe found a heavy mackinaw that fit him, and a boy's coat he thought would do for Ruth. He offered to pay for them, but the woman behind the plank table noted his grimy clothes and haggard face, and said, "No, sir, you just take them!"

Joe said, "Thanks very much. We only got out with what we had on. Lady, do you know if there's anyone here from the bank?"

She turned and called, "Mr. Mays! Here's a man wants to talk to you."

A young red-headed man left his post dispensing coffee from a restaurant urn, and came to Joe. He said, "I'm Bill Mays. I'm a teller at the bank . . . or at least I was. There isn't much bank left. You're Daly, aren't you? I guess you've had more than trouble than any of us. You and Mrs. Bemis. What can I do for you?"

Joe said, "It's her I wanted to talk about. Her account rather. What's the chance of her getting her money?"

"She withdrew her own account. But if you mean her husband's private account . . . I'm afraid the prospect is very bad. As the widow, it would go to her, of course. But he died intestate, and that alone means a long delay. And now, those Mexicans cleaned us out . . . all our cash; and all our records went up in the fire. It isn't certain that we'll ever open again . . . and far less than certain that she'll ever get the money. We'll do our best, but it's an impossible job to get it all straitened out. At best, it would be months."

"Well, I kind of expected it," Joe said. "I hate to tell her. That's all she had in the world."

He walked back to Paul Contreras' house. Concha answered his knock. She said, "You gonna fall down, you don't get some rest."

Joe said, "How's Camargo?"

"He's one tough *pocho!*" she said. "He wake up. He's hungry. I feed him soup an' drink of whiskey. Now he wanna get up an' go."

As Joe walked to the room where Camargo lay, Ruth came out of the other bedroom. "I heard you come in," she said. "Where'd you go?"

He showed her the two coats and said, "I went out for these. Camargo's awake. Come on in."

Concha started to follow them into the room, and Joe faced her, searching for polite words, not wanting to hurt her feelings.

She studied his face, then said, "Okay. Is private. Concha don't wanna hear no secrets." She went back to the kitchen.

They went into the room. Ruth sat on the only chair, and Joe leaned against the wall.

Camargo seemed to have gotten older, even in the two hours he'd been lying there — new lines deeply graven in his hollow cheeks, and sparse whiskers showing black against the gray skin. He said, "Listen, Joe, you been acting like we not friends no more. If I know somethin' you wanna know, I gonna tell you. You save my life this morning."

"Okay, Santos. Did you kill Dutch Hauser?"

"No, I never, Joe. How 'bout you?"

"Not me, Santos. Why you think I came all the way to El Paso trying to find you?"

"Well," Santos said, "I never really think you do it. Other people got good reason to shoot that son of bitch."

"Then why'd you run for it?" Joe asked. "Almost as bad as confessing it, running that way."

"Not if you Mexican, Joe, in Spanish Wells. You don't get no fair trail there. An' that sheriff, he only gonna b'lieve what he want to. You never change he's mind. An' Cal Morgan gonna lie, he gonna, too, 'cause I tell Pritchard I gonna kill that bastard some day."

"They had me convinced, too," Joe said. "Only when I went with Cal to tell the sheriff you'd cut out, Kincaid wouldn't listen. He said I did it, because I had that trouble with Dutch in Spanish Wells. He had a warrant for me and I ran for it, too, because I couldn't prove I didn't do it. Then *Cal* took a shot at me. Now why the hell, if Cal thought *you* did it, would he shoot at *me*?"

"I tell you, Joe. Cal don't want you around, 'cause maybe sheriff take you in and you talk, and sheriff figure out Cal done it. 'Cause Cal done it, Joe! You din't do it and I din't do it! So Cal don't take no chances. Maybe sheriff think I done it, but if he can make sheriff think maybe you done it after all, then nobody gonna look Cal's way."

"What about Pritchard, Santos? Why not him?"

" 'Cause he wasn't there, Joe. He come in after. Anyway, I don't think he got the guts. He run things, an' Cal an' Dutch do the work, 'cause he got the brains an' they stupid."

"Run what things?"

"Aw, listen, Joe, don't make jokes! You know we runnin' guns to Pancho Villa from that ranch."

"So that's it," Joe said.

"Why, sure," Camargo said. "I was lookin' for good place near the *frontera*, where we could hide guns and slip them across. You know, ever since Pres'dent Wilson make law for no more sellin' guns to Villa, we have to get 'em somewhere."

"Who's we?" Joe demanded.

"Pancho Villa. Well, not really him. My cousin, Jesús Manuel Castro, he tell me. And he get money from Pancho when I have to pay for guns and pay off Pritchard. So I talk to Pritchard, and he like the idea. We get guns from all over. Me and other men buy them lots of place, and have them deliver to Spade Bit Ranch. An' pretty soon Pritchard makin' a lot of money, and he got too many cowboy around, somebody gonna find out all right, so he fire everybody but Cal an' Dutch, an' sell his cows. Guns come in automobile, sometimes on train, marked machinery. An' Cal an' Dutch an' me, we take 'em to different places on the *frontera*, when I get word from Castro. Everything goin' fine, only Dutch Hauser, he spoil it."

"Wait a minute," Joe said. "What about Tom Kincaid. Did he know what was going on?"

"I don't know," Camargo said. "But I think he know, all right."

"Santos, why'd you run away from me in El Paso? I couldn't do anything to you. I just wanted to talk to you."

"I think maybe you comin' to get me, Joe. I don't know; maybe that sheriff make you deputy or somethin'. You tell Florencio Vidal there was warrant for me, din't you?"

"Well, yes, I did, Santos. If you heard I was trying to warn you, maybe you'd talk to me. Actually, far as I know, the only warrant is for me. I don't suppose you'd come back with me?"

"I can't do that, Joe! Anybody see me this side of the line, I'm dead, after what happen last night! If I gonna go back, Cal an' that sheriff gonna lay me right into my grave, anyway."

"Yeah, I suppose so. So why did somebody have to kill Dutch Hauser?"

"He make too much money, Joe. An' he want more . . . he got swell head, an' he can't keep he's mouth shut. He throw his money around Spanish Wells, an' he take train to El Paso an' buy them fancy clothes an' get drunk in whorehouse. The he tell Pritchard if he don't get more money he's gonna tell the gover'ment. Pritchard was plenty worry, Joe. He tell me we gotta do somethin' about Hauser. Cal, he don't like it, neither. He try to get Hauser, he won't do that. So Cal always go with him an' try to stop him from talkin' when he's drunk. An' they have fights, too, 'cause Dutch, he don't like for Cal followin' him around all the time. I hate that son of bitch, too, an' I woulda kill him myself, but I know if police an' sheriff comin' round, why then we gotta stop runnin' guns to Pancho Villa.

"When you come, I think maybe Pritchard hire you to kill Hauser. An' I really thought you done it, too, Joe. That's why I din't kill you at that Santa Ysabel. Anybody that kill that son of bitch, why he's my friend."

"I guess you took a chance, there, didn't you, Santos?"

"Yes, I take big chance. If any of them Mexican see me let you go, they gonna shoot me quick, you bet."

He paused and looked at Joe's face. "We all even, now, eh?" When Joe didn't answer, he went on: "If you gonna work on somebody, you work on Cal. He ain't got no guts. They couldn't just kill Dutch, 'cause how they gonna explain it? But you come along, an' you an' him have that fight in Spanish Wells with whole town watchin'. Everybody gonna say, why, sure! That stranger shoot Dutch!"

"Well, you've given me something to go on," Joe said. "You need anything, Santos?"

"Well, maybe you make me cigarette," Camargo said.

Joe found Bull Durham in Camargo's jacket pocket and rolled him a smoke. He and Ruth went out.

She said, "You can clear yourself, now, can't you!"

"I'll sure have a try at it," Joe said. "If that sheriff would only listen to reason! But I'll have a little talk with Cal Morgan. If I don't get anything out of him or Pritchard, I'll go on to Prescott and get Mike's lawyer on it."

"Joe," she said, "let's go to Prescott first, and work from there. I'll have the money to pay the lawyer."

Joe didn't have the heart to tell her, not just then.

Concha cooked a fine lunch. Paul Contreras came home about five o'clock, riding one rawboned Tarahumara mule and leading the other. He put them into the walled patio behind the house. When he came in, he said, "I borrowed two saddles." He threw his hat into a corner and sat at the kitchen table. "Columbus is famous," he said and handed Joe the *El Paso Morning Times*.

The headlines screamed for war with Mexico. Column heads demanded investigations, called the Thirteenth Cavalry a collection of cowards, called for court martials, and said that General "Black Jack" Pershing would command a punitive expeditionary force into Mexico and had promised to bring Pancho Villa back in a cage, like a wild beast.

On the back page was a short article about the escape of Mrs. Harry Bemis and Mr. Joe Daly, from the massacre at Santa Ysabel. The picture was so poor, Joe was sure no one would recognize him.

After dinner, Joe was about to ask if he and Ruth could stay the night, when Contreras said, "Mrs. Bemis, you look awful tired. Why don't you go to bed? I won't be here. You can sleep with Concha."

Joe said, "You're not going tonight! Can he ride?"

"He says he's going to. His leg look pretty good. He won't be safe till he's across the line."

"How are you going to get him past the guard post?" Joe asked.

"I'm not," Contreras said. "The Mexicans cut the fence, east of town."

Ruth went to bed. Concha banged things around in the kitchen. About eight-thirty Joe helped Contreras to get Camargo out of the house and onto a mule, where he clung dizzily to the horn and said, "I'm feel fine! So I tell you again, Joe, *buena suerte!* Good luck! It work pretty good last time I tell you, eh?"

"*Muy buena suerte*, Santos," Joe said. He swung the gate open, and they rode out and turned south on Wisconsin Street.

Back in the house, Concha told Joe, "I put clean sheets on bed where he was."

"Thanks, Concha! You're a number one, first class angel!"

"Fancy words gonna get you no place," she said and grinned slyly at him. "You gonna kiss her good night? I wait. Maybe *I* gonna use that other bed, eh?"

Joe said, "Concha, you've got a heart of gold and a dirty mind. And you said yourself, I'm too tired. I'll be out in a minute."

He opened Ruth's door and, in the light from the hall, saw her sleeping as relaxed as a kitten, her dark hair spread on the pillow. It was going to be very hard to wake her and tell her that all she had in the world was whatever was left from her three hundred dollars.

As he looked down at her, the memory was strong in him of their desperate struggle across the bitter desert, of El Buey frying on a bed of coals and Concepción Osuna shrieking and dying, of the nights when he held her close to keep her from freezing, of the shared miracle of a drink of bad water and a half-cooked leg of goat, of a trip to a looted safe in the talus of a mine dump, of the treachery of a thieving husband, of a stolen, gem-studded rosary buying the help of a small, tireless Tarahumara — and, most insistently, of a night in a firelit cabin where she had given herself to him and suffered agonies of shame afterward.

Well, there was no way around it, she had to be told about the money, and he might as well get it all done at once and tell her he was riding out in the morning leaving her homeless and friendless and almost destitute. he felt like the original, one-of-a-kind son of a bitch.

He knelt beside the bed and put the back of his hand against her face. She sighed and put her hand over his, but didn't come fully awake.

He couldn't do it.

He pulled his hand away and made a cowardly retreat into the hall and shut the door.

TWENTY

Joe got up early Friday morning and knocked on Ruth' door. He got a sleepy answer and went to the kitchen where Concha was getting breakfast. She said her hus band had not yet returned. Joe borrowed a towel and hac a bath. Ruth was at the table with Concha when he came out.

When they had breakfasted on chorizo and fried egg with a sauce that nearly took the roof off his mouth, Joe said, "Ruth, I've got to talk to you." They went into the room where she had slept, and sat on the bed.

Joe said, "I guess there's no way to tell you this, tc make it easier. Yesterday afternoon I talked to the telle at the bank. The place is a complete wreck, and all thei records burned, and the money gone. It'll be month before you get anything, and chances are you never will."

He wasn't sure what he had expected she would do o say. She had pretty much gone to pieces whenever they'c been in physical danger, but he remembered that she hac shown nothing but courage in the face of the shock o Harry's treachery, and had stood up to every hardship o hunger and cold and terrible tension and uncertainty.

She looked down at her hands folded in her lap. At las she said, "What can we do now? There's no money for a lawyer for you. Do you really think you can force the truth from Cal Morgan?"

Joe said, "That's not the point! I can raise what I need. Mike Burnham will let me have it, or I can sell the ranch. But what about you? What are you going to do?"

She said, "I don't know, Joe. I haven't thought about it. I'm out of my trouble. You saved my life a dozen times, and now I can't do anything to help you."

It came out then, and he didn't know whether he really wanted it that way or not. He said, "Well, you can't stay here. You've got to go somewhere. You'd better come with me . . . if you want to. I'm going back to the Spade Bit Ranch. Or you can go to Prescott. I'll write to Mike. He'll take care of you till I get there. He can find you a job."

Her face shone as if there were a light inside. She said, "I want to go with you, if you really mean it. But, Joe, you don't have to do this. I'm not your responsibility."

He grinned at her, then, and pulled her off the bed. "Come on, let's ride!" And to his surprise, a great weight lifted from him that he hadn't known was bearing him down.

She was actually gay and laughing, as though they were starting on a holiday, when they said goodbye to Concha.

They walked to the livery stable, with Ruth commenting that they weren't ready for a long ride, she didn't have the clothes, they needed blankets and food.

"It's a long ride to that ranch, isn't it?" she asked.

"About a hundred miles," Joe said. "We can pack enough on the horses. We'll ride to Deming today, and get what we need there. There're no stores left here."

The saddle for the roan was almost as fine as the one that had bought the help of Julio in the Tarahumara village. The bridle was silver mounted, with braided reins hooked to a spade bit. The bit worried Joe. Brownie wouldn't like it, and Ruth didn't know how to handle it.

When he had paid the hostler, he saddled the roan and put it through a few figure-eights in the corral. This was a reined horse with a mouth like velvet. It changed leads like a machine. Its owner was probably still smoldering in that heap of bodies down by the tracks.

There was the usual tightly-woven serape over the saddlebags, which contained only a handful of rifle cartridges and two spare horseshoes and a package of jerky. The ornate saddle scabbard was empty.

Joe shortened the stirrups for Ruth. He said, "Go easy on this one. Whatever you do, don't put any pressure on the bit. You just mention to this boy what you want him to do, you don't haul him around."

She had trouble, as always, getting the wad of skirt and underskirts comfortably adjusted. The roan was suspicious of the woman and all that clothing, but he was such a gentleman that he made no trouble.

The thirty miles to Deming was slow going, because the roan was also distrustful of the few automobiles among the wagon traffic carrying supplies and relief workers to Columbus.

They got to Deming in time to buy supplies and blankets and two one-gallon canteens. Joe also bought a hatchet and tin plates and cups and a skinning knife, a coffee pot and knives and forks and two rubberized army ponchos. He bought a wool shirt and socks for Ruth, but ran into an argument when he asked what size pants she wore. She said, "I won't wear pants!"

"Didn't you wear them at the mine?"

"Never! Our Mexicans would have been horrified! And Harry, too!"

Joe said, "Please use your head. You'll be comfortable in a union suit and Levi's and boots. Put all that stuff you're wearing into the saddlebags."

Grudgingly she conceded, and let the clerk measure the swell of her hips and the narrowness of her waist. The clerk blushed and said, "We got nothing to fit that!"

Joe said, "She can lap 'em over the waist and roll up the bottoms. Now let's see some boys' boots. And longjohns."

They had dinner in a Chinese restaurant and rode about eight miles northwest, paralleling the Santa Fe Railroad. At dusk they made camp — with separate beds — in the lee of Black Mountain.

In the morning they left the railroad and cut northeast across a tremendous sandy flat dotted with yucca and maguey and sage, passed between the lower end of the Burro Mountains, and a big hump to the southwest, then turned north across a wide plain. The Burro Mountains, on their right, swelled higher and higher. They stretched out their food and used boiled water from a couple of cattle tanks. Ruth said the saddle and gait of the Mexican roan were pure luxury, compared to the wooden Tarahumara saddle and the bone-wracking gait of that mule.

On the third day out of Deming, they crossed the shallow Gila River. Joe said, "We'll see Spanish Wells pretty soon, and the Spade Bit is ten miles past it, up in those hills. We'll camp this afternoon, and I'll go there about three in the morning."

"All right," she said, "but I'm going with you. You expect me to wait around camp and not know what's happening to you?"

Joe knew it was futile to argue.

They rode to within about a mile of the Spade Bit. It was about three in the morning, and there was no moon, but the sky was light with starshine, and their vision adjusted to the gloom. Joe said, "From here on don't talk. Stay behind me. We'll hide the horses somewhere and walk the last of it."

He reined Brownie off the road and led the way among the juniper and pinon and after half an hour, stopped and dismounted. He tied the horses to a tree and slipped the bridles and loosened cinches and checked the loads in his Colt's. They went slowly up a rise and looked over. The bunkhouse and cookhouse and blacksmith shop roofs reflected the sky, lighter squares in the darkness. A horse whinnied in the corral. The ranch house was out of sight over a swell of ground.

TWENTY-ONE

oe waited ten minutes, but could see no movement in esponse to the horse's challenge. They made their way o the corral, and two horses snorted and moved around nd a mule ambled up to the fence. No one came out of he bunkhouse. "Goddamn it!" Joe whispered. "Nobody ere! You think you can find the horses if there's any rouble? Because if there is, don't stop to ask questions, ust go!"

"I couldn't get back to them," she said. "What are you oing to do?"

"I don't know, yet."

He sat down and took off his boots, then stood up and ulled the gun. He made no sound as he walked to the oor.

The hinges squealed when he turned the knob and ushed the door inward. Somebody muttered. Joe stood ense, the gun poised in his hand. He held the pose until he man inside began to snore. Cal Morgan's bunk had een the second on the right, but whether it was Cal in here, and whether he was in Cal's bunk, there was no elling. Joe slipped inside and slid his feet across the loor an inch at a time.

He found the table, and located the lamp above it. He olstered the gun and used both hands to take off the amp chimney. He got a match from his shirt pocket, got he gun in his left hand, and wiped the match head alight n the seat of his pants. The man in Cal's bunk lay face o the wall, still snoring.

Joe lit the lamp and put the chimney back. It was Cal, all right — he could tell by the white hair.

He switched the gun to his right hand and crossed to the bunk, crouched, and suddenly clamped his hand over Cal's mouth.

Cal jerked and threw his arms around, and Joe jammed the muzzle of the Colt's under his chin. Cal's pale eyes stared wildly as he jerked his head and grabbed Joe's left wrist. Joe whispered harshly, "Quiet down Cal!"

Cal quit struggling and slumped and seemed to get smaller. Joe took his hand away and said, "You know better than to yell. Get up!" He stepped back, and Cal sat up, staring like a man seeing a ghost. He was in his longjohn's and his right arm was in a plaster cast from the upper arm to his wrist.

Joe said, "Get over to the table!" and hauled him out of the bunk.

Cal squalled and said, "My arm! Watch my arm, will you?" He stumbled across to the table and sat down. Joe saw his holstered pistol hanging from a nail at the head of the bunk.

Cal shrank back as Joe stood above him. "You're Joe Dyer!" he said, as if he didn't believe it.

Joe said, "Where's Pritchard? Up at the house?" and Cal nodded.

"If you holler for him," Joe said, "Then there's no point in keeping me quiet. So I'll plug you."

He went to the door and waved his hand outside, and stood there watching Cal until Ruth came in. Cal hardly seemed to notice her, but kept staring at Joe with his mouth working.

"Ruth," Joe said, "go over and sit on that bunk. Take that gun and hold it. And don't say anything, not a word."

She followed orders, and Joe sat at the table across from Cal. "That arm pretty sore?" he asked.

"It's killin' me!" Cal said. "That's what *you* did to me! It come out my elbow and smashed the bones. I'm gonna be crippled."

"That's what you get for shooting at people," Joe said. "So now, you talk. Tell me why you cut loose at me, when you said it was Santos Camargo that shot Dutch, or whether it was your own idea."

"You don't make no sense," Cal said. "First you say I knew Camargo done it, then you say I did it. And I'm not talkin'. You got nothing on me."

Joe reached across and whacked the plaster cast on Cal's arm with his gun. Cal squalled, high pitched and quavering, and clutched the arm to his chest, rocking back and forth.

"Start talking," Joe said, "before I tap you again."

Cal drew a shuddering and there were tears in his eyes. He said, "I was sure Camargo done it, but when we met the sheriff and you pulled your gun on him, I thought you were tryin' to kill him, and why would you do that if you weren't guilty? I just cut loose, that's all."

Joe said, "You keep on lying, I'll bust that arm all over again." He raised the pistol, and Cal shrank back.

Across the room, Ruth said, "Joe, don't do that!"

Joe said, "Keep your mouth shut!" and to Cal: "You better start over. You shot Dutch, and I know why. And you tried to hang it on Camargo. Then when you saw that Kincaid still thought it was me, and had a warrant for me, you figured you'd take advantage of that. Gun me down, and it was all over. Kincaid would have his murderer . . . but dead, so he couldn't talk, or stand trial where a good lawyer would get you tangled in your own lies and get the truth out of you."

"*No!*" Cal yelled.

Joe said, "Quiet, you son of a bitch! I'll rap again!"

Cal said, "That ain't the way it was! Camargo done it! I told Kincaid, after you run out. He knows it now. I just kind of lost my head when you knocked him off his horse and started ridin' away. Camargo done it because he hated Dutch, that's all."

Joe laughed at him. "Go ahead," he said. "I'll get a pencil and paper and set it all down, and you'll sign it. But maybe you ought to know, I brought Santos Camargo back from El Paso. He's talking to Kincaid in Spanish Wells right now. I expect they'll be out here about daylight. Now, you want to change that story any?"

Cal stared at him accusingly, like a child who has been unfairly treated. Joe said, "I know all about the gunrunning, and Dutch yelling to Pritchard for more money and getting drunk in town and bragging and throwing his money around. Of course, you had to get rid of him! It was just a question where and how, and who would do it. And I came blundering in and fixed it all up for the bunch of you – the stupid grubline rider that had the fight with Dutch in front of the whole town of Spanish Wells. Made to order, wasn't I?"

He waited. Cal looked from side to side and started to speak, and couldn't seem to get any words out.

Joe said, "I don't really need anything from you. Sheriff Kincaid's got it all by now. You'll get a trial before they stretch your neck. And if the sheriff was in on it, if Pritchard was paying him off, why you've got all the less chance. He'll see damn well that you hang, to shut you up."

Cal stared at him as though hypnotized, and said, "It wasn't me! I was too drunk! Pritchard done it! He knew he could hang it onto you. He stood outside there, lookin' in the window, and waitin' for me and Dutch to get back from Spanish Wells and get to sleep. He saw the whole thing – you an' Dutch cussin' each other, an' you knockin' Dutch down, an' Dutch layin' there drunk."

From the doorway behind Joe, Frank Pritchard said, "Joe, lay the gun on the table and get up and walk away from it." Without taking his eyes from Joe, he said, "Lady, you put the gun in the bunk and come over to the table, or I'll kill him."

Joe put the gun down and stood up. Ruth came to the table, and Frank Pritchard came in, as he had the morning Dutch Hauser was murdered — shirt outside his pants, and his hair on end.

Joe said, "What do you do, spend your nights looking in the bunkhouse window?"

Pritchard grinned. "Huh-uh. I heard Cal scream, just like I heard the shot the night he killed Dutch." He stuck Joe's gun in his waistband, sat down, and hiked his chair close to the table. At his order, Ruth sat next to him, and Joe across from him next to Cal. Pritchard propped his elbow on the table and kept the gun on Joe.

Cal said, "Frank, you can't get away with it. You said we'd lay it onto Joe here, and Camargo wouldn't ever come back, and you and me would peddle off the rifles in the cookhouse and blacksmith shop, and split the money and I could ride out."

Pritchard laughed. "Good try, Cal, but you aren't smart enough to lie me into a murder charge the way you did Joe. Right after you shot Dutch, I heard you yell "I shot the son of a bitch!"

"No, I never! Cal was almost crying. "I said. '*He* shot the son of a bitch!' I meant Joe, 'cause I thought he done it then. I never thought about it bein' you till you told me."

Cautiously, Joe began to push his right foot across under the table, an inch at a time.

Pritchard said, "Cal, you're in a rut. First you said it was Santos Camargo, then it was Joe Dyer . . . and now you say me! You try telling that to Kincaid and you most likely won't even come to trial. He appreciates the payoffs I give him. He wouldn't want that to come out in any trial. You might try to run for it while he's taking you to town, and he'd have to shoot you. What our Mexcian friends call the '*ley de fuga*.' "

"You're so goddamn slick an' smart!" Cal said. "He found Camargo and brought him out from El Paso, and he's in town right now spillin' all he knows to Kincaid."

Pritchard lost a little of his self-control. He said, "I talked to Kincaid on the phone, not ten minutes ago. He didn't say anything about Camargo being there!"

"Phone?" Joe asked.

Pritchard recovered his calm. "A precaution I took after you and Camargo ran away. In case you should come back maybe a little mad about what happened. Cost me quite a bit to string the line and put in the batteries and the phone. So, you see, Dyer, it was clever of you, but Kincaid would have mentioned Camargo if he was there."

"Why would he?" Joe asked, "If Camargo is giving him an open-and-shut case against you and Cal?"

Joe's slowly moving foot brushed lightly against Pritchard's, under the table, but Pritchard didn't notice. Joe carefully raised his foot and got it under the rung of the chair.

"Very plausible," Pritchard said. "Only I don't believe it. The sheriff has a good thing in the gunrunning. If Cal hadn't panicked tonight, we could start operating again. But I'm sure Kincaid will find us another partner, after Cal is tried and hung."

Joe said, "Kincaid might have second thoughts after he hears my testimony."

"What testimony?" Pritchard demanded.

Joe tensed his right leg, pressing his foot upward against the chair rung. He said, "Well, really not testimony . . . just a question for the jury. How could you have heard Cal say that, after he shot Dutch, if you were asleep up at the house?"

Pritchard's eyes narrowed. "Yes," he said, musingly, "I slipped there, didn't I?" His eyes swung to Cal. "Cal, he hasn't got Camargo. Camargo wouldn't come back here to be picked up on a murder charge. This boy is bluffing, and he's guessed too much. He came here and sneaked in and began to browbeat you, and I heard a shot, and came down to the bunkhouse, just as he was going to kill you. I shot him, and he fired a wild shot and killed the woman. Isn't that the way it was?"

Cal stared at him, and a grin crept slowly across his face. "Why, yeah!" he said. "You got it!"

Joe jerked the chair from under Pritchard and dumped the table over on him. Thrashing his arms wildly, Pritchard dropped the pistol and crashed over onto his back. Joe clubbed the cast on Morgan's arm with his fist. Cal screamed and Pritchard tried to throw the table off. Joe snatched up Pritchard's fallen pistol, grabbed Ruth's hand, and ran outside with her.

Pritchard was cursing wildly and Cal yelling with pain. Joe pulled Ruth around behind the corral and pushed her down flat and gave her the gun.

"Stay right here! If one of them comes around the corral, shoot! Don't hesitate!"

"No! No!" she said. "You need it!"

"I've got one hid out," he said, and sprinted for the back corner of the bunkhouse. He dropped to his knees and threw aside the board covering the opening where he had hidden his carbine over two months ago.

The carbine wasn't there.

Pritchard flung the window up and poked his head out. Joe dropped and tried to make himself small against the building.

"Pritchard said, "We found it a long time ago, Dyer." He laughed. "You might as well bring the pistol in. It's nearly daylight, and Kincaid will be here, and we'll hunt you down. And the woman. Man or woman, it's no difference to Kincaid."

Joe began crawling toward him, along the baseboards of the bunkhouse.

"You know, Dyer," Pritchard said loudly, "he doesn't like you much, and he does have that murder warrant."

While he talked, Joe crawled a little closer.

Pritchard said, "Cal, take the lantern out to the corner of the bunkhouse. He's right here somewhere."

His voice rose in excitement. "By the corral! By the corral, Cal!"

Joe thought furiously, Damn her! I told her not to move!

Pritchard thrust head and shoulders out the window, raised his arm and fired toward the corral. Joe leaped up and grabbed his arm and threw all his weight on it, pulling downward. Pritchard came cartwheeling out, his heels crashing against the sash, and slammed heavily down on his back.

He groaned and rolled over and got to his hands and knees. Joe kicked him in the face. Pritchard's head snapped back. He dropped the pistol and swayed, his head drooping. Inside the bunkhouse, Ruth shouted something Joe couldn't understand, and two shots went off. He seized Pritchard's collar and belt, heaved him nearly erect, and ran him head first into the bunkhouse wall. Pritchard dropped face down, loose and sprawled.

Joe scrabbled for the dropped gun and couldn't find it. He backed up three steps, ran, and dived headfirst through the window and rolled up onto his feet.

Ruth was backed against the wall, holding a smoking pistol in both hands. Across the room, Cal Morgan had his good hand stretched so far up it almost touched the rafters.

"I *missed* him!" Ruth said. "I missed him *twice*!" She gasped for breath, the pistol shaking in her hands. "He was getting the lantern, and I knew Pritchard would be able to see you, and I came in and he ran to the bunk and tried to get the pistol there. So I tried to shoot him!"

"Good girl!" Joe said. "If he moves, plug him. You can't miss forever."

Cal said, "Lemme put my hand down!"

"You just keep it up there!" Ruth said.

Joe got the pistol from the bunk and ran out.

Pritchard had found the dropped gun and was standing knock-kneed, braced against the wall, trying to raise it. Dawn was breaking, and Joe could see him well. Joe approached cautiously and ordered, "Drop it! You're no good to me dead!"

Blood ran from the corner of Pritchard's mouth. Joe slid toward him and said again, "Drop it!"

Pritchard's eyes weren't focusing. He muttered, and tried to raise the pistol with both hands. Joe slugged him — a full-arm swing with his left fist. Pritchard twisted sideways and fell on his face.

About seven o'clock, Pritchard had regained consciousness and was lying in the bunk where Joe had put him, with his wrists and ankles tied with bailing wire. Cal Morgan, similarly bound and tied to his chair, sat at the table. There was no fight left in him. There never had been very much, Joe thought.

Ruth sat across from Cal, pistol in hand.

Joe had found his carbine in the ranch house. He asked Ruth if she was afraid to stay there and watch Cal, and she said she'd shoot him if he moved.

Joe took the carbine and walked the quarter mile to the ranch gate and got down behind a rock.

An hour later, Sheriff Kincaid reined his horse through the gateway, and Joe raised up and said, "Unbuckle your belt with your left hand and drop it. Get your carbine out of the boot and drop it, too."

Kincaid knew better than to gamble. He complied. Joe stepped into the road and said, "We'll go to the bunkhouse."

"Frank never told me what to expect," Kincaid complained. "Just said something was goin' on down at the bunkhouse, an' I'd better get out here. Didn't figure on seein' you."

Cal Morgan talked freely for an hour. Frank Pritchard, not very coherent, protested feebly and called Morgan a liar, but he wasn't very convincing, perhaps because Kincaid most likely already knew the whole story. He knew it was finished, too, the gunrunning and his payoff money. Joe thought the sheriff was not a man to hold to loyalties when the pay stopped.

Kincaid said, "No hard feelin's, huh, Dyer? I had to hang it onto somebody. A sheriff don't keep his job if somebody don't hang for a murder in his county. I figger on keepin' mine."

"It doesn't really matter, then," Joe said, "whether you've got the right man or not?"

"Not a hell of a lot," Kincaid said. "But I expect I got the right one this time. An' you know? I hate to see the county spend all that money for trials and jury fees and transportation for witnesses and all that. Hell of a waste. Well, help me catch up a couple horses."

"What about me?" Joe asked.

"You?"

"That warrant," Joe said.

"Oh, yeah," Kincaid said. "Well, now. . . ."

Joe said, "I've got Santos Camargo for a witness."

"Yeah," the sheriff said. He rubbed his hand down his walrus mustache. "Well, I can't very well haul you an' Pritchard both in for the same murder, can I? Forget the warrant."

"I'll give you my address, so you can get hold of me when the trial starts," Joe said. "For my testimony."

The sheriff stared at him woodenly. "Needn't bother about that, neither," he said. "I got a case without you. It ain't real healthy for you around here. Was I you, I'd keep away."

"Yeah," Joe said. "*You* catch up the horses."

Kincaid walked away.

The sheriff rode out, herding his mounted captives along, with Cal white-faced and scared and Pritchard lolling in the saddle, still confused from the beating Joe had given him.

Joe and Ruth, arm in arm, watched them go.

Joe said, "Let's get out of here as quick as we can. There's grub in the ranch-house kitchen. Fix some breakfast, will you? I'll go get the horses and find Mabel's pack saddle."

She smiled for the first time in many hours. "Oh, yes! Let's go!" She turned to go to the ranch house, then turned back and asked, "Where are we going? Prescott?"

"Well," Joe said, "I thought maybe Lordsburg. If we push, maybe we can get there before all the preachers close up shop for the day. I'm going to need a hard-rock miner at the claim, and a cook at the ranch. And it's a lot of work, making up those two beds every day."

She beamed and threw him a kiss, and trotted around the cook shack to go to the ranch house. Joe walked up the slope and down the hill and into the pinons to get the horses.

Brownie and the roan were half asleep under the tree. He tightened the cinches and slipped on the bridles, then coiled his lead rope and tied it to his saddle. He took the end of the *mecate* that was tied around the roan's neck, and mounted and lifted his reins. As Brownie stepped out, Joe looked back through the trees, and saw that they hadn't come very far from the road last night. He could see a piece of it through the tree, and dust still hanging in the air from the passage of Sheriff Kincaid and his two captives.

From quite a way along the road, a shot sounded far away, Cal Morgan screamed, "No! No!" and in a few seconds, there was another shot.

For a moment, Joe thought he'd ride over there and take a look. Then he thought he wouldn't. It was far enough from the ranch so Ruth couldn't have heard.

****